hell, dream, and nothing in between

A Novel

Written by: b.p.

ISBN: 979-8-9993022-4-3
Third Edition

Cover design and photography by Maddie Haug
Printed in the United States of America

This book is dedicated to Didi,

I've thrown caution to the wind.

ACKNOWLEDGMENTS

I must first start off by thanking my angelic mother who not only did all the editing for this novel, but drew the inside art, and helped me with everything else in between. I could not have created this book without you. You were my *mon complice* who had the magic abilities of turning my explosive brain coherent. I love you mom, you are not only an art piece yourself, but you are the reason this book has become tangible. I must also thank my dad, whom I adore uncontrollably. You are the most amazing and supportive human-being on the planet and I learn from you every single day. I would not have had any of the opportunities that I have had in my life without you. I can't thank you enough for allowing me to blossom at my own pace and continuing to water my roots even when the direction was unclear. I love you so much. I hope to grow up like you one day. And to my brother, who was one of the very first people to read my novel when it was at its most deranged place. You are the best brother a girl could ever wish for. Even though you are younger, you have protected and supported me with wisdom beyond your years. I am so glad I could include your artistic touch to this novel as well, your beautiful drawing of the Archivaldo Wing. You have talents beyond your fingertips. Thank you for everything.

Thank you, to Didi and Grandad. Who are both up in heaven now. Your love story was my greatest muse for my entire life. I wrote this book while living in your house, surrounded by your art. I carry you both with me every single day, spreading what I learned from your insights into my own little corner of life. I love you both, endlessly. Thank you, to Mimi and Pop-Pop, I find joy in just hearing your names. You have both taught me how to buckle up and get what I want out of this life, as well as the power of laughter. I love you both, oodles, and boodles. And thank you, to the rest of my devoting family. You guys are my *raison de vivre* and my artistic inspiration. I can't thank you guys enough for reading my manuscript when it was in its baby stages and still finding faith in it. I am beyond lucky for the family I was born into. Thank you to Lindsay and Maureen, you guys were also major helping hands in crafting this story into what it is today. And lastly, thank you to all my friends. You know who you are. I am overjoyed day in and day out that I get to behold such amazing friendships. You have all fervently supported me in all my highs and in all my lows and it's because of you guys, I am filled with such immense peace and joy. Never stop being yourselves. I have collected the most amazing human-beings along the way, and I wouldn't trade those friendships for the universe. Thank you all so much. I am filled with so much gratitude and so much love.

p.s. thank you to the late Charles Bukowski whom Cutty B. Sands is greatly inspired by. Your angst against the world was never healed but your poetry has left many heard, and for that I hope you're resting xxx.

"An intellectual says a simple thing in a hard way. An artist says a hard thing in a simple way."
- Charles Bukowski, *Notes of a Dirty Old Man* (1969)

I muttered to myself, "can the whole world be one person?"

The gas station cashier glanced up from his stool. "Is that Cutty B. Sands? Who you're quoting?"

Startled, I looked over to him. "…what?"

He nodded. "Yeah. I believe it is."

"How do you know that?" I asked. It's not as if I was quoting a line from Forrest Gump.

--

What follows, is a recollection of my memories, me, Nathan Whitlock, age 42, and how the trajectory of what is about to unfold, makes this minor gas station interaction so significant in my life.

Chapter One: the first meeting
Date: June 13th, 2016

You'll have to forgive me. I have a long history of telling cashiers my business, eating uninspiring food, and expressing how I feel using a string of vague metaphors. In fact, that's exactly how *this* story begins.

--

To avoid becoming a cliché, suicide was ill-advised. "Lonely alcoholic kills himself." That's a story nobody reads. Death by natural causes however… "Mysterious man is struck to death by Sacramento's failure to keep the city safe from falling lights." *That's* a story that would sell.

This was the very reason I was standing under a streetlight at 8:05 on a Monday morning; in hopes it would come crashing down onto my head and end the impending doom that would be the rest of my day. Sobriety. It's a fun one.

I was walking home from an early AA meeting. Sobriety had manifested itself into insomnia which was quite the alternative for a man who had slept through his mother's funeral.

But because I was awake and unfortunately still alive, I was desperately attempting to light my cigarette against the irritating wind that found humor in sending briefcases flying, toupees peeling off, and skirts airborne, revealing the lack of underwear worn in this city.

I sighed, tossed the cigarette, and stood under the streetlight another minute or so, for good measure. But when the universe decided that it wanted to torture me another day, I continued my downhearted stroll.

"Maybe tomorrow?" I yearned.

And that's when I stumbled across a little gas station on the corner of Alfalfa Plant Rd. and Brunk Rd. painted a dull yellow. I wasn't one to particularly be interested in small stores nor the color yellow, but there did happen to be something that caught my attention.

"$2 cof e and don ts"

Even in my worn-down, cynic state of mind, I could rejoice at the idea of cheap coffee and donuts. As someone with unnurtured tastebuds and no concept for cuisine, this was a pipedream.

I greeted the cashier. He was a burly man with a wicked five o'clock shadow. One that alluded to his lack of a romantic life. He greeted me back with an empathetic look on his face. Touché.

Slightly humbled, I carried on to the task at hand: bland gas station food.

And that's when I met Luna Elrod.

A pair of very nice-looking legs adorned in fishnet tights and black boots were sticking out of the refrigerator doors. The legs were desperately trying to reach something in the back of the fridge, given they were climbing the shelves. I kept watching as I poured milk into my coffee (I drink my coffee black).

After somewhat of a struggle, long, crimped, blonde hair slightly tucked into a fur coat appeared triumphantly holding a can of root beer.

It wasn't your typical gas station outfit.

In fact, no one should be wearing a fur coat over a light pink slip dress during a California summer.

And then she turned around.

Hot coffee overflowed my mug and poured down my hand.

She was uncomfortably attractive. She was the kind of attractive that made you feel slightly perverted just for looking at her. Her face alone gave you regrettable thoughts. It made you question your morality, made you unwise. Like you wanted to tell her to put more clothes on when she was wearing a winter jacket, like you wanted to tell her to cover up, as if it was her fault how she made you feel.

I felt intoxicated watching her, as if someone had taken me against my will and poured all the liquor in the store down my throat. I felt entirely-

"Can I help you?" she asked, clearly uncomfortable by my loss of social awareness.

"Oh, uh-, no... sorry, I just came for the donuts," I responded in a taken-aback stammer, coffee spilled all over the countertop, running down to the ground.

"Is that who you came for?" she asked, pointing at my genitalia.

"What?!" I looked down and grabbed hold of my crotch that was now covered in coffee.

"I'm kidding," she said, grabbing a donut, "they aren't *that* good."

And then I stood frozen in deep fear and attraction, gripping onto my pant zipper as she walked past me, purchased her donuts and root beer, and then left.

Chapter Two: routines are a required regiment.
Date: June 13th, 2016

You are allowed sixty minutes to wander. After said hour, you are officially either regrettably in debt or clinically disoriented. There are far too many self-proclaimed "wanderers" in this state and after a certain point, one must accept the fact that they are indeed, lost.

After an AA meeting, I allotted myself one hour to saunter like a lost hippie before it was time to order a black coffee and get my shit back on track (in both ways). When it comes to sobriety, routine is necessary. If I didn't do the same mantras every day, I'd find the time to think, and when I found the time to think, I'd find the time to drink.

What my day's looked like:

Hardly sleep (involuntarily).

Attend an AA meeting at 7:00 am (somewhat voluntarily).

Wander until 9:00 am (voluntarily).

Black coffee and dry nourishment (extremely voluntarily).

Head home and turn on my favorite album, *The Psychedelic Sounds of the 13th Floor Elevators*. Start at-home rituals to the beat of the drum. Lead into afternoon rituals. End on the night's rituals.

Repeat.

Some would consider that obsessive compulsive disorder. I however considered it sobriety as homicide: a never-ending demise.

So, on this day when I wandered into the trap of a beautiful diversion at that peculiar gas station, I had to then carry on with myself as if it was a normal regular day. Because it was, of course.

Cue The Psychedelic Sounds of the 13th Floor Elevators

Track one: You're Gonna Miss Me.

The track that set off the regimen for the day.

Each day begun with one quick peek at myself in the mirror (today also required a pant change). Nothing crazy, just long enough to make sure I was still there. I was no tragedy; a tall, white man with a healthy abundance of tangled brown hair. It wasn't a bother to look at myself, but I could have done without the added sober weight and disheveled undertones.

Brush my teeth. Eat burnt toast. Brush my teeth again.

Track two: Roller Coaster

Coffee time (again). But unfortunately, without the habitually added brandy and complimentary joint. I had to lean all my problems strictly onto caffeine now. I turned the coffee pot on and off two times before starting the brew. Then, while the coffee was brewing, I would wash the two cups, two plates, two forks, two knives and two spoons I owned. (Try not to think about the rogue blondie).

Track three: Splash 1

Lean against the counter and drink the coffee.

(Try desperately not to think about the rogue blondie).

Track four: Reverberation

Read calendar. (Recklessly think about the rogue blondie). Plan.

Date: June 13th, 2016

GET A JOB!!!!

Side note: You've probably assumed that I'm poor. Well, regrettably for the image you've painted in your head, I am not. My apologies for bursting your stereotyping bubble. When my mother passed away, she left me with a vast amount of trauma and an even larger amount of cash. I have never fully been aware of how my mother acquired so much money, expensive jewelry, and iconic, eclectic rock paraphernalia, but regardless, I could have lived the rest of my life not working a single day.

But since becoming sober, you quickly realize that boredom is *not* your friend.

And as a guy with very little talent and even less of an interest in hobbies, my top priority for the day was finding a very time-consuming distraction.

(And try desperately not to think about the rogue blondie).

Track five: Don't Fall Down

Fifteen jumping jacks. Ten crunches. Five pushups. Repeat twice. Grip onto the sink in agony.

Track six: Fire Engine

Smoke a cigarette in the shower. Deodorant. Get dressed.
One last cup of coffee. One last cigarette.

The album reached its end at 11:27am every day. This was a sullen reminder that there was an outside world that needed to be had. One that was not quite as predictable as my morning routine.

I grabbed my wallet, tied, and retied my shoes twice, wiped them on the doormat two times, knocked on the wall once, and then once again, and then left to find a job. But not before checking if the door was locked twice.

The world felt more controllable this way.

I began my unconfident amble to find a job, when I realized suddenly, I had forgotten a very important part of the plan: I was entirely unaware of *how* to get a job. I had planned which side of the street to walk on, and which lunch spot had the dimmest lighting, but I had failed to plan what the destination was. Or what to do once at said destination.

This is shameful to admit, but I've already confessed to my wealth and to my addiction tendencies, so what's one more… I had never worked before. Granted, I'd pulled together a string of random operations throughout my life, such as writing book reports for the kids in my class, or selling my mother's Adderall, but I had never worked an actual job.

I never had to.

Instead, I spent most of my time getting various degrees.

And drinking.

I assumed jobs were just like puppies that you could pick up on a rogue sidewalk outside a bodega. But considering my legs were now twitching and turning like nervous schoolboys, I realized this was, in fact, not the case.

This isn't the roaring twenties. Where the hell do you even go to find a job?

Look at you? You think you would be hirable anyway?
You couldn't find a job if it hit you in the face.

Uh oh. This is what I called relapsing foreplay. And it all started with some good, ole, dirty talk.

What's going to happen if something goes haywire, Nathan? Do you think you'll be able to handle all that pressure?

And what are you going to do if they do hire you? It's not like you have any experience or skills in anything.

It had also just occurred to me that it was the anniversary of my mother's death. This was the justification portion of foreplay. If mourning the loss of my dead, inebriated, tumultuous mother were the qualifications for allowing myself a drink… consider me anguished.

And then the longing, pulsating thirst that only a cold, frothy beer could quench, arrived. The erection portion of foreplay.

Being seven months sober doesn't make much of a difference when you've been seduced and led into the bedroom by the sensual hands of dependency.

I pulled out my phone to google maps a nearby bar (as if I didn't know where every bar within the ten-mile radius of my neighborhood was on its exact coordinates). Perhaps the absolute lousiness of the app might guide me to a Catholic Church, and I'd be forced to repent my sins instead of relapse.

Nonetheless, there I stood. Anxious. Seduced. And google mapping a nearby bar.

Classic.

I arrived at the *The Little Shack* in fifteen minutes after standing under a couple of streetlights. I opened the door to the bar with far too much confidence and groove that I thought to myself, *hey, maybe they could hire me here?* I certainly knew how to pour a drink.

I approached the bartender. "I'll take whatever's on tap, thanks, oh, and are you guys hiring?"

The bartender shook his head, rolled his eyes, and turned to pour my beer.

"Bummer," I muttered, looking around to see if I could catch anyone in AA slipping up.

The bartender handed me my drink.

And right on cue, just as I was moments away from a delicious embrace, a strong Mongolian accent shook the shack. "Nathan!"

"Shit."

And now would be a good segue to talk about my AA group.

My AA people were an acquired taste. But you should know, they were all I had.

Elizabeth was a fifty-eight-year-old fast-fashion enthusiast. She couldn't quite grasp the concept of child labor laws and she found joy in murder podcasts (her hobbies were morally questionable). Elizabeth also used to drink herself into oblivion during her kids' dance recitals, resulting in her joining the five-year-old ballerinas on stage. The PTA moms eventually had enough and rallied outside the school with signs that said, "Mother's Against Elizabeth's Drinking!!!" I'd personally suggest going about an intervention in other ways... but then again, what do I know.

Mateo was a seventy-four-year-old Veteran who served during the Vietnam War. Mateo was visually a flabby mess. He had ridiculously giant knuckles and a large amount of elbow fat. Mateo suffered PTSD from the war. He had violent nightmares and a toxic relationship with knives (which are difficult to avoid if you like to eat, and men like Mateo certainly like to eat). He once had a full breakdown outside a William-Sonoma's because he said the knives were calling him slurs. Said they had a bad temper. After that he could no longer walk on the same side of the street as a kitchen store (which is debilitating if your wife likes to shop). Mateo drank because it was the only thing that could subside the hallucinations. He drank because it was the only thing that would help him fall asleep. But then his drinking became just as violent as his PTSD.

Daniel was a fifty-one-year-old construction worker. He was very passionate about the earth being flat and proving that we never went to the moon. Daniel switched his addiction to conspiracy theories and the entire group was collectively trying to get him to start drinking again.

Sofia was a very attractive Hispanic woman. She was forty-five but didn't look a day over thirty. Especially with the fake tits her seventy-five-year-old fiancé bought her. Most of the group wanted to sleep with her (this included Elizabeth). Sofia started drinking when she first miscarried. She started drinking even more after her second miscarriage. And even more after she was told that she biologically could not have children. And then when her husband left her for a younger, more fertile woman, she couldn't stop. Until her current fiancé sent her to Ocean Hills Recovery (did I mention his age?).

Max was my personal favorite (to pick on). Nobody knew his age because it changed all the time. He had diabolical bleach blonde hair and looked like a regular at Glo Station Tanning. He was a member of some sad, unnatural, garage band that refused to play anything other than Nirvana covers. The days I felt like relapsing the most were the days he forced his band to perform for us. He claimed that he was a "rolling stone who was poisoned with elation for the flask." In my words, he was a punk kid who had one thing promised for him, and that was skin cancer. I was also not entirely convinced he even had a drinking problem. Or knew what the word 'elation' meant.

Xavier was a forty-two-year-old pharmacist. His job was so stressful and the massive student debt he was in sent him into a very passionate and very intense affair with Vodka Red Bulls. You couldn't help but feel bad for the guy. All he wanted to do was help people, but he couldn't even help himself.

Landon was the AA Chairperson. The director of meetings. He was practically our Jesus, in fact, he looked like Jesus. He got sober at a Buddhist temple in Southern Thailand which was unfortunate for us because he was always trying to align our chakras and encourage us to do things, like, tell the truth, and use excessive details in our stories. He also strongly believed that opening our third eye would be the ultimate, all-longing, universal orgasm. Whatever that meant, but I didn't think I wanted to experience it with him.

And then there was Strong Jim. My best friend. Jim was an intense Mongolian man with the physique of a mountain lion. He had dark slick hair that sat like a perched peregrine-falcon that had just given birth to his oddly ovular shaped head. He was alarmingly loud and loved sweet treats. But mostly, he was my best friend.

(Don't worry, you won't have to strain yourself to remember all these names. I will remind you with context clues. Such as, Mateo, the one with the elbow fat).

So, as I was saying, right on cue, as the bartender handed me my cold, frothy beer, the door swung open and a strong Mongolian accent roared, "Nathan!"

"Shit." I put down the beer.

"What the hell are you doing?" he asked.

My eyes darted around the room. "Obviously? I'm applying for a job."

"Where? At a rehab facility? Because that's where you're going if you take a sip of that."

I groaned. "Cock block."

He reached in his pocket and pulled out a twenty-dollar bill, placing it on the bar top. "Let's get out of here. The beer sucks anyway."

I met Jim about three or four years before this. Although, when you've spent the last ten years of your life drunk, it's hard to decipher timelines.

I was sitting at *The Little Shack* by myself, ordering the strongest drinks on the menu. Round after round. The band *Rush* was playing on the stereo and anytime *Rush* comes on you are required to order another drink. My mother's orders. Neil Peart was just getting into it on the drums when this ginormous man encroached upon me.

What is this strange man doing? I thought. Of course, I didn't think much at the time. And when I did, it was in bad taste. Your vocabulary and tongue muscles go away when you drink, which is why Landon encourages us to use exhaustive details in our storytelling (this being unfortunate for you).

And then, out of all the open spots available in the pub, this mountain of a man sits down on the stool right next to mine. "I'll take any Craft Non-Alcoholic Beer you guys got," he ordered.

"Are you allergic to a good time or something?" I asked.

He slowly turned his massive neck muscles to face me. "Yes."

"Well, that's a mood killer," I responded.

"You look drunk," he said.

"Good," I said, "because I am."

"Are you always this drunk?" he asked.

"What's it to you, non-alcoholic, giant man?" I responded.

He didn't say anything after that. Instead, he turned the rest of his body to face mine and slowly sipped on his non-alcoholic beer for the rest of the night. Observing me. I had nothing more to say either considering my tongue was thick enough to hang at the dry cleaners. So, I did nothing to stop him.

After that, for weeks, he came to the bar and sat next to me. He would just sit, sip, and watch.

"Do you not have cable?" I asked once.

No answer. I hadn't cared to continue the conversation because I hadn't cared about anything.

Until one night when he said, "you should come to a meeting with me."

I glanced his direction. "Like... a sex thing?"

"No."

"Then what kind of meeting?" I asked.

"Alcoholics Anonymous meeting."

"Wait a minute," I put my drink down, "you're an alcoholic? Then why the hell are you always in a bar?"

"Do you want the long story or the short?" he asked.

"Preferably neither-"

"Okay," he said, "I'll give you the long story."

Jim's daughter died from cancer when she was six years old. His wife couldn't get out of bed for months, their home was filled with the faint smell of plastic toys and spilled apple juice, and people kept bringing over their sympathetic homemade recipes. There wasn't anywhere he could go that didn't remind him of her, especially his home. Until one day when Jim stumbled across *The Little Shack*.

A bar was the one place that didn't prompt him to think about the loss of his precious girl. It was the one place people couldn't find him to bring their casseroles and their condolences.

Maybe his pain wouldn't exist if no one else around him knew about it.

So, every day, day and night, Jim just sat at the bar and drank. He drank until beer could no longer be an acceptable coping mechanism and his wife now had to worry about losing another family member. The only issue, however, was that it took him years to get clean because he couldn't find anywhere to go that didn't make him think about his daughter. And thinking about her made it hard to stay sober.

But one-day, ironically enough, he realized, the only place he could go that didn't make him think about his daughter, was the *The Little Shack*. The bar was the only place that didn't make him want to drink.

And this is how the non-alcoholic beer came to be.

It took Strong Jim awhile to convince me to go to a meeting. I didn't believe I had a problem. I thought a drinking issue was like an STI, in the way where it would eventually go away. Rather, it's much more like an STD.

Finally, one day, Jim said if I went with him to ONE meeting and I absolutely hated it, then he would personally buy me a round of beers. I was sold.

We went on a Tuesday morning, at 7:00 am. I had yet to go to bed. Landon was shamelessly far too eager to accept me. I had the normal rundown; introductions, ostentatious detail about getting sober, yada yada… I was completely checked out, nodding my way through until I could get the free round of beers.

But then Xavier (sad pharmacist) spoke. "I had a good friend tell me once, he said, Xavier, addiction is a disease. It's a noose with a slow grip and killing yourself for all to watch is a vicious act."

I hadn't realized I had been tying my own noose.

So, is it possible I found myself at *The Little Shack* because I knew there was a substantial chance that Strong Jim would be there to stop me? Well, perhaps I'm not as foolish as one would expect.

Chapter Three: a brief interlude
(Primitive childhood memories)

Now, to whet your appetite, because I am sure you're just dying to know who I am, Nathan Whitlock, telling this strange, depressing story that certainly started off invigorating about a girl in a fur coat, we must go back to where it all began. Childhood memories.

--

My mother, Cathy, had me when she was seventeen. My father is unknown. Cathy had a wide assortment of men under her belt, and she claimed all sorts of stories like, having a threesome with Mick Jagger and Lori Lightning one "hot, steamy, summer in the Cayman Islands," or "making out with Robert Plant behind an In-N-Out." Needless, it is arguable that I am the spawn of the world's greatest rockstar (but given my stocky build and lack of talent, I highly doubt it). It's more likely I come from a roadie. Or an innocent sound technician. Or perhaps, just a lonely night with a bottle of Sauvignon Blanc and an unoccupied phone line.

The day I was born she asked the obstetrician where the nearest fire-station was, to which a mortified surgeon called security on her. "Nobody has a sense of humor anymore," she said as they rolled her down to get questioned by CPS.

Fast forward to when I was eight and old enough to understand the concept of a womb. Cathy informed me over pancakes and oats that she had originally planned to abort me, but her religious and formidable father made sure that did not happen. Cathy was a riveting storyteller and I always found myself enthralled to find out more.

"What happened?" I asked, on the edge of my seat.

"He locked me in my room and threw away my car keys to prevent me from making it to the clinic," she answered, sipping her Pisco sour.

"Bummer," I responded.

"Truly."

She was equally as glamorous as she was insane. She had exquisite taste in books, music, and fashion, but opposingly so when it came to things like interior design or... lifestyle.

The nights when she wasn't passed out drunk, she would read to me *The Old Man and The Sea* by Ernest Hemingway. She would hold my hand as she read, and I would wonder if this moment would last forever or only for the next few hours.

"I want to be just like Hemingway when I grow up," I would say.

"No, you don't, honey-love."

"Why? He was extraordinary."

"That's because he was in a tremendous amount of pain, honey-love," she would say, "most extraordinary people are."

A gentleman approached us once at the grocery store and inquired if we studied the bible. "Honey-love, praying isn't going to make you any less gay," my mother said to the man before turning to me and saying, "if you ever want to experience the touch of a man, all you need is a little lube and a consenting partner. No hell flames involved. Unless you become a pyro, of course."

I was ten.

Then when I was a little older, sixth grade if I recall correctly, I had a tummy ache. She took me to a back alley behind a Walgreens where she met with some strange looking character and then handed me some suspicious looking gummy that tasted much like bitter grass. The next day, traumatized, I asked her why she didn't just get me Pepto Bismol, we were right by a Walgreens anyway. "It's always better to go the natural route, honey-love," she said, "remember that."

I nodded mournfully, thinking that was a bit of advice I'd rather forget.

And when I was eighteen, grappling with my own sobriety, and delivering the valedictorian speech, she stumbled up on stage drunk, grabbed the microphone from me, and said to the audience, "love is the glue that will tie us all together, but Principal Dan is the man who will tie me up later!"

After that, I never told her about the rest of my education.

It was an odd juxtaposition, her as a mother. She was so beautiful, and so full of adventure. Her contagious energy had a gravitational pull, one that outweighed the laws of human nature. But she was also a mother. My mother. And that was a role she never quite wanted to fulfill.

Half mom. Half friend. Half there. Half gone.

And when she could never be a full piece of anything, I started to resent her.

Somewhere around the age of thirteen or fourteen, I arrived home from school to find Cathy in her favorite position: comatose on her adored green plush sofa, a bottle of Grey Goose loose at her fingertips. *The Psychedelic Sounds of the 13th Floor Elevators* filled the apartment with "waves of eccentricity," as she would call it.

I never knew if she was going to wake up and make me a grilled cheese or if I would have to call 911 again. When most kids were learning how to tie their shoes, I was learning how to find a pulse.

On this day, when I came home to find her in her natural habitat, I sauntered over to check her wrist, dropping my backpack down on the floor before kneeling. Even on the days I called 911, I always found a pulse. So, I wasn't worried. It had become second nature at this point. A routine such as brushing one's teeth.

But this time, there was nothing.

No beat.

I checked her neck. Nothing. Her other wrist. Nothing. I put my head to her chest hoping to feel a rhythm. Nothing.

The only sound penetrating the living room was the voice of Roky Erickson.

I dug around the couch to try and find her flip phone, but it was nowhere to be found. I ran over to the kitchen and grabbed the jungle-green wall telephone, but it had been disconnected.

I had experienced fear before, but nothing to this extent. I wanted to grab her and shake her back to consciousness. I wanted to cry and rip my hair out. I wanted to run down to the police station and scream for help. I wanted to pick up her limp body and drag her down the block screaming.

But instinct must be hereditary because instead, I grabbed the bottle of vodka and I chugged.

And then I sat down on the orange and pink retro carpet (that my mother swore by, said it could cure cancer) and I drank more.

I drank until *The Psychedelic Sounds of the 13th Floor Elevators* turned into my mother's heartbeat. As the turntable scratched on, so did my mother's bloodstream. If the music was alive, so was my mother. That's what the vodka told me. That's what the vodka *assured* me.

They were Cathy's favorite group, and in that moment, they became mine. My mind felt at ease with the combination of their tunes and the vodka. I was alleviated. I now knew that there was a way to numb any pain. To ease any fears and anxieties. No matter what happened, I now knew that there was a way I could handle life.

And then my mother woke up.

And made me a grilled cheese.

She never wanted to die.

She loved life more than anyone I knew.

Not a sober one. Or one with responsibilities. But her idea of a life. The one she selfishly created on her own.

She wanted to drink expensive red wine, fuck anything that could hold a guitar, listen to as many records as she could. She wanted to spin in circles around our 70's styled apartment, under the disco ball she hung in the living room. She wanted to dance like the strobe lights that flashed shades of green and purple in the dining room. She wanted to strut around in Dolce Gabbana gold strappy heels and Vanessa Mooney corset rompers. She wanted to entertain, not only men, but the moon and the stars.

I wanted to hate her. It would've been easier to hate her.

When various men came in and out of the apartment like it was a cheap motel. When she was so drunk, she couldn't remember the lyrics to *Strawberry Fields Forever*. When she swam naked in pools after snorting white powder off keys. When I had to wear headsets around the house because uncanny people played their instruments too loud past my bedtime. When I feared that she may leave me before I knew how to turn on a stove and make my own grilled cheese.

Yeah, it would've been easier to hate her.

But how could I? When her laughter filled the house with exuberant, vibrant energy that could only be felt and not explained. When she would grab me by the arms and spin me around, dancing with me until I fell to the ground in sheer joy. Or when she read every single book to me in our public library, so she found a way to get access to the next town's library. Just to keep reading something new.

It was hard to hate her when she could make you feel like the world existed strictly for enjoyment.

So, when alcohol finally rid her of her beauty, and her joy, and her excitement for the world. And when her electrifying parts were no longer there to pull its weight.

I could finally just hate her.

Her death was not nearly as glamorous or dramatic as her life was. She was forty-seven and died from alcohol poisoning on a Tuesday at 3:03 pm. She didn't quite make it to happy hour that day.

I got the call an hour after she was found. The only thing that bothered me was that I had nobody to tell.

I walked to the liquor store and told the clerk, "My mother died today."

He responded, "I'm sorry, Pal. I just want to let you know though; we have a special today. Half off Miller."

"Nobody likes Miller," I said.

"I know, that's why it's half off."

"Okay."

I bought three cases of Miller.

Cathy's mother died before she was old enough to walk, leaving her to be raised by her father. He was an English professor who fell into the commanding idioms of the bible, believing life was meant to be a prophecy of suffering. Cathy inherited the love for literature and rebelled lustfully against the rest. Not long after she popped me out, ran away with a newborn baby, a bottle of her father's Heritage Cognac, and a middle finger that couldn't have been stopped with a chainsaw, her sinful ways sent her father in cardiac arrest before the endearing age of fifty-two.

So, when she followed in her fathers' departed footsteps and died before a decent age, she left me, completely and utterly:

Alone.

I was thirty, single, drunk and had enough money to bury myself with when she died. Thanks to whatever illicit behavior sent my mother into riches.

Physically, I started to replace her. I'd wake up mornings not remembering how I got home or what I had done that night. I'd check my phone just to see what day of the week it was. Sometimes I'd wake up with more than one person in my bed. Strippers, prostitutes, bar tenders. One time I woke up face down on the ground because there was a morbidly obese woman and a heroin addict named Sara in my bed (I still have no explanation for that one. But I'd like to think I wasn't involved). Other times I'd wake up in a park, or the back of a bar, or in a museum storage closet next to a naked woman.

My routines were *slightly* different during this time. I'd wake up, crack open a beer to subside the headache, then I'd pour myself a glass of whisky (I figured, if it was dark enough, it had the same effects as coffee). If I woke up with a gash or cut (which was not unusual) I'd pour vodka on the wound and then dip my bloody fingers in the bottle to clean my hands.

I didn't do laundry or dishes. I hardly ever bathed myself. I'd fall asleep in my clothes and shoes, and in the morning, I would take a Lysol Lemon All-Purpose bottle and spray myself, then I would take the bar of soap from my sink and wash my pits and privates. If a glass plate was dirty, I would throw it out until I had no plates left and was forced to use the countertop as a dish.

But the thing was, I was going to bars that smelt like sandalwood and butterscotch. Bars that had holes in the walls from neon signs that had fallen. Tiffany-stained glass lamps hung from the ceilings and deep burgundy stools lined up against the dark walnut wood bar-tops. They were small with warm aromas. They were the type of bars that had special beer on tap. The type of places that gave their ciders names only small businesses would take the time to create, such as "Sunday Smiles," or "Happiness Prescription." *The Little Shack* even had a non-alcoholic beer named after Strong Jim.

They were places you felt safe. Places you felt snug.

You couldn't become an alcoholic in places like that?

31

And besides, I was just grieving, right?

I was going to get it together soon. I just needed time. Right?

And that's the thing about alcohol. She's a siren. She knows how to lure you to her and once you fall in love, nothing else matters. It doesn't matter if she makes us sloppy, or nauseous, or inarticulate. It doesn't matter if she makes us angry, or dumb, or foolish.

Because she knows how to trick us into thinking that she's all pleasure.

In the moment we think, *it can't get any better than this.*

She sings her sweet lullaby and plants her pretty little trickery onto anyone who shows faint signs of vulnerability. She gives us a companion. She makes us feel good, warm, confident, and alive. She strokes our egos until we become dependent. She sings and sings that lullaby until we can't physically live without her. Until she becomes our beautiful little ritual.

And *boom*, that's when she owns us.

When you're drunk, it feels thrilling to cross a line. To make a choice that might be a mistake. The idea of danger used to be something that exhilarated me. But the more you drink, the more you continue to cross that black line. And the more you keep crossing, the more that line starts to get grayer and grayer.

And then one day you look around, and you realize, you've been entirely swallowed by the gray.

Drinking only on weekends? Okay.

Drinking only at night on the weekdays? Okay.

Drinking during the day only on Fridays? Okay.

Drinking during the day if no drugs are involved? Okay.

Drugs involved? Okay.

Drinking. Drugs. And having intercourse with married Pilates moms? Okay.

Drinking. Drugs. Having sex with a Pilates mom and stealing a wing off the Archivaldo Monumental statue outside the mayor's office? Okay. (I still have that, by the way).

It feels euphoric at first. The pain doesn't exist anymore. You don't abide by the rules that make you suffer.

But euphoria doesn't last forever. That kind of thrill only pursues if you can feel fear. And when you no longer feel fear, there is no longer fleeting morphine that comes with rejecting the mundane nonsense of it all.

And so perhaps, you start to miss the black line.

But by that point, it's too late.

The black line is long gone.

When you're an addict, the grounds of logic do not apply. Facts will very well register within us. "Drinking doesn't solve your problems," "drinking will destroy you," "drinking every day of the week makes you an alcoholic."

But the truth is, logic will not soothe us.

And an addict must be soothed.

So once again, the siren sings.

--

That's why for some people, a meeting might be as simple as sitting in a chair across from others they can't stand. Or across from people that drag on pretentious, corporate bullshit. But for people like Elizabeth, Mateo, Daniel, Sofia, Max, Xavier, Jim, Landon, and me,

it's how we pull ourselves out of the siren infested waters.

Chapter Four: the tumultuous task of finding a job
Date: June 2016

I called Jim the next day and told him I needed a job. I said, if I couldn't do it with the help of beer, I needed to do it with the help of a man shaped like one (he had broad shoulders and a long neck, it was meant as a compliment). Despite his offense, he came over immediately. (Strong Jim was a professional WWE wrestler back in the day. Now he owns a wrestling gym. Needless to say, he was always available).

"What about the library?" he suggested.

"You think a library would hire me?"

"No."

"Well then why the hell would you suggest it?"

"I really do think you would like it though," he continued, "you like all that literature woo woo and silence suits you."

I nodded in agreement.

"And the books would keep you distracted. You could bring home a new book every night. You wouldn't even have time to think about drinking."

"Then why the hell would you suggest it?!" I asked again, upset that this new revelation may not unfold for me, but Jim kept teasing it anyway.

"No harm in applying," Jim said, shrugging.

I sat on that thought. When you're in recovery mode, you feel like a fish out of water (or a drunk out of liquor) running around looking for your next habitat. Maybe Shakespeare could be my next vice? I mean, could obsessing over *King Lear* ruin my life too? It seemed a much safer bet than booze.

"Maybe." I responded.

"Do you have a resume?"

"Do you?"

"Why the hell would I have a resume?"

"Why the hell would I?"

"Okay, okay," Jim put his hands up in surrender, "let's go make you one."

"How?"

"I don't know?"

We had to go to the library anyway, to create the resume (I got rid of my computer after I got clean. For reasons beyond a simple explanation. And Jim feared that his absolute incompetence when it came to technology would send him into a relapse. So, we both remained computer-less homes). Therefore, it became: two large and helpless men sitting around a small computer screen, trying to turn a template on the internet into something convincing. It was an artform, attempting to turn the aimless jobs I've had in the past into something appealing and virtuous.

"What can I say for drug dealer? *Distributor of valuable merchandise?*"

Jim smacked his head. "How do you have eighteen different degrees and no valuable work experience?"

I shrugged. "Because I spent all my time getting eighteen different degrees."

"Who do you have as a reference?"

I looked at Jim as if he had just told me my mother walked in.

"A reference." He said again.

"As in…"

"As in who they can call to make sure you're not a pervert or a thief! Jeez."

I shrugged again.

Jim sighed.

"Can I put you down?"

He shook his head. "No. I know you are both a pervert and a thief."

"Shoot."

"Put Landon's number down. He doesn't know how to speak ill on the behalf of others."

"Oh. Great idea," I said.

A couple minutes (hours) later, we printed the final product and held it up in the air.

"Ta-da!" Jim said, smiling ear to ear.

"Wow," I said, "this may just be the most motivational and simultaneously unethical day of our lives."

Jim shrugged. "A little light fraud never hurt anybody."

I smiled. "We did it, Jim. After all that hard work, we did it."

"Well congratulations, you were able to convince a piece of paper that you're employable. Now you have to convince her," Jim pointed at the woman in the corner whose nametag said *Librarian*.

I took a deep breath. This was going to be quite difficult.

"You're hired."

"What?"

"You're hired." The Librarian whose name was Susan said, "you have a PhD in literature, I'm not even sure why you are applying for this part-time job."

"But you don't even know me? I could be a criminal."

"We need all the help we can get."

"But are you sure? You haven't even called my reference."

Susan gave me a strange look. "Hey pal, aren't you the one asking to be hired?"

"Well-"

"Okay, who's this?" Susan pointed to Jim.

"That's Jim," I said.

"Okay Jim," Susan said, "is this man somebody you would recommend for hire?"

Jim shook his head. "No."

"Okay," Susan said, "when can you start?"

"Um."

"How about right now?"

I looked nervously at Jim who was giving me two big thumbs up.

"Brilliant," she smiled, "then let's get you started."

Susan grabbed me by the arm and started pulling me to the non-fiction section, explaining the lack of intelligence that goes on in that corner and my new duties. Jim sauntered off into the abyss, leaving me to fend for myself in the wooden establishment that was filled with what *hopefully* would be my next vice.

Chapter Five: the alcoholic gets a job
Date: June 2016

My part-time job quickly turned into a full-time (please let me work as much as possible) job. The less time I spent alone in my apartment, the better. For the obvious reasons, and because, quite frankly, my apartment could've been used in an ad for an anti-depressant drug.

Light gray walls are sensible for a single man like me in his thirties, but quickly become dismal once you add in the matching gray furniture, gray rug, gray couch, and gray pillows. I had assumed, if everything was the same color, it went together. Clearly, I have no indication behind the mindset of an interior designer. But I suppose I had a previous lust in my eyes for anything that could cause a serious sense of misery.

The real star of the joyless one-bedroom home, however, were the psychedelic rock posters that hung carelessly around the walls, begging to be ripped down and burned because they couldn't fathom the embarrassment of being seen in anyone's room besides a coming-of-age teen boy with a sparkle in his eye and a chick at his hip. Neither of which, were seen in this house.

A large stereo system kept the noise in the exterior of my apartment rather than the interior of my mind. I'm sure my neighbors understood that.

And to make matters worse, a large (stolen) wing from the Archivaldo took up so much space it made my living room look like a closet. It was hard to walk around without the threat of getting stabbed by metal feathers, but there was something that kept it from flying away.

My fridge worked hard at keeping microwavable meals, off-brand soda, plain hummus (not even the kind with creamy tahini in the middle), carrots and yogurt cold. The pantry was stocked with Oreos (on brand), white bread, classic potato chips (off brand) and Bugles (on brand). And I had two cups, two plates, two forks, two spoons and two knives.

Like I said, it could've been used in an ad for Lexapro.

But I couldn't change anything. Any alterations could have thrown off my routine. So, I didn't dare risk it. Besides, I didn't mind waking up to Jimi Hendrix on my wall every morning. At least I had someone to share my coffee with.

And it didn't matter now that I was hardly there anymore.

My mornings as an employed, sophisticated man, now looked like this:

cue *The Psychedelic Sounds of the 13th Floor Elevators.*

Track one: You're Gonna Miss Me.

Black coffee. Jumping Jacks. Crunches. Pushups. Cold shower.

Track two: Roller Coaster

Brush teeth. Bagel with cream cheese. Brush teeth.

Track three: Splash 1

Comb hair. Get dressed. More black coffee.

Track four: Reverberation

Scheduled mind-wandering time.

Track five: Don't Fall Down

Check to see if there's any black coffee left in the pot. Make more.

Track six: Fire Engine

Grab my wallet. Tie, and retie my shoes two times. Wipe them on the doormat twice. Knock on the side of the wall once, and then once again, and then leave my apartment. But not before making sure to check if the door was locked twice.

This schedule and my sobriety were a dire combination. It was a symbiotic relationship. And working helped give me some purpose to want to continue it.

I was like a busboy, but for literature. I organized the books, put away any strays, handled the returns, helped with checking out if needed, and cleaned the shelves.

Every now and then, I'd come across a book that I read as a kid with my mother. I tried not to think about her, but it was hard not too when reading was the main connection we had (besides alcoholism). I was doing as Jim suggested and taking home a new book every night. I spent so much time reading and working that I was succeeding in having very little time to have thoughts of my own. This was a major advantage when it came to prospering in my sobriety. I read almost every book in that entire library. Susan was right, the non-fiction section was mediocre, at best.

Speaking of Susan, we were becoming quite good friends actually. However, I lack confidence in that statement as I never really had female friends before (outside of my AA girls. But they were required to be my friends).

Susan gave off intense widow vibes. She was vastly unattractive and not afraid of indulging in a solid carb or two. And she must've been in her early to late fifties given her refusal to admit that she was a lesbian.

Susan had no taste for fashion and a fear of life. You could tell by the way she held herself up in the library that it was the only place she could escape the modern-day tragedy she probably called a Saturday night. Susan was the kind of woman who made a meatloaf on a Tuesday evening and called it spontaneous. Susan was the kind of person who would kiss her female "roommate" on the lips after the "roommate" brought her forgotten Tuna sandwich and then get upset when you referred to said "roommate" as her "girlfriend."

She was limited in her mannerisms, using the same few phrases, such as, "boy, that'll be a story for later," regarding nothing of interest, or "a papercut is literature infecting your veins," regarding me not being able to hold a book without mishap. She was predictable, tedious, and had a horrible haircut (that makes two of us). But she was cool.

Okay she wasn't cool. But I liked her.

She was nothing you ever aspired to be, yet, simultaneously, she was probably happier than you. A mere juxtaposition between uninteresting and joy. She was the kind of person who was so entirely authentic that you would never desire to be her. You saw her fears, and her inner dialogue, and the mustard on her sweater. You saw her guilt-less gluttony. You saw her hole up in the corner reading a book on a Friday night.

But what'd you fail to see was that Susan had no problem being Susan. And Susan didn't try to become a mass production of human likeability seeking approval from the outside world.

And that was probably something that equated to happiness.

I don't know why Susan took it upon herself to take me under her wing. Maybe it was because she thought my constant shaking and unexplainable sweat outbreaks were because I was nervous. Maybe because she saw the way I counted the books over and over again. Or maybe it was because I was always asking to pick up extra shifts. Either way, Susan took a liking to me. And either way, I was okay with it.

"I've never had such a boring job before," I said once.

"I won't take offense to that," she responded.

I didn't know how to explain to her that what I had meant was, 'drinking happened to consume most of my life, even as a teenager, so I never got to experience the mundane ways of being an employed kid with something to prove.' So, I didn't respond. And we continued working on in silence.

That might've been why we got along so well. Because Susan never took what I said seriously or got offended by my ignorance. And most of the things that came out of my mouth never did seem to say what I meant. So, we both just carried on.

She told me about the time she saw Cher in a grocery store but was too scared to say hello, so she hid behind the cereal aisle and watched her from behind the cracks. I told her about the time my mom didn't pick me up from school, so I went to a sports bar down the road and ordered a beer at the age of fourteen. We both told each other many things. But I never told her I was an alcoholic. And she never told me she was a lesbian.

I guess there are certain things people seem to be ashamed of. For no reason at all.

Outside of my working life, Strong Jim came over every Sunday for football reruns. He always brought two large pizzas and a pitcher of root beer. We called it, Sober Sunday.

"When are you gonna get rid of this shithole?" Jim asked one Sober Sunday, in between pizza bites.

"Never."

"You should start coming over to my place on Sunday's, it's too depressing here."

I threw him a roll of Oreos. "I don't want Cindy seeing how rowdy we get."

"I think my wife can handle it."

I got up to connect the TV to the stereo system. "But you don't have this," I said, motioning towards my speakers.

"But we *do* have hand soap."

I rolled my eyes.

"How's the job?" Jim asked, ripping open the roll of Oreos.

"Good, actually," I said, sitting back down.

"You can thank me for that later," he said, smirking to himself.

"And for all your help with being such a supportive reference?"

Jim held his hands up. "Look, I'm an addict, not a liar."

I laughed, shaking my head. "How is Cindy?"

"Drier than the Sahara Desert."

"Wow! Okay. That took a sharp right."

"I don't think she's attracted to me anymore since I've put on the sober weight."

"Come on Jim, that can't be true," I said, "maybe her, like, pheromones are off?"

"Do you mean hormones?"

"Hormones? Women have those too? Jeez, they're complicated."

"I know," Jim shook his head, "I don't think I'll ever figure them out."

"What are we going to do about it?" I asked.

"Well. We certainly can't drink about it."

I chuckled. "Been there, tried that."

Jim laughed. "I'm still trying to figure out the female anatomy. I'm forty-three and I'm starting to think I'll never find the sweet spot."

"Oh, I know where it is like the back of my hand."

"How?"

"My mother," I said, "at my sixteenth birthday party she had 'pin the finger on the female external genitalia' hanging on the wall and really reinforced to everyone how crucial it was we all got it right. Blindfolded and all."

Jim looked over at me, mortified. "Your mother is in hell."

--

Life was un-seemingly okay in June.

This story will also be told through Luna Elrod's Journal entries in chronological order.

Her journal was given to me, and as the ethical storyteller I am, I owe it to her to give her side of the story as well.

Because as we all know, there are always *two* sides to every story.

Luna Elrod Journal Entry
Date: June 11th, 2016
(Two days before we met)

I can fly.

I am soaring over the entire population of flightless birds.

Am I the only one who has discovered her wings?

I will walk to the edge of Mount Whitney, spread my wings, and jump. I will find a family of Blue Jays, nestle in, and eat berries and seeds. I'll find the tallest peach tree in all the land and burrow my yearning teeth into the forbidden fruit juices of the forest.

I'll soar into the arms of Christ the Redeemer and listen to tumultuous sounds of Brazil, as Rio de Janeiro fires up for the night. And then I'll find a Japanese maple bush and dance barefoot around it, protecting it from any strong winds, encouraging the growth of the shrub.

My morning croissant tastes sensational.

The salt and the butter have assorted themselves together in a way only a hopeless mixologist could dream of.

Strawberry jams lingers on my tongue. Teasing my tastebuds. My mouth can't stand to be alone. She is an elated animal ready to be seduced by her source of nourishment.

I watch my neighbor pluck up weeds and wonder what I can do to help. Where can I best provide the weeds themselves a suitable home? Does my neighbor prefer green juice or tea?

I have an insatiable appetite for the world. There is no time to sleep, no time to rest. There is too much to see, too much to watch, to hear, to taste. I must suffocate all five senses until they are paralyzed with exhaustion.

I don't remember when I last slept. Was it three days ago?
I've been busy wandering the streets of Sacramento, watching as the
streetlamps cast spells on the nearby lovers. I fly to the top of one and light
my cigarette with the flame of the night. I am a cat, prowling the empty
streets of the night as the obedient dogs of the universe lay compliant next to
their owners.

Too much to do that the other humans won't understand.
Too many places to fly.

Luna Elrod Journal Entry
Date: June 12th, 2016
(One day before we met)

Sometimes, I sit in my car, and I watch as the other cars drive by and I think, my god, this is the most beautiful thing ever. The way traffic moves in such a linear fashion, one car after the other. Someone in front of you and behind you always. You are at the constant center of the pickle jar of life, driving past a different soul, a different mind, a different beauty, of someone you may never meet. You look over, barely considering the hair color of the person right next to you. Barely even wondering what their name might be, or who their first love was, or what color makes them feel the most alive.

I look over at the person next to me at a red light and I wonder who their first kiss was, and if they liked it. I wonder if I'll ever see them again, or if maybe I already have. In a past life? In a future life? Tomorrow at the grocery store? Where are they all going? What will happen to them within the next five minutes of their life?

I look in my rearview mirror and I consider the life that exists in the four wheeled object that goes in motion directly behind me. What a beautiful thing, to get to see a world full of busy and curious people, moving at the speed of life, bumping to the sound of their own music.

What does the person in front of me like to eat on a Tuesday after work? What is their favorite movie? Are they religious? Do they have a partner? Do they prefer their coffee hot or cold? Do they have any pets?

Every day we get in the vehicle of life, and we drive past people we may never love. What would happen if I crashed into one of them? Just to say hi. I think that may be a nice gesture, but fate probably prefers to work alone.

And when you hear an ambulance? Everyone pulls over. There is nothing more beautiful than an entire society collectively working together to help someone. When you hear a noise, a simple noise, it conducts the entire orchestra. The orchestra of life, and we are the band. Extraordinary! To see everyone pull over on the side of the road due to the cue of a sound is a miraculous site to witness. There is something outrageously wonderful about watching cars move past you and getting to indulge in the riddle that each vehicle brings you.

There is something exceptional about the mystery of someone who will only be in your proximity for less than a moment.

Luna Elrod Journal Entry
Date: June 13th, 2016
(The day we met)

I must've fallen asleep, but sleep is for those who I watch over. My wings were made for flying, not resting. The sun was already rising. So was I. Not a minute to lose.

I couldn't rid my mind of the street name I walked past earlier. Alfalfa. A perennial flowering plant, used for grazing. So, shouldn't that be what one does? Graze the street of the flowering legume?

I wasn't sure what time it was, but there was none to waste. I put on the only sensible outfit I could find for the breezy weather: my beaver coat and remarkable boots. One should always dress like they are ready to walk the Met.

Once I arrived at my destination, I sat down on the curb and observed. Daises grew from the cracks in the sidewalk. I followed their trail straight to a beaming, bright yellow gas station that laid its roots on the block corner. The daises flourished right outside this extraordinary store.

Of course. This is what Alfalfa wanted me to see.

The glorious grazing of Alfalfa led me straight to a brilliant, rugged adventure.

Once inside I continued my search for greatness: pink donuts, hot coffee, bubbling soda, salt & vinegar chips galore! How wonderful.

However, amidst my grazing, I stumbled upon quite another brilliant, rugged adventure.

He was very tall. And very handsome. Although, he could have used a haircut and some caffeinated eye cream. But nonetheless, it was hard not to notice those wide-set blue eyes. I mean, considering he had quite the staring problem.

It's not unusual for men to look at me, but they usually try to retain at least a hint of subtlety. The assholes are the ones that mutter out pathetic words of flattery.

But this one didn't seem to fit in either of those categories. He was very conscious of his decision to unabashedly stare at me. But in utter silence.

I felt sorry for him. Like he was looking for something he lost. And he looked at me as if I might know where to find it.

Those are the humans that never find the ability to fly. Those are the humans that I watch over at night.

Chapter Six: barefoot blondie
Date: July 2016

Have I made it clear enough that having a routine is vital for me? A **rigid** routine. Well, Luna Elrod, completely and utterly, destroyed all sense of a routine I could get my rigorous hands on.

--

I saw *her* on my tenth shift.

She was sitting in a corner chair by the fireplace wearing a very familiar fur coat and knee-high black boots. I thought my imagination was pulling a prank on me. The last time I had seen her, I almost relapsed hours later. Was my brain trying to find a creative way to relapse again? It had been a while since I dipped my toe in some relapsing foreplay. Maybe my mind was role-playing?

I spent the entire shift avoiding eye contact.

But then, she kept coming. And I mean like, *multiple* times a week.

"Susan."

"What Nathan?"

"That girl over there... in the red dress... do you see her too?" I asked, slightly hiding behind a bookshelf one morning.

"What?" Susan looked in her direction. "Barefoot blondie?"

"Barefoot blondie?"

"Why are you asking me if I can see her? Is that an old joke?"

"Why did you just call her barefoot blondie?"

"It's her nickname."

"She has a nickname?"

"She used to come to the library barefoot until the establishment reinforced that she wouldn't be allowed back until she stopped. Now she just keeps a pair of shoes in the bathroom closet- are you going to answer why you asked if I could see her?!"

"What?! How long has she been coming here?"

"Nathan, I don't know? For as long as I can remember? Since I started working here maybe?"

(Fuck)

"What's her actual name?" I asked.

Susan laughed.

"What's so funny?"

"Her library card says 'Iris Moore', but we don't think that's her actual name."

"What? Iris Moore? Why?"

"There's no information on an Iris Moore in this area."

"Where do you think she got the name from then?"

"Cutty B. Sands."

"Cutty B. Sands?!"

"Yep. Iris Moore is a character from his first novel."

"So?"

Susan pointed over to her. "If you didn't clench your eyes shut every time you had to look in that direction, you'd notice that she's always reading something he wrote."

I gave Susan the "seriously" look, and then braced myself. I glanced over quick enough to catch a glimpse of the book she was reading. *Broad in Daylight.* Written by none other than the man himself, Cutty B Sands.

"Don't you guys do background checks or anything? If she has a fake alias, don't you think that's something you would want to know? For legal purposes? Especially if she's pretending to be a fictional character?"

"Nathan, it's a library card. Not a government ID. And besides, she's our most loyal customer."

"Library books are free though-"

"Nathan, it's not that deep. Let it go!"

(Fuck)

She recognized me too.

Every time she came in, she smiled and waved at me. I never reciprocated. I mean, how could I? She was a livewire that needed to be imprisoned for fraud. I couldn't let that kind of behavior derail me.

Usually, I tried to hide behind one of the library carts. But she always found me. She'd come up to the cart I was squatting behind and wave, completely unaware of the fact I was hiding from her. I'd close my eyes and wait for her to go away.

Then one day in late July, she spoke to me.

"Can I have that book?" she asked.

"What book?"

"The one that you're trying to cover your face with. Moby Dick."

"Oh, uh," I moved the book out from in front of my face, "it's not very good."

"I'd like to find out for myself," she stuck her hand out.

"You know it's about a whale and not a-"

She stood there and waited for me to regret what was coming out of my mouth.

"Yeah. Here you go," I gave her the book.

And then she skipped off to her chair in the corner, like there was nothing else in the world for her to be doing besides disturbing my work.

She irked me. And she confused me. And to be confused was to be curious. And being curious was something that I avoided like the plague. Curiosity was an anxious and bothersome feeling. It created an annoying internal dialogue. Like I had another person living in my head who couldn't stop obsessing over her.

"I wonder what she's going to read today."

"Doesn't she have a job?"

"What the hell is she doing here again, and why is she dressed like that?"

"She looks quite lovely in that blouse-WHAT IS SHE DOING?"

"For god's sake, does this woman have a job?"

She sat in that corner chair, mindlessly turning page after page of whatever book was her newest infatuation while I stewed, shelving books, slowly being boiled in a liquid of questions and emotions that I was not comfortable with. Slowly being taunted-

"I think you're wrong."

"What?" I almost dropped the book I was holding.

"The book," she held it up, "Moby Dick. I thought it was brilliant."

"Well then you must be a patron of the arts." I said, bitingly.

"What's your name?"

"Mine?"

"I'm Luna." She held out her hand.

I examined it for an awkward amount of time before slowly reaching out and shaking it. "Nathan Whitlock."

"Huh," she said, "I didn't peg you as a Nathan."

"What did you peg me as then?" I asked.

"A Dick." She smiled.

I frowned.

"See you tomorrow, Nathan?" she started to walk away, "I can't wait to hear what the next book you *don't* recommend is."

"Wait!" I called after her, "your name is wrong on your library card! That's fraud!"

But she didn't hear me, or rather, she absolutely, did not care.

Luna Elrod Journal Entry
Date: July 20th, 2016

I find comfort in knowledge. I also find comfort in knowing some things can never be accomplished. Like reading every book in a library. It keeps my mind busy. And calm. It's my favorite place to be.

The colossal window that doubles as a front door of The Sacramento Public Library is a portal into thousands of imaginations. Once inside, you no longer belong to the human-race. The ceilings stretch up to the bright skies, its roots are embedded in the dirt and seeds of Sacramento's land. You have now entered a world of minds. Skin doesn't matter here. Only curiosity.

The library is home to every type of intelligence.

A CEO, smoothing his business suit, getting ready for a sweaty handshake. A woman dressed head to toe in Prada, hoping to be seen for her brands and not her heart. A distressed mother, over-tired and under-paid. A homeless man seeking warmth amongst the embracing manuscripts. A skipping child, so beautifully oblivious of the pain that surrounds him.

Now inside, everyone is no longer what they try to be.

They are anything and everything.

They are now, simply, a wild, inquiring, intellect amongst generations of others, ready to put ego aside to jump into someone else's psyche.

And the souls that disguise themselves as books are packed into gorgeous oak-brown shelves, cuddling each other to keep warm as they await their next visitor. Round tables line the room with puffy blue padded chairs that lead straight to my favorite area of the entire library.

The fireplace.

A dark, handsome, limestone stretches from floor to ceiling around the mantel. The fire roars throughout the entire day and into the early night, speaking only to someone with a listening ear. She whispers sweet everything's into my curious mind, filling my heart with warmth and ecstasy. Four vintage, maroon chairs sit before the fire, warming their laps for their awaited company. I always settle into the far-left seat, it's the shaggiest chair. It's the warmest chair. It's the most spoken too chair.

It's just about the only consistency in my life.

The entryway of the library, is gapping and open, allowing for the best people watching. You can see everyone, and observe anyone, even those on the outside.

I recognized him the first day he came in.

It's hard to forget eyes like that.

I knew right away, that was the guy from Alfalfa.

I was up on the second level, leaning against the railing, watching the world, when he came in.

He's a tall man. Tall and unkempt.

He anxiously fumbled inside.

He was nervous and uncoordinated.

I could see his palms sweat from yards away.

And he was with a very large, and loud man.

But, to my surprise, I found myself observing this brilliant, rugged adventure, yet again.

As if we were two magnets being drawn towards each other.

He's negatively charged.

And I'm positively charged.

There was an invisible force that could not stop pulling my magnetic energy towards his.

But why?

Chapter Seven: to kill her or thrill her?
Date: August 2016

I did my best to avoid her.

I covered my face with any broom, book, or Blu-ray disc I could find. I switched lunch breaks whenever I saw her come in, forcing Susan to eat her cold cut sandwiches warm. I walked the halls like a nervous agent on the look-out for a crazy, rogue blonde who somehow had the ability to appear out of no-where and look incredibly, and effortlessly beautiful.

But regardless of my stealthy efforts, Luna had taken an unrequested interest in me. And she was better at finding me than I was at hiding. She saw how nervous and troubled I became when she was around, and that power poisoned her (or at least, that was my assumption). But it was obvious. I was an insecure, tongue-tied, nonentity, and it amused her. Or rather, it seemed; aroused her.

One of those two. Or possibly both.

But she was an unpredictable safety hazard, and I was not going to let her get in my head and throw me off my routine. I had a good thing going, a stable thing going. And from just the simple, short encounters I had with Luna thus far, she was not good nor stable.

And I was not going to let her mess with me.

Or my routine.

--

But oh, she tried.

Luna Elrod Journal Entry
Date: August 9th, 2016

There's never the question of *what now?* in a library.

My brain feels as if it's been hardwired to constantly ask myself, *what now? What now? What now? What now? What now? What now? What now? What now? What now? What now?*

Questions with no answers become exhausting after a while.

But in a library, there's always a "now."

And now... there's an even *bigger* "what now," and I think it might be a little more fun than a book.

Our 'relationship' was nonverbal. We hardly spoke during the month of August. The contact we made with each other was entirely registered in telepathy... and flabbergasting behavior. I believe that it wasn't quite *me* Luna was interested in, but rather, the reactions she could get out of me.

She'd come in wearing low rise-jeans and a shell-pink thong up around her hips. Her crescent moon tramp-stamp was always in view. She would find where I was working and shuffle through the books that were in my cart, the books that I was *trying* to put *away*. She would smack on her gum, grab it out of her mouth and twist it around her finger knowing damn well that I was the gum in between her teeth. I wanted to take her shell-pink thong and strangle her with it.

I'd go outside for a smoke break, and she'd already be out there, barefoot, and cross-legged on the sidewalk, dragging on a cigarette. She'd look up at me when I'd come out and smile, saying nothing with her mouth but everything with her eyes. I'd stand on the other side of the library beam, leaning against the post, searching in my mind for an innovative way to get a faster buzz so that I could leave her presence quicker. I wished the wind would blow smoke from my cigarette in my eyes so I could be blinded by her attendance.

I walked past her once as she was entering the bathroom and she turned around and said, "hey, I'm going in there to make love to Mark Twain."

"Okay." I said, all the color flushing from my face.

And then she shut the door and pretended to have an orgasm.

As much as I loathed her for coming into my territory and detonating it, it was... fairly obvious that I was wildly drawn to her.

Which is why she was having so much fun teasing me.

I'd find myself standing behind a bookshelf, staring at her, losing myself. She made me reckless. I could stare at her without looking away and feel shameless about it. And she would stare right back, looking at me from behind whatever book she was reading.

I couldn't look at bread in the grocery store for longer than a few seconds before becoming flustered and worried that the sour dough would criticize my existence. But Luna was an emotional aphrodisiac, and I had no self-control when it came to indulging in her.

And that's exactly why I fucking *loathed* her.

She had these round baby-blue eyes that could sink any sailor. Her mouth was light pink and so plump you could rest a cigarette on her upper lip. Her hair was always tangled from running through the Sacramento breeze and her cheeks were always slightly red. She had freckles on her nose and cheeks that were designed like the constellations in the night sky and a glow in her skin that made the library seem dim. She had taken the beauty out of the universe and injected it into her face.

But that wasn't even what entranced me so abundantly. Her beauty wasn't even close to the most fascinating thing about her. When I looked into her eyes it was like I was falling off a raft into a deep blue sea. As if I lost my balance and fell into a body of water that wouldn't be held responsible for drowning me. The library held multiple generations of stories and words of wisdom in every language, but it felt slight compared to the universes that laid beyond her eyelids. There was no telling where you'd go when you glanced her way. One look in her direction and you were sucked into a riptide of different galaxies.

One look.

One look and my routines were thrown off.

One look and poof. There goes the stable life I had created.

One look. And my life was over.

One look.

I racked my brain for ways to make it stop.

To put it to rest.

I could quit.

I could move towns.

I could move states.

I could move countries.

I could change identities.

It had to stop.

Luna Elrod Journal Entry
Date: August 13th, 2016

I'm used to people watching me. I'm used to people eyeing me with their tongues out like panting dogs.

But nobody's ever watched me the way he does.

I can't figure it out.

I can't decode it.

He looks at me as if he's trying to see past my beauty and into my mind.

He looks through me.

He looks *into* me.

What is he looking for?

The looks, the cigarette breaks and the gum chewing continued. For weeks.

I continued to fall off my raft into those eyes. Into an endless cycle of drowning.

And then one day, at the end of balmy August, Luna was reading *Gone with The Wind*. She was staring at me through the top of her book as I shelved lost literature. I was mid not-responding to Susan because I couldn't focus. Luna and I wouldn't break eye-contact from each other.

I was debating on whether I wanted to kill her or thrill her.

Thrill.

Or.

Kill.

Kill.

Or.

Thrill.

Thrill and Kill?

Those were the three words that were playing on a loop in my head.

Luna was sitting in her usual spot, wearing nothing but a pink mini dress. The world felt calm for a moment. Susan talking about her broken boiler. Luna and I not parting from each other's glances. When suddenly, right there in the middle of the library, Luna spread her legs, wide, open.

Right there.

In the middle.

Of the library.

"Oh my god."

"What is it? Is that book damaged?" Susan asked concerningly.

"Jesus Christ."

"I know, it's so horrible that people return books vandalized. Criminals."

"I-"

"Leaves me winded too."

"I'm sorry Susan, I- I have to go to the bathroom."

She wasn't wearing any underwear.

Chapter Eight: these cigarettes aren't killing me fast enough
Date: August 2016

"You saw this girl's fallopian tubes?" Strong Jim asked, addled.

"Jeez, Jim, you really need to figure out the female anatomy."

"Holy shit," he said, "what did it look like?"

"Jim?!"

"I'm seriously asking!"

I shook my head. "I mean?! This girl… Luna. I can't explain it."

"You don't need too," Jim said, "just do her."

"What?!"

"I mean if you don't, Susan will."

"Jim?!"

Jim sighed. "Just saying, you're always talking about Susan being scared of excitement when you're the one in reality terrified of it."

"Yeah, yeah." I mumbled, ashing my cigarette.

Jim and I were walking to AA together. It was 6:43 am. We often took the long way when we felt we might be a bit early. There was no need to over-achieve in an AA meeting.

"Have you ever noticed that bookshop?" I asked Jim, pointing over to the brick building just past our favorite coffee shop.

"The one that has tetanus and typhoid? Yeah, they need to tear that down."

"Why haven't we ever gone in there before?" I asked, "I think it looks quite nice."

Jim's eyebrows became erect. "What are you drunk?"

I gave him a disagreeing glance.

"You're just uterus happy," Jim said, shaking his head.

"Whatever." I said, as we arrived at the meeting.

AA was hosted in a giant recreational room with blue carpet, an array of red chairs, the left-over trace of stale coffee, cream cheese, and an aroma of bad breath. Nothing else was notable enough except the few windows that brought in an unnecessary amount of light. Nobody wants a dewy morning glow on their face as they recount the time they threw up on their child after a relapse. There was far too much sun in a room that held so much darkness.

"How's everyone feeling today?" Landon asked, "are our chakras aligned?"

Jim and I always had bets going on who would roll their eyes first. The loser had to buy the winner pie. We typically never lasted longer than five minutes before someone caved. (I happened to be the loser this time after the chakra comment).

"Mine are not," Elizabeth the fast-fashion-enthusiast said.

(Mine either, Elizabeth).

"Why is that?" Landon asked.

"Confusion." Elizabeth's red hair fell over her face as she looked down at the ground.

Landon took a sip of his tea, mentally preparing himself for her daily soap opera. "Elizabeth, more description words please."

"But how?!" She exclaimed.

"Find what you're trying to say deep in your gut. Look beyond your conscious self, into your third eye. And then tell us what you are confused about."

I glanced over at Jim who was scrolling Twitter. Looks like we'd both be buying each other pie today.

"I simply don't know!" Elizabeth said. She had a weird temper that came out at unusual times, usually when she was frustrated about her feelings. And she was always frustrated about her feelings.

"That is understandable, Elizabeth," Landon responded gently.

"Really?" Elizabeth asked, shocked by Landon's lack of prying.

Landon nodded. "Yes."

The room settled a moment before he continued. "Usually, we don't recognize how something made us feel until after the dust has settled. That's why emotions can be so confusing."

Silence.

"And things that can't be labeled can make sobriety scary."

Loud silence.

"What do you do then?" I asked to my own shock (and everyone else's).

Landon looked over at me, stunned at my participation as well. "Well, it's quite simple. You allow yourself to be confused, or to feel an emotion that you can't quite understand yet. And just let it sit."

"How?" I asked, again, to my own shock.

"Is there something going on with you Nathan?" Landon asked.

"Me? What? No?" I laughed defensively.

"Any feelings you're confused about?"

"No!" I shouted, now suddenly finding myself contributing to a weird temper at an unusual time.

"Okay…"

I looked around at the group who were all giving me nods of disapproval. "Well, okay," I said, shifting my position in my chair. *How can I turn this into a metaphor, so I don't have to get **too** real*, I thought.

"I've recently started gardening-" I commenced.

"Gardening?" Max (skin cancer) chimed in.

Landon shushed him. "Let him finish."

I nodded. "Yeah. And I hate it. I think... It's just the whole herbage thing. It's so extraneous. Plants. I mean, they are always there and always in the way. And why do they require so much attention? But it's like I can't stop. I can't stop planting the damn plants. Because the end result is so... *so* beautiful. But why are the responsibilities to get there so taxing?"

The room looked at me like I was slowly turning into a Hibiscus flower.

Jim nodded his head. "I hate herbage."

Landon started laughing to himself. "You have mixed emotions about... gardening?"

I nodded, biting my thumbnail.

"Okay." He said, adjusting himself. "What else about gardening scares you?"

I swallowed. "What if I suck at it? And I end up killing all the flowers?"

Landon took another sip of his tea. "Nathan being sober is supposed to give us life. Not take it away. And life is about failures."

I didn't respond, instead I just sat on the edge of my chair staring directly at his teacup.

"So," he continued, "have a willingness to fail."

I nodded, no longer having a willingness to continue this metaphor. "Okay."

The room was silent.

I nodded again. "Okay."

And then Sofia (hot Latina) held her middle finger up. "To herbage," she said, "we can take on any damn plant that comes our way."

"To herbage," the entire group responded, saluting with their middle fingers.

Chapter Nine: a willingness to garden
Date: September 2016

I started playing the record *The Psychedelic Sounds of the 13th Floor Elevators* backwards. Did you hear that? I started playing the damn album <u>backwards</u>. Take *that* for a routine.

Track six: Fire Engine

Black coffee. Jumping Jacks. Crunches. Pushups. Weights. (*Multiples* of all four) (What? I wanted to look good).

Track five: Don't Fall Down

Warm shower. Put cologne on. Spin in approximately 180 degrees. Start the coffee pot. Comb my hair. Put my (freshly washed AND dried) clothes on. Hip thrust. Pour myself a cup of coffee.

Track four: Reverberation

Spark a cigarette. Sip my coffee. Slide across the floor in socks.

Track three: Splash 1

Free hanging mind wandering baby. (But only for one track).

Track two: Roller Coaster

Rigorously minute-by-minute plan out my day... (baby steps).

Track one: You're Gonna Miss Me.

Toss the cigarette in the sink (like a bad ass) ... and then, in a chaotic frenzy, collect it, and properly put it out in the ashtray. Head out the door. (Check to make sure it's locked twice).

I would bring Susan coffee every morning. She loved it.

"Nathan, seriously. Please stop bringing me this shit coffee."

"So... add more sugar tomorrow? Got it."

"I will fire you," Susan said, holding the coffee cup like it was a grenade.

"Where do you want me to start today? Fiction?" I asked.

"What's got you in such a good mood?"

"Good mood?" I asked looking around, "says who?"

Susan stopped what she was doing. "Don't tell me it's that girl."

"What girl?!" I asked, all too defensively.

"You know what girl. The one you're always looking at when you're supposed to be doing your job."

"I have no idea what you're talking about."

Susan squinted her eyes at me. "Start in non-fiction today."

I backed away, my hands up in surrender. "Alright. No more coffee for you then."

--

Despite Susan being correct in her assumption, (which was a mental challenge for later), I had to focus. I practiced all night how I might approach her. I had to walk up to her in a sort of subtle, nonchalant way. In a way that read, "hey, I know I just recently saw your external female genitalia, but I respect you, and I appreciate you, but I also find you... attractive, and slightly scary."

Believe it or not, there aren't many approaches that give off that vibe.

I couldn't frighten her, but I also had to prove that I was worth her time. It had to be a light approach. I couldn't encroach upon her like Jim did when he met me. But I also needed to speak to her with proper decency, and in a manner that wasn't entirely off putting but also not too overbearing (you can see why this needed to be practiced all night).

I was ready to plant some damn herbage.

Even if it meant responsibilities.

Landon was right, sobriety was supposed to give us life. Not take it away.

And this was the most alive I had felt in a long time.

I was going to go for it.

But she never came.

This wasn't unusual. Luna never came on the same day or at the same time. Her appearances were as predictable as car crashes. Different hours of the day and uncoordinated days of the week.

I just had to keep preparing my approach until she showed next. It had to be soon. Luna always came multiple times a week.

So, I went home and practiced my greeting some more.

The next day my shift started at 10 am and ended at 9 pm. She never showed.

So, I went home and practiced my walk-up some more.

Then the next morning my shift started at 9 am and ended at 5 pm. She didn't show. So, I went home and practiced my approach some more.

The next day, my shift started at noon and ended at 8 pm. She never came.

So, I practiced more.

A week passed, then two weeks, still no Luna.

I kept practicing.

Sometimes I would dart off to the bathroom to get some practice in just in case she came strolling through at any moment. Every now and then (every five seconds), I would look at the doors, waiting for them to go flying open and reveal a barefoot, celestial being.

But that didn't happen.

Susan would drone on, talking about her latest chicken pot pie recipe or about how her "roommate, lady friend" liked their home hot and she liked it cold, and how they simply couldn't agree on a temperature.

"Mhm," I'd respond, or "oh wow."

I couldn't focus on anything except the disappearance of a rogue blonde.

"Have you seen, uh, barefoot blondie recently?" I would ask.

"Nathan? No? I'm trying to tell you about the mallard I saw the other day, it was magnificent."

"Okay, but uh, where do you think she's been?"

"Who knows? Probably mucking around with the mallards in a dirty lake." Susan would say.

I shrugged. "Or maybe she's just sick."

I couldn't help but lie awake at night and fantasize about *Gone with The Wind*. Or about the wind in her hair. Or about how maybe the wind would blow her to me like how it blew cigarette smoke in my eyes.

I'd look over at a bookshelf during a shift and imagine she was standing behind it, laughing away at some slashing murderous novel or bending over in her shell pink thong. I wish I hadn't taken that shell pink thong for granted. I wish I hadn't-

"Nathan?"

"What?"

"I asked you to put those books away twenty minutes ago."

"Oh, sorry Susan."

She wasn't coming to the library anymore.

And so, no flowers grew.

Luna Elrod Journal Entry

Date: September 1st, 2016

Luna Elrod Journal Entry
Date: September 2nd, 2016

Luna Elrod Journal Entry
Date: September 3rd, 2016

Luna Elrod Journal Entry

Date: September 4th, 2016

Luna Elrod Journal Entry

Date: September 5th, 2016

Luna Elrod Journal Entry

Date: September 6th, 2016

Luna Elrod Journal Entry

Date: September 7th, 2016

Luna Elrod Journal Entry
Date: September 8th, 2016

I haven't been able to leave my bed unless I've found myself in utter despair for food or wine, or perhaps to pee somewhere that isn't in the empty water bottles under my nightstand.

There's a hot, maple incense burning on my nightstand. I sometimes poke myself with it in the wrists and the thighs, in a last-ditch attempt to feel something.

I don't know if I've lost my job or if I've been evicted. I can't check my emails because my computer is on the other side of my room.

If only I could shove the hot end of the incense stick through my ear and into my brain to jolt it awake, then maybe I'd find the wits to care.

No reason to leave here except the mere urge to get out of bed and find something to kill myself with. There is hardly a rope I haven't fantasized about, magically growing legs, finding its way to my neck and slowly but marvelously tightening its polyester hands. Finishing the job that I couldn't.

All I can do is lie about and hope for a natural disaster to strike Sacramento and its infestation of flightless birds.

Chapter Ten: An immortal resurrection
Date: October 2016

My record sounded better starting from track one anyway.

Every day that passed, my coffee pot retained less and less leftover caffeine. Every day that passed, my cigarette packs emptied quicker.

I was going to meetings around six times a week. I found myself needing the meetings more than usual. As fall was rearing its ugly head, so were my inhibitions. Being in the library felt like a hangover from the most exciting drunken daydream of my life.

I was desperately searching for something to give me the same buzz that she did.

Jim and I were still hosting Sober Sunday, although, we were now going to his place. He said he'd rather have Cindy's 'undiscovered female bits' in his face dusting the television during the game instead of feeling the melancholy that was my apartment. It was a hard point to argue with.

We didn't have to watch reruns anymore which was nice, but it didn't matter much anyhow, because Cindy would bring us chips and soda just to stand right in front of the television during the biggest point of the season.

"Cindy!!!" We'd both yell, trying to see past her.

"*Thank you*," we'd both say upon her motherly look of disapproval.

I must admit however, I liked going to their place. The exterior of their home was a French, plain blue. They had a Keurig, Rae Dunn Coffee mugs, full rolls of toilet paper, *and* dish soap. I was used to ripple acrylic lights, neon colors, and washing my dishes with hand-crafted sage soaps made from gypsies at the farmer's market. Their home was so different than any place I had ever lived before. It felt so… *homey*? Not a usual sentiment I felt while at home. And Cindy made some mean soft pretzel bites. She seemed eager to host.

And I was happy to assist.

I decided to bury Luna once and for all. She wasn't coming to the library anymore, so I took it upon myself to fantasize about all the ways she could have died. I settled on carbon monoxide poisoning. Luna seemed like the kind of person to accidentally leave a stove on overnight.

It was for the best. I got a taste of the excitement Luna brought me from afar. I didn't need to see where the excitement could take me if she got too close.

So, good riddance and rest in peace.

I was eleven months sober and that's where I was going to put my focus. Not some fishnet wearing siren who thought shoes were optional.

Until October 11th

10:12 am.

Historical nonfiction: where I was dusting books when the door swung open.

She walked in.

Her presence loud enough to wake the dead from within the history department.

Her blonde hair causing a scene as she marched her way inside.

I nearly became the dust particles I was sweeping up.

She's alive? I thought. *So much for carbon monoxide poisoning.*

I looked for an exit sign.

She wasn't barefoot. And it didn't look like she had just run there. Thick, cobra black leather boots don't make for a good run, I'd presume. But they do make for a shocking entrance. A black mini skirt and black top hardly covering her chest matched the startling aura she was emitting. And of course, as did her fur coat.

She was sucking on a neon blue lollipop. I could see her stained tongue from across the building.

She saw me staring at her.

She walked towards me.

"Fuck, fuck, fuck," I muttered, scurrying to pick up the duster and turn my body away from any danger.

I could hear her heels approaching rapidly.

Once the noise stopped, I knew she was right behind me. I refused to turn to acknowledge her presence.

"Ahem."

I didn't move.

"Ahem."

I dusted the books in front of me very precisely.

"AHEM!"

…I turned fifty-degrees. Enough for her to only see half my eyebrow.

"Do you have a problem with my outfit?" she asked once she could see part of my face.

"Why would you assume that?" I muttered, dusting rigorously now.

"Because you can't even look at me right now."

"Obviously I'm busy."

She sucked on her lollipop for a good minute. "Busy re-locating dust particles? Sounds invigorating."

"Dusting is the top threshold of fun I can handle," I responded.

"It's a damn good thing you aren't looking at my outfit then," she said.

"Yeah. Good thing indeed."

"Alright."

"Alright."

"Bye then."

"Bye then," I whispered back in a mocking grumble.

I was so furious at this tiny woman for reasons that were completely arbitrary. She owed me nothing, yet I still felt like I had been fooled.

Luna Elrod Journal Entry
Date: October 11th, 2016

I'm not sure why, but I was expecting a warmer welcome.

A typical man, receiving the attention I have served them, would've taken it by now and utterly slaughtered it.

But he won't budge. He won't move.

He almost seemed… annoyed?

At first, I thought what I always thought, that he was breathlessly compelled by me.

But now I am starting to believe that he simply, just, isn't interested.

He simply would prefer to fly elsewhere.

She sat in her chair for an hour. Turning page after page of her book as I shifted around inside myself, trying to get comfortable in what felt like a liquid abyss. She wasn't looking up at me or acknowledging my presence whatsoever. Instead, she just sucked and chewed and flipped pages.

How many god-damn lollipops was she going to eat?

I was now aggressively shelving books in a fury, trying to collect my thoughts and maintain reasonable actions. I had done so much work in my sobriety to stay sensible. I needed to thoroughly plan out everything I said and did before I made any hasty decision-

I stormed right up to her. Not an approach I had practiced.

"Do you need something?" I asked in a threatening manner, standing over her.

She glanced up from her book. "No? Do *you* need something?"

I hovered over her for only a second more before I said, "sorry," and turned to leave.

"Do you like Cutty B. Sands?" she asked as I was turning around.

I froze.

She unwrapped another lollipop and put it in her mouth while she waited for me to answer.

"I think the better question is why do *you* like him so much?" I responded.

"He's cynical and straightforward. Sometimes I need people to be that way with me."

I scratched the top of my head and then turned to leave, but instead found myself blurting out, "so does that have anything to do with your disappearance?"

She put her book down. "Are you stalking me?"

"No?" I said, far too defensively.

She crossed her legs. "I was on a sabbatical."

Not really what I was thinking, I thought. "Are you a teacher or something?" I asked.

"Why are you so interested?" She asked.

"I'm not."

"Okay."

I was frozen staring at her again.

She stared back, biting the remnants of the current lollipop that was in her mouth.

"So... are you teacher or something?" I asked again, idiotically hoping for a different outcome this time.

"No."

"Oh."

The silence and staring continued.

"What do you do then?" I asked, unable to now stop myself.

She squinted her eyes and evaluated me as if I was something she might consider chewing on next. I waited patiently for her to finish. "I'm a bartender at a Burlesque club on Third Street." She finally said.

"Oh," I responded. I guess that made sense given the hours she was at the library.

"I'd ask what you do, but I already know," she said.

And then she picked her book up, flipped the page, and started reading again.

Luna Elrod Journal Entry

Date: October 11th, 2016

Huh?

Chapter Eleven: little red riding hood
Date: October 2016

"Nathan... is that an entire coffee pot you're holding?" Landon asked, his eyebrows alert.

I looked down. He had paused me mid-rant about something that probably involved other people's joy. "Yeah?" I shrugged.

"How much coffee have you had to drink today?"

I shrugged again. "I don't know? A normal amount?"

"What's a normal amount to you?"

"Like, a pot and a half?"

"Woah!" everyone in AA blurted out.

"What?" I asked, disrupted amid my vent session.

"Why don't you try cutting back a little on the caffeine intake, okay?" Landon suggested.

"I can't do that."

"Why not?"

"Because I need it, I have a job now."

"Your job should not require *that* much caffeine, Nathan." Landon said, concerned.

"Okay well, I'll get a headache if I stop."

"And you'll die from a heart attack if you don't," Xavier (legal drug dealer) added.

I held my coffee pot up in cheers.

"Nathan, Xavier is right," Landon crossed his legs, "you really should try cutting back, all that caffeine isn't good. I mean listen to you right now, you sound insane."

Wow. So much for a gentle approach to healing. I thought.

"If you can quit alcohol, you can most definitely kick the caffeine habit too," Xavier said.

"Yeah, yeah." I shrugged them all off.

What the group was failing to see, other than future health conditions, was that the flutter effects from the caffeine was a much safer alternative than what was previously giving my heart pitter patters. So, the coffee was not going to go anywhere.

The conversation I had previously with Luna wasn't exactly how I had planned our first real interaction to go. It wasn't quite the charming and darling fairytale I had worked up in my mind.

But that was nothing in comparison to what was happening now.

Halloween was approaching and that meant terrible *terrible* things for Sacramento's Public Library. Luna wasn't missing a day now, as if she was seeking revenge on the institution. I found myself nostalgic of the time she had died from carbon monoxide poising. Her current disposition was much scarier than death. Or any haunted house.

Her October behavior began tastefully, I suppose.

First, she came dressed as Little Red Riding Hood. This involved a modest black dress and a red cape. It was *almost* sweet. But then, she came as a cowgirl, in pink cowboy boots and a matching hat. Only, this cowgirl was missing *a lot* of denim. Then she was a nurse, but not one you'd find in a hospital. Or at least one you'd count on to save your life. Then suddenly, she was a pirate. But this pirate was wearing spandex, fishnet tights and a corset that covered almost nothing of her chest. And before I knew it, she was dressed just in lingerie! Not even sure what the costume was supposed to be!

It was a Wednesday at 12:03 and she was wearing a baby blue bustier, a skirt so small I could hardly even notice it, and knee-high socks with bows on them.

Mind you, she wore this to a public library.

I hid behind one of the bookshelves and watched her from the cracks exactly how Susan watched Cher.

I felt like a hunter in the woods, watching a cunning deer.

"Woah, look at her boobies' man, that's crazy."

I whipped my head around and saw two pre-pubescent boys kneeling next to me, also spying on her from behind the bookshelf cracks.

"She's so hot, dude. I wish I could grab those."

"Hey," I whispered firmly at them, "don't talk about women like that."

"Says the old man spying on her," said one of the boys with pubic hair on his face.

"I'm not spying on her." I said, defensively.

"It sure looks like it, creep," said the other one.

"You're the creeps spying!" I hissed.

"Well maybe she shouldn't dress like such a slut and I wouldn't look," said the former boy, his voice cracking.

I pointed my finger at him. "Listen here, you schmuck. Shut it before I ring you by the neck so hard you won't even have the vocal cords to speak such overtly foul words. Do not step foot into this library again until you learn how to respect women."

Terror formed in the two boys' eyes as rage took over mine. They were stuck in fear until the one with the deficient facial hair burst out laughing. "Did he just say *schmuck*?"

The other one followed suit, howling. "What, are you ninety-five?"

And then they walked away, grabbing onto each other to try and hold themselves up as they guffawed.

"Perverts," I whispered to myself.

"Nathan."

"Uh-" I jumped.

"I'd scold you, but those two boys deserved it," Susan said, standing behind me.

"I wasn't spying."

Susan raised an eyebrow.

"I wasn't!"

"So, what was with the crouched position and your head in-between the books then?"

"That's my preferred organizational method."

"Mhm."

"Whatever."

"We have bigger problems anyway," Susan said, nodding her head in the direction that Luna was in.

I glanced in her direction and concurred.

"I do have to go say something to her, don't I?" she asked.

I looked back over at Luna. "I mean... this is a public library... with children and creeps and families and the Amish..." I answered, "so *maybe*?"

She nodded nervously. "It's not slut shaming, though," Susan said, "it's just the principle of it all."

I nodded. "Right. It's just the principle of it all."

"Okay," she exhaled, "here I go."

I watched as Susan delayed the inevitability of this conversation by fixing every tilted book she saw along the way. Luna was sitting in her chair by the fireplace, her heels up on the ottoman.

I'm not ready to die, I thought.

The reason for the collective fear among Susan and I was not only because of Luna's choice of costumes, but also because of her peculiar manners. She was throwing books on the ground when she didn't agree with the plot or the "character development," she was stomping around in her platforms, threating to set fire to the undeserving literature. She *actually* stole candy from a baby reading Dr. Suess and told the kid to "try reading something a little more academic like, Nineteen Eighty-Four by George Orwell or your brain might rot like your teeth from that candy." And she even lit a cigarette with the flame from the fireplace and smoked it right there, in her chair, all while dressed as a pirate.

So, you can understand Susan's fear when it came to telling her that her outfit was too inappropriate to wear at a public library.

I couldn't hear Susan by the time she was talking to Luna, but boy could I see it.

Susan, hands clasped, brooch tightly pinned to her heart chakra, closed her eyes as Luna got out of her chair, threw her book down and screamed, "SLUT SHAMER. SLUT SHAMER. SLUT SHAMER."

Frightened for my life, my heart thumped more then, than it had from the entire coffee pot. But I couldn't move.

I stood frozen in deep fear and attraction.

In hindsight, maybe it was best I didn't come running to Susan's aid, considering Luna's reaction towards my non-compliance. Luna looked at Susan one last time before stomping away and coming up to me. "And you! You're nothing but a pathetic, feeble, coward!" she shouted.

"Oh." I responded.

Then she took both her heels off, threw them on the ground and stormed out.

Susan came up to me clutching her brooch. "Nathan. I'm having heart palpitations."

"Me too," I said, watching Luna leave.

--

The horrible truth about this situation however (and this is not pleasant to admit), was that, when Luna Elrod called me a pathetic, feeble, coward, it gave me more adrenaline, more confidence, and more pleasure than any substance or alcoholic drink I'd ever tried in my life.

I was also completely and utterly outraged.

And very turned on.

Luna Elrod Journal Entry
Date: October 28th, 2016

My mind is a ravenous, uncontrollable ocean.

My mind isn't mine; it never has been.

My mind is an ocean, thrashing at the shore.

Exciting at first glance, calling you towards it,

but once you get a taste of its wrath,

once it slaps against your unknowing body,

it scares you far,

far away.

I wasn't expecting to see her again. I figured after her meltdown she would disappear again.

But she was there when I arrived the next day.

However, she wasn't dressed in costume, or thick platform boots, or lingerie of any sort. She wasn't even barefoot.

Her hair was up in a loose ponytail and a giant sweatshirt unveiled itself down to her knees. I hadn't been aware she owned normal clothes.

I should mention before the narrative slips out from underneath me; my mother was a fashion guru. She taught me three things in life: music, literature, and fashion. If there was one thing I was confident about by the age of ten, it was that peep-toe booties and color clashing was ghastly.

So, the reason I draw so much attention to the detail of Luna Elrod's wardrobe is because, well, it's the one thing I may really understand about women. It might just be about the only control they have in a world that forces their identities on them.

So, when Luna showed up on this day wearing a hoodie and leggings, I knew she felt as if she had lost all control.

I tried to act normal (by hiding behind a bookshelf and pretending I didn't see her), but of course, she found me still.

"Hi."

I flinched, I squeezed my eyes shut, and waited for the wrath.

When nothing came, I opened my eyes.

Her blue seas were unusually still.

"Hi," I said, gripping onto the book cart.

We remained silent for what should have been an awkward exchange of nothing to say but was curiously comforting.

And then I went back to shelving books.

And she went back to her chair.

She read for a while. I watched her from afar.

And then before she left, she found me again.

"What are you doing after this?" she asked.

I looked at her with a blank expression.

"Do you want to get a coffee or something? I know a place."

And for some godforsaken, unknown reason, I nodded.

--

It was one of those venues with vegetation that hung from the ceiling as if it was a groundbreaking idea to have plants dangling in your face as you were trying to enjoy the precious moments you would get your buzz.

Herbage.

Always there and always in the way.

Just another thing that made plants so *fucking* great.

But of course, Luna seemed right at home.

I ordered a black coffee and a plain bagel with minimal cream cheese. "Make sure it's minimal," I said to the barista.

Luna nudged me. "Say thank you."

"Thank you." I grudged.

She ordered an iced vanilla latte with two pumps of hazel and caramel drizzled on top.

"Coffee is a necessity not a dessert." I said.

"Sometimes a necessity is a dessert."

"Mhm."

"You know there is so much more to the world than black coffee and plain bagels."

"This is fine. Nothing is more predictable than a cup of black coffee and a bagel with cream cheese."

"'Minimal.'" She said, mocking me.

Luna Elrod Journal Entry
Date: October 30th, 2016

Queen has made her move. Still waiting on pawn.

Chapter Twelve: vanilla iced latte with two pumps of hazel and caramel drizzled on top
Date: November 2016

Due to circumstances that led me to chain smoke, engage in weeklong benders, and seek self-loathing poetry in college, I was very familiar with the man Luna Elrod loved. Cutty B. Sands.

Professionally, Cutty B. Sands was a poet and an author. When he wasn't partying or sleeping with unstable women, he was writing about it with a hostile aggression that left his work wildly unsettling.

He never wrote a single piece of work sober.

His work was a sad attempt at making something out of his hurt.

To him, pain and love were the strongest emotions in the world. And he had a hard time deciphering between the two.

Nobody liked Cutty B. Sands. Except for Luna Elrod.

Sands was like a cigarette. He was thrilling and rousing to consume. But the after-effects he left you with were much more dire than the original buzz was worth. He made you see the world through a cold, hard lens. One that often left you stripped naked in front of a mirror wondering who you were in this world. And that's not necessarily something a guy like me prefers to participate in.

Luna however, had a strange admiration for this man for much deeper reasons than one could imagine.

"What's your favorite book?" Luna was sitting in my book cart as I was trying to put first editions back where they belonged. She was kicking her feet as if this was a pleasant park bench.

"I don't have one."

"Oh, come on. I don't believe you."

"I don't have a favorite anything."

"That is such a lie! Everyone has a favorite book."

"Not everyone."

"Mines *In the Vein of Feeling Something.*"

"Never read it."

"I know you have."

"I don't prefer anything written by Cutty B. Sands."

"You seem like the kind of man that doesn't prefer anything."

I certainly didn't prefer the way my mind was keeping me up at all hours of the night. Pondering over her. Distracting me in the way where your mind can think of nothing else.

"If you love him so much, why don't you go sleep with him," I asked, shoving a book into its place.

"I can't Nathan? He's dead."

"How do you know?" I asked, taken aback.

Luna shrugged. "I just assumed given the last novel he ever wrote was a manifesto of his suicide."

"What made you think that?"

"That was just my interpretation. I mean the man kept standing under streets lights until one of them would fall on his head."

I shrugged. "Maybe he just had a flirtatious relationship with death?"

"Maybe he flirted a little too hard."

"Or maybe he's just brainstorming?"

Luna raised an eyebrow. "I thought you didn't read anything of his?"

"I don't, I'm just assuming." I said, defensively.

"Uh huh."

I rolled my eyes.

"What are you doing?" she asked.

"I'm working?"

"Do you wanna get out of here?"

I looked around. "Luna, hello? I can't just leave my job."

"Okay," she said, hopping off the cart, "I'll catch you later. I have to go find a post office."

"Why?"

"Because Nathan? I have a calling to soak in the ambiance of inscribed letters that have the potential to change someone's day, yet alone life."

"Why?" I asked, again.

"Because Nathan! Who are the mysterious souls that will receive words filled with love? Or pain? I'll never know, and neither will the postal workers who are responsible for sending off those momentous messages." She shook her head, "they probably carry the weight of the world on their backs while they hand off those little white envelops to strangers whom they will never fully understand. I have to go carry some of that burden."

"Or they just work as a means to survive and will probably end up quitting later because it makes them miserable."

"Catch you later!"

And off she went.

"Wow."

Startled, I jumped. "God, Susan, you really have to warn people before you sneak up."

"I've been standing here the entire time." Susan said.

I looked around, remembering Susan had also been there. "Oh... right."

She furrowed her eyebrows. "Well, I appreciate you not leaving in the middle of your shift to go frolic around a post office."

I nodded.

Susan sighed.

"For the record though," I said, "my shift ended an hour ago."

I woke up the next morning to the smell of freshly baked éclairs. I rolled out of bed, offended at first that a smell so impregnable would have the audacity to linger at such seedy corners. But when I looked out the window of my apartment and noticed a mom-and-pop bakery for the first time, my nostrils and my heart opened. Without further ado, I went across the street, ordered a bunch of pastries, and took them to my AA meeting.

"What, are you in love or something?" Mateo asked when I was placing a cream pie down on the table.

"What? No?!" I responded aggressively.

He laughed, grabbing a donut. "I'm kidding, you'd never be in love."

Max leaned over and grabbed an éclair, "you do seem... happier though."

"I'm fucking not!" I shouted, "can't a guy just bring a damn pastry to a damn event?!"

"I'm not sure if I'd go as far as to call this an event-" Max started to say when Elizabeth leaned over the table and observed my offerings.

"Cream pie?" she said, utterly disgusted.

"Did you say cream pie?" Jim asked, lunging at the table.

"Cream pie, Nathan?" Elizabeth said again, "not yet a pie, not quite a pudding. Just a pathetic attempt at trying to fit into both parties. No use."

"Damn, what did cream pie ever do to you?" Daniel asked.

"Jim seems to like it," Xavier said, pointing to Jim who was cutting a slice larger than the mass of Mateo's elbow fat.

"Jim likes anything that has the word cream in it," Elizabeth rolled her eyes.

"It's a shame he can't make his wife cream anymore then," Mateo said, digging into the pie himself.

"Alright guys!" Landon said, stopping the direction of this conversation as quickly as one could, "let's get this meeting started, shall we?" He pointed with a strict finger to the chairs in a circle.

"... if we must," Jim said, looking over at the pie, begging it to not grow legs and run off before he could finish it.

There was nothing substantial to report about the first half of the meeting. It was mostly the usual: Max trying to harmonize while Landon talked and a lot of crying coming from Elizabeth.

But things took a turn when Strong Jim opened his big mouth.

"Any life updates?" Landon asked.

"Nathan has a girl," Jim said, smirking.

I shot my head up. "What the fuck?" I mouthed across the room at him.

"I knew there was a reason for the cream pie!" Mateo exclaimed.

"There was no reason for that cream pie other than to ruin my day," Elizabeth said.

"There was no bloody reason for that pie other than the fact I was trying to support a small business," I declared.

"Yeah right," Sofia snickered, "since when have you ever supported a small business?"

"When he lied on his tax forms last year," Max said.

Landon shushed everyone. "Do you want to tell us about her?" he asked.

"There's no *her* to tell," I said.

"Come on," Daniel said, "we have nothing else to talk about."

"Uh," I clenched my nose, "how about your alcohol addiction?"

"Oh, come on," Sofia agreed, "stop being such a bebé and tell us about this girl."

"I have a crush," Elizabeth said.

"Elizabeth!!!" Everyone shouted, directing their attention back at me, but for once, I was okay with Elizabeth's blatant lack of social cues.

"It is a non-judgmental zone," Landon said, shrugging.

"I'm sure as hell judging," I whispered to myself.

"We are waiting..." Sofia said, turning over her nail file.

I looked over at Jim who now had the cream pie in his lap, nodding as if none of this was his fault.

"Alright fine!" I said, knowing they were never going to let this go. "I have a friend."

"He likes her," Jim added, fork in hand, cream pie all over his face.

"Is she hot?" Mateo asked.

I sneered at them both. "It doesn't matter. She's younger than me, she's out of my league, and she's extremely reckless. None of those are in my style."

"You don't *have* a style." Sofia said.

"How much younger?" Daniel asked.

"Like… ten years." Jim responded for me.

"So, what, she's 26? That's attainable," Daniel replied.

I shook my head. "She wouldn't go for me."

Daniel shrugged. "Yeah, you're probably right." (About the first time we ever agreed on anything).

"You're wrong," Jim said, "she showed him her… V word."

"Her vest?" Xavier asked.

"No, *tonto*, her lady bits." Sofia said, flicking her nails at him.

"What?!" said everyone in the room.

"Well, that's a new addition to the story," Daniel said, sitting back and crossing his legs.

I glared at Jim again, wanting to shove his face into the empty tin he was holding coated in leftover whipped cream. "You guys wouldn't get it," I said, "it wasn't like that."

"You're right," Jim said, "I wouldn't. My wife hardly shows me hers."

"We know!!" everyone exclaimed.

"I think I get it," Landon said suddenly, nodding. "I think this is the 'gardening' you were so afraid off."

"What? No?" I expressed, stuttering, "that was about actual plants."

"Nathan, you've been sober for over a year now. You're allowed to date."

"No, I don't think so." I said, shaking my head.

"Yes, I think so." Landon responded.

I continued to shake my head no.

"Remember what we said about herbage?" he asked.

I waved my finger 'no.'

"To herbage!" Jim exclaimed, raising the cream pie tin.

"To herbage," the rest of the group chimed in.

After the meeting, Jim and I ended up at a hole in the wall café. It was the kind of place that was right up my alley: beige walls, no posters, no knick-knacks. *No* herbage. Hardly four options on the menu, those of which held virtually no flavor, and an aura of depletion that could only be fixed by caffeine. Usually, I would have been embracing the minimalism, but my mind was all over the walls.

"Sir?" The barista looked at me, "what can I get you?"

"Oh sorry," I said, gathering myself, "can I just get a vanilla iced latte with two pumps of hazel and caramel drizzled on top?"

"Uh…" the barista stammered, "I'll check to see if we have caramel."

"Did you just have a stroke?" Jim asked me, a look of terror on his face.

"What? Why?"

"What the hell did you just order? Caramel on coffee?"

"Oh." I looked at the barista who was now rummaging around for caramel. "Fuck. I don't know why I just ordered that."

Jim looked concerned.

"Found some!" The barista exclaimed.

"He actually doesn't want any of that," Jim said, coming to my aid.

"No, actually," I thought for a second, "I think I do."

"Really?!" Jim and the barista replied at the same time.

I shrugged. "Figured I'll try something new."

"Okay…" they both said, the barista unconfidently starting my coffee.

"Hey Jim, can I ask you something?"

He nodded, grabbing his order of black coffee and a croissant.

"Do you agree with them?"

"With whom?" he asked.

"With our AA group? The whole *herbage* thing."

Jim ripped into his croissant. "I wouldn't have brought it up if I didn't."

I gave him a wrathful look.

He shrugged. "There's power in numbers."

I sighed. "That's the last time I tell you a secret."

"Here's your caramel, uh, hazel, vanilla latte?" The barista said, handing me the iced cup as if it was an atomic bomb.

"Thank you," I said, grabbing it.

I took one sip and threw the rest out.

Carmel does not belong in coffee.

Luna Elrod Journal Entry
Date: November 10th, 2016

If only he could see the universe in the way I see him.

If only he could see himself in the way I see the universe.

If only he could see me.

But with his eyes shut.

If only...

Chapter Thirteen: burlesque clubs and hipsters
Date: November 2016

I was sitting alone in my apartment, gnawing on my upper lip so much it started to bleed.

Was I crazy? Maybe. Possibly. Most likely.

Was I making this all up in my head? Maybe. Possibly. Most likely.

I couldn't, I decided.

She was unpredictable. I knew myself; I needed a rigid routine. I needed security. I needed comfortability. I needed safety.

Luna was none of those things.

Thirty minutes later I was in my car on my way to Third Street.

"I'm a bartender at a Burlesque club on Third Street."

I had no idea if Luna actually held a job. I had never even been to Third Street before, or if I had, I don't remember. But I was about to find out.

She lied about her name on her library card. Why would she tell the truth about this?

But *how hard* could a Burlesque club be to find?

I clutched the steering wheel and kept trying to convince myself to turn around.

When I arrived, I fell back onto my car due to the insufferable number of lights on the street. This was the first sign that I did not belong here. The next sign was the clusterfuck of hipster bars, thrift stores, modern-day vinyl shops (not the ones that smell like incense from the counterculture movement, but rather the ones that smell like non-toxic air fresheners), and women ages sixteen to sixty all in crochet crop tops.

It was a cauldron of wanna-be's and had-been's all trying to bring back the freedom of the sixties by enforcing more ethical rules than ever before.

It seemed a little faux pas. I didn't expect someone like Luna to work on such a poser block.

I should've just gotten back in my car and driven away.

There was no reason for a man like me to be on a street like this.

But I couldn't help myself.

Curiosity was a drug Luna had slipped me and I was not known for bypassing temptations.

I sauntered up and down the block a couple times, trying to keep strides with the hipsters buying rainbow-scented candles. But I didn't see anything that had the potential to be a Burlesque Club. I figured Luna had been pulling my leg. Where would there be a seedy Burlesque club on this street? It had to have been a joke. A decently funny one, actually. Why would there be lingerie and booze mixed in with handmade jewelry and veggie burgers? Haha Luna.

And why the hell had I even come?

This is exactly the sort of behavior I was trying to avoid in the first place. I turned to head back to my car, but fate caught me off guard.

Gold lingerie poking out of a girl's jeans struck me like lightning on a metal rod. I turned just in time to catch the smeared blue glitter eyeliner that darkened her face. She didn't look as if she had just been chowing down cauliflower tacos and talking about her feelings.

"Excuse me," I said, holding a hand up to stop her.

She slowed down and looked at me. "Make it quick."

"Sorry, I just happened to notice the-," I stopped myself, "never mind. Do you by chance know if there's a Burlesque Club around here?"

She sighed. Unpleased. "I'm not supposed to tell."

"Oh?" I said, confused by the dramatics.

She squinted her eyes at me. "But... I am *oddly* attracted to you."

"Okay?" I replied, "so is there a Burlesque Club around here or not?"

She rolled her eyes. "Canterbury Tales. Walk towards the back. You'll find a security guard standing near the men's bathroom. Tell him Jane sent you."

I looked at her in shock. "What's with the theatrics? Isn't Burlesque legal?"

"Look man, my shift just ended, you can either front up the money for the time you're taking out of my night or fuck off to the club. Doesn't matter much to me."

I nodded. "Okay. Have a good rest of your night, Jane."

She frowned. "I'm not Jane."

I frowned. "You're not? Then who is?"

"Just go get a drink man!" She declared and then walked away.

"I won't be doing much of that," I whispered, watching her storm off.

Canterbury Tales was not how one would imagine the passageway to a Burlesque club to present itself. It was an elegant white building with quaint black shutters wrapped in twinkle lights.

I stepped inside expecting to be greeted by the hands of an aristocrat at happy hour but rather was met with the gaze of Hamilton writing the Federalist Papers, a pair of D cups photoshopped to his chest. Not that it was much of a difference between the two, but I wasn't quite expecting the deep saturated red walls and protruding tits.

Inside was like a Russian tea doll. Every step I took, a new set of ornamentations exposed itself within another. Each embellished with their own jewels. It was not the quaint outside I had seen previously.

The lights were dimmed low and house music kept the young crowds' eyes jarringly wide (if they had played this kind of music in my day, it sure would've kept me out of bars. Shame).

It was surprisingly easy to avoid any unwelcome thoughts that I was under a roof meant for the pouring and serving of alcohol because I was only thinking about one thing: Luna.

I shoved my way through the crowd until I found the security guard standing by the men's bathroom. I walked up to him, hoping to God that the woman on the street wasn't setting me up for embarrassment.

"Jane sent me," I said, still unsure who Jane was or what the passcode was even all about.

"50 bucks."

"50 bucks?" I asked, astonished.

"50 bucks."

"Alright." I reached into my pocket.

I handed the guard the money, he nodded, and then opened the men's bathroom door (and when I tell you, I'm not sure what I was expecting, I mean, I sure wasn't hoping to have just paid fifty bucks for a couple of unwashed urinals and a broken soap dispenser, but, what I was engulfed in suddenly, was surely, not what I was expecting). At all.

I was met with the gaze of a hundred waitresses (alright it was more like 10 but still, it was a flabbergasting amount). They were in black dresses lined up against a spiraling red carpet, holding champagne bottles and smiling as they stood proper and poise, gesturing you to enter.

"Champagne?" they all asked as I walked past.

I shook my head.

"No. Thank you."

"No. Thank you."

"No. Thank you."

"No. Thank you."

The carpet lead inside the lounge which smelt strongly of spicy amber and dirty martinis. The velvet red walls and solid gold floors were nothing in comparison to the large piano encrusted with a silhouette of a woman in nothing but a top hat. A man with black glasses and a stovepipe hat passionately played the ivories.

Women dressed in lingerie performed on a grand stage with feathers while the audience sat in tight rows. Each a respectful guest nodding along to the music with a cigar in one hand and Galilean binoculars in the other.

An elegant mixture of professionalism and eroticism so compelling I nearly forgot I was in a room with my addiction.

Waitresses walked around taking drink orders, carrying gold trays with flutes. They flaunted around in black corsets and mini top hats, floating around the room as if on an escalator, carrying heavy trays as if they were clouds. I would've been seduced by the shimmering champagne that was spilling down the rim of the glasses, but amid the boozy haze,

I saw Luna Elrod.

Her long blonde hair draped over her shoulders like a cape. Her smile looked like the moon in the distance of a J.M.W. Turner oil painting. I was a ship in a black sea being drawn to her light. And just as I started to float over, I saw her nametag.

Jane.

I was a fucking fool.

Who was this girl?

I was no man to mess around with a woman who ran barefoot through the streets of California. I was no man to mess around with a woman who dressed in lingerie at public libraries and had names like hats.

Was Luna even her real name?

She clearly didn't want anyone to know who she was.

So, why was I so hung up on trying to find out?

She was a stranger to everyone except the universe.

And it needed to stay that way.

I turned to leave.

I was awkwardly dodging my way through tiny humans dressed in corsets and top hats when I heard it.

"Nathan?"

Fuck.

I thought about running, covering my face, or slamming my body on the ground like I was in a psychotic break.

But instead, I remained frozen, facing the door. Staring ahead like I couldn't see a small blonde in front of me, saying my name.

"Nathan? I can see you."

Fuck.

I slowly lowered my eyes to her level. "Luna! What are you doing here?"

She put her hands on her hips. "Cut the shit Nathan."

"Sorry," I said, "I was just leaving."

"Leaving?" she questioned, "the show hasn't even started yet."

"I like to leave those types of things up to the imagination," I replied.

"Enjoyable things?"

"Preciously."

"Well enjoy your own fantasy then." She retorted.

"I will. Jane." I said, shocking both me and her.

Her eyes widened and then looked down at her name tag. "Nathan-"

But I wasn't staying to hear anymore.

Chapter Fourteen: the inching tide
Date: November 12th, 2016

It was well past midnight. I was sitting on the curb of the library, ash and anger burning in my chest when headlights pulled up.

Fuck.

I put the cigarette out.

She got out of the car and walked towards me.

"How'd you know I'd be here." I asked.

"You're a pretty predictable guy."

"News to me."

She sat down on the curb next to me and held her hand out. "Cigarette?"

I laughed dimly, opening the box of Marlboro's. "You know, I think you and I are the only two people in this state who smoke these things."

She took one. "That's because everyone else here is getting their buzz from starvation and narcissism."

I lit her cigarette.

It was habit. The one she hadn't broken yet.

"Well," she said after a long stretch of silence, "I should go."

She put her dart out on the edge of the curb.

I stood up after her. "Why'd you come?"

She shrugged. "I'm not sure actually."

I chuckled. "Okay."

She smiled. "I think maybe... I just wanted to make sure that you were okay."

I shrugged. "Why wouldn't I be?"

She pointed at her nametag.

"Ah," I said, taking another drag. "I guess I was just *informed* is all."

"Okay," she responded, "but on what exactly?"

My eyes wandered, looking for an explanation. "...on you, I guess."

"Oh."

We stared at each other. Silent.

"Okay, then." She turned to go.

"Wait," I said, I grabbed the inner part of her arm, "Luna-"

"Nathan, it's okay." She said, trying to pull her arm away.

"Wait, please." I said, holding it tighter.

She yanked her arm from my grip. "Nathan, please. I get it. You're not into me. It's fine."

I looked at her confused, grabbing her arm again when she started to turn. "What?"

"Can you please let go?"

"What?" I asked again.

"That's what this is all about right? You're worried I'm into you and you're not into me, so you don't want to continue to lead me on? I respect you for that, but I got it. Now let me go."

I couldn't help but laugh out loud.

I laughed so hard I nearly fell over.

She looked at me outraged and perplexed.

I kept laughing.

"Nathan?!"

"Luna," I said, guffawing, "are you serious?"

"Serious about what?"

"You think I'm not into you?"

"Well obviously you're not, otherwise you would have done something about it by now!"

"Luna," I said, "of course I'm fucking into you?"

She still looked agitated.

"I'm way too fucking into you!"

No response.

"I mean jeez! Your hair! Your lips! Your legs and that fucking body you can't seem to keep to yourself! Of course, I'm into you! And those goddamn eyes, that laugh, and goddammit, that crazy ass mind of yours?! You make me go insane! I mean absolutely insane!"

No response.

"You really think that's the reason I've been avoiding you? Are you kidding me?" I kept laughing, grabbing my forehead. "I mean, from the second I laid my eyes on you in that gas station I lost myself in your tidal waves and I haven't been able to find my way back to shore ever since! And that's the problem! That's the god damn problem Luna!"

No response.

"For fuck sakes Luna, I can't just go running around with some girl who disappears for months at a time and has multiple fake aliases. That would not end well for me. I promise. I mean fuck, look what you made me do tonight? Do you understand how dangerous you are for me?"

An unknown expression crept its way around her face.

"That's what this is all about, Luna. Okay?!"

My unraveled heart was tangled around her feet, keeping her from leaving. My pulse was the only noise that filled the space between us.

Until she finally just nodded and said, "okay."

"*Okay?*" I asked. "That's all you have to say about that?"

She nodded. "Yeah."

The silence pursued again.

"So," she eventually said, "I guess I should go then."

I nodded.

She nodded.

But nature is more powerful than man. And sometimes a moon's gravitational pull causes the ocean to create a tide, pulling dead carcasses into the unknown territory of the sea.

"No," I said.

"No?" she asked.

"No."

Her eyebrows bunched together, asking for an answer. "What do you mean no-"

And then I kissed her.

She tasted like cherry candy and cigarettes.
She tasted like the whole world.

Luna Elrod Journal Entry
Date: November 11th, 2016

Sometimes, I imagine going down South, finding a dock, and falling backwards into the deep, dark, blue waters.

I imagine my head filling up with the kelp and the fish of the sea. I picture the little anchovies scavenging around in my mind, watching my thoughts as they fill the ocean with liquid entertainment. I picture my body dressed in white silk, floating through the water effortlessly, like everything finally feels easy, soft, and gentle, as if my body belongs to the sea.

My mind isn't mine. It never has been.

My mind is an ocean, thrashing at the shore. It's exciting at first glance, calling you towards it, but once you get a taste of its wrath, once it slaps against your unknowing body, it scares you far, far away.

My mind is an ocean. So beautiful to look at. So free to the eye.

People want to swim in her, people want to dip their feet in her, but they won't go out too far, they won't enter without a life jacket or a safety raft.

Eighty percent of her is unexplored.

Eighty percent of her is entirely untouched.

My mind is an ocean. She is completely uncontrollable.

She never knows when she is going to crash or when she will be still. She has no idea when she will be shark infested or when she's safe to swim.

Only mother nature can tame her, and she seems to celebrate her defiant ways.

So, every now and then, when a scuba diver comes through, and this scuba diver wants to explore, he wants to swim all around you, and he is wildly aware of the riptides, and the sharks, and the currents,

      but he dives in anyway...

      you let that scuba diver swim.

Chapter Fifteen: oddly shaped oases
Date: November 12th, 2016

We stood at the foot of Folsom Lake. I watched as the black and gray turpitude of the night was slowly replaced by the beauty of the reddish, orange, and yellow sunrise. The water brushed against my toes, lustfully demanding my attendance.

"I can't do it Luna," I said, backing away.

"You're kidding me. Right?"

"It's too much, I can't."

"Nathan, this was your idea! You asked me to help you with this!"

"I thought that if I was with you, I would be able to do it."

"Why do you want to do this again?" she asked.

"Because" I said, "I want to conquer my biggest fear."

"That's why we came? Because it's your biggest fear?"

I nodded. "Swimming in an oddly shaped oasis at night is my biggest fear."

Her face scrunched up at me. "God, that is such a niche, weird fear."

I bit my bottom lip, hoping she would suggest we leave. But Luna would never suggest leaving. That's most likely why I brought her here.

"I highly suggest that you do some reconsidering of your fears," she said.

I looked at her. "Are you going to help me with this or not?"

"Okay, sorry, yes," she took a deep breath, "I'll help you."

"Okay."

She nodded. "You know what I do when I'm scared?"

"What?"

"Nothing. Because I'm not a fucking pussy."

And then she ran straight into the dark, murky water.

Her body a star amongst the orange sky.

Fuck.

She jumped in.

I closed my eyes.

She came up and screamed for me to join her.

I took my socks off, folded them neatly, and set them on the ground.

"Okay," I exhaled, "I *am not* a fucking pussy."

I went running into that water faster than if someone had said "free wine" at an AA meeting.

Luna was floating on top of the water. Her bright hair luminescent amongst the opaque water kept me running.

I felt like a kid with a mason jar on a mission to catch a firefly. If I could capture such a delicate creature and be near it's light for only a night, I was going to try.

I grabbed her and threw us both underwater.

"What if a fish eats me?" I asked, soaking wet, clinging onto her.

"It would spit you right out," she laughed.

I shoved her head back under water.

--

The stars that warmed the sky from the previous darkness slipped away as the sun continued to rise. It was a pallet that required no acquired taste. Just pure beauty.

"They're so beautiful," I said.

"I love that," she responded.

"Love what?"

She didn't respond at first, but then she turned her head to look at me. We were still floating on the water that was now warm against my back. "I love that those stars could fall out of the sky at any moment and kill us. Yet, we lay back and call them beautiful anyway." She finally said.

I thought for a minute before responding. "I suppose we have a choice then."

"Which is?"

"To find the fear in uncertainty or the beauty."

"And what do you choose?"

I watched as the blue sky emerged. "I think I just decided."

Luna Elrod Journal Entry
Date: November 12th, 2016

Do I think that his biggest fear is actually 'swimming in an oddly shaped

oasis at night'?

No.

I think his biggest fear is swimming in a *different* body of water.

One shaped more like a girl.

Chapter Sixteen: the logistics of dating
Date: November 2016

I laid on my bathroom floor and stared at the ceiling until my shift started.

What had I done.

At work, I stared at the books, unable to decipher any other thoughts besides: *What had I done.*

"Take me on a date."

"Huh?"

I snapped out of my trance and saw Luna standing in front of me.

"Huh?" I said again.

"Take me on a date."

I paused. "…how?"

Her eyebrows furrowed. "What do you mean how? You know what—never mind. What are you doing tonight?"

"Uh," I stuttered, "I'm busy."

"No, you're not. Pick me up at seven."

What had I done.

"Jeez, you look like I just told you that your mom died. It's just a date." And then she turned around and walked away.

"Wait!" I called out after her, "I don't know where you live!"

But she didn't hear me, or rather, she absolutely, did not care.

"That's going to be awkward when she finds out your mom really did die." Susan chimed in after Luna was gone.

"Thanks Susan," I said, coming out of my second trance of the day.

--

I was not going to pick her up at seven. Or go on a date with her.

There was just no way.

So why was I furiously chucking shoes and ties around my closet, looking for something to wear after my shift ended?

Because I was not going.

So why did I put on a navy-blue wool tailored suit, dress shoes, and a white tie?

Things were completely out of control.

Before I could find the will power to control myself, I was spraying cologne, brushing my teeth two times, and swinging my hair around like Jim Morrison at the Whisky a Go Go.

And then hoping in my car.

What had I done.

I had no idea where Luna lived, so my impulse was to drive to the library. I drove at eighty miles per hour in hopes that if I drove fast enough it might make this inevitable experience end quicker.

Or kill me.

When I arrived, I put my head on the steering wheel and counted to two hundred.

I'll just drive away, I thought, *I still have time to leave.*

But I still opened the car and got out.

I never have been great at listening to my craving control.

I stood out front and lit a cigarette. Waiting. But when no one showed up, I walked to the back. No one.

I sighed.

It was a sigh of relief, but when it left my body, I didn't feel any solace.

I guess I was just a man in a navy-blue wool tailored suit, smoking a cigarette outside a closed public library. That's all I needed to be.

I turned to head back to my car when I met the gaze of a very bright and cosmic sign on the back door.

Come in, Nathan. Door is unlocked.

I put the cigarette out and opened the door.

There she stood. Draped in a long, beige, French-retro dress loose at her hips. Her hair in a loose ponytail.

Big gold hoops and gold bangles chimed on her wrists and ears.

Warm vanilla and rose wafting from her ethos.

Barefoot.

She was more beautiful than the universe.

I was unable to respond to such a magnificent site.

It was physically impossible to process.

"Isn't she beautiful?"

That's when I noticed Susan, standing next to her, holding hairspray and a tube of lipstick. I wasn't aware that Susan was acquainted with either of those two artifacts.

"Susan?"

"I was helping Luna get ready for the date!" She said with a big smile.

"You know how to do that?" I asked.

Her eyebrows furrowed. "I am a woman you know."

"Hi." Luna said, her lips perked up at both sides of her face.

"Hi." I replied.

Silence.

"Are those for me?" She asked.

"What?" I looked down at my hands. In a mere trance, I must have picked some daises out of the ground.

"Oh," I stammered, "yeah-"

"Daises are my favorite," she said, smiling.

"I saw them outside the library, I must have thought you'd like them." I said, handing the messy bunch to her.

"I do like them. I was the one who planted them."

Of course she was.

"Oh," I stammered, "sorry for ripping them out of the ground, I-"

She laughed. "It's okay Nathan. I love them."

"You might need a permit for that," Susan said, an eyebrow raised at Luna, "I don't know if it's legal to go around planting flowers on public property."

More silence. Our eyes never left each other's gaze.

"Alrighty," Susan said after a while of uncomfortable longing, "let's get you kiddos on a date."

"Oh yes, I, uh, I made a reservation at The Waterboy," (I must have made those being held at gun point… obviously).

"Scratch those," Luna said, "I have a better idea."

Chapter Seventeen: A yellow gas station
Date: November 2016

She blindfolded me with my own tie and then drove me frighteningly to what I thought would be my death.

"Ta-da!" she exclaimed finally.

"Can I take the tie off my eyes now?" I asked.

"That's the entire point of the phrase, 'ta-da'?"

"Well, I just wanted to make sure you didn't mean-"

"Nathan! Just take the damn tie off!"

"Okay, okay," I said, pulling it down.

I was standing at the corner of Alfalfa Plant Rd. and Brunk Rd., right in front of the yellow gas station.

A shade of yellow that was now seemingly brighter.

This seemed to be a corner of the universe that had the ability to revive a beating drum inside me that had long been silenced. A pocket of the world created just for me.

Containing the very few things I found beautiful:

Luna.

Food.

Bad coffee.

Wine.

Candles.

And.

Wait wine?

(One should always disclose allergies before dining with another).

I stared at her in silence.

"Well, are you going to ever sit down?" she asked.

"Oh," I hadn't even noticed I was hovering over her, "right." I sat down on the blanket, feeling uncomfortably large and ungraceful next to her.

And then I noticed them. The innumerable daisies growing from the cracks in the sidewalk.

Everywhere.

Blossoming in between us.

Wherever Luna was, daises seemed to follow.

I pointed. "Did you plant those too?"

She giggled. "No. But this is where I fell in love with them."

This is where I fell in love with you.

"Luna, I-" I had to tell her. To warn her.

"Wait," she said, "let me go first."

I closed my eyes and clenched my fist. This was not going to be effortless.

"I wanted to say-"

I could see the condensation dripping down it's precious neck, the frosty glaze that was mesmerizing my gaze. In a moment filled with so much beauty, there was only darkness staring into my eyes.

"I'm an alcoholic." I interrupted her.

She stopped what she was saying.

"I am an alcoholic," I said again, "and I am a year sober."

Silence. The silence that always seemed to fill the area we were in when we were with each other. Most of the time it felt like the silence was louder than actual words.

And then she grabbed the wine bottle and threw it across the street.

We watched as the glass shattered in the road. The liquid seeping down the gutter.

"Problem solved then," she said.

And for the first time since I had met her, I thought,

Luna Elrod is going to be the life of me.

Chapter Eighteen: a swan trapped in a cage
Date: November 2016

I'll spare you the specifics of the rest of the night because, well, I don't know you that well and it would make me uncomfortable to tell you about the details of my sexual escapades.

Maybe later if you buy me a drink. (Kidding).

But let's just say, we went back to my place.

And there wasn't much more talking that occurred. Or eating.

And certainly, no drinking for that matter.

There was hardly a cigarette smoked (I think you get the idea).

Being around Luna made me realize how uncomfortably conscious I was. It was painful being constantly reminded of my surroundings and my human-like tendencies and persistently trying to ward them off.

Luna just absorbed everything around her.

Taking it all in and turning it beautiful.

She let the wind blow her where mother nature thought she should be.

So blissfully unaware of her role as a flawed human.

No attempt to control her mankind defects.

She let the essence of her feelings and the gravity of the world decide things for her.

Meanwhile, I let the pain of my past decide mine.

--

Two in the morning.

My car windows down, a cigarette clenched between both our tired mouths.

Luna put her head out the window.

I shut my eyes for just a second.

These moments of silence with her were the first bits of quietness I had in my sober life.

No pain. No fear.

Just silence.

A silence that only alcohol could have created prior to her.

Luna's hair was gone with the wind. Her laugh heard but not seen.

The sadness in my eyes. Heard. But no longer seen.

"Is this it?" I asked, pulling into a dark parking lot.

She laughed. "I have no idea."

"What? What do you mean you have no idea? You directed me here!"

She kept laughing. "I'm not very good with directions in the dark," she grabbed my arm, "but let's go find out!"

I put my car into park before she could pull me out of the moving vehicle and followed behind her.

Once we got to her apartment door, she nodded. "Yep. This is it."

"Okay," I said, "well, have a good night."

"Wait!" She stopped me, "don't you want to see my place?"

Luna Elrod Journal Entry
Date: November 13th, 2016

Nathan has a wing in the middle of his apartment.

How is it then,

he hasn't learned how to fly?

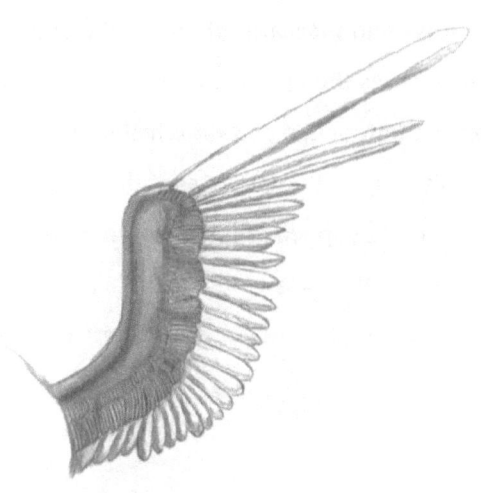

Her place was as organized as her thoughts. Half her walls painted pink, and the other half looked as if she never got around to finishing the job. A long, velvet green couch embroidered with an array of flowers took up the entire living room and daises were everywhere. Half of them dead and the other half thriving to an extent that was boastful.

A white canopy with twinkle lights hung from the ceiling in her bedroom over a mattress on the floor that couldn't be bothered with sheets or a duvet. A green nightstand stacked with the remains of what used to be candles stood taller than her bed. She seemed to have more pillows than mattress, considering throw pillows were the main attraction. Lighters were left around the room as tripping hazards and a typewriter sat overturned in the middle of the floor.

Books piled up in every corner.

A fluffy bathmat was soaking on her wet bathroom floor, given she had no shower curtain. *Cutty B. Sands* stained in red lipstick was written across her bathroom mirror and shampoo bottles scattered all over the ground. Eyeshadows and mascaras claiming the entire countertop.

Her kitchen was the epitome of a European hostel. Dry pasta was all over the counter, an untouched sourdough starter sat in the sink, and ceramic glassware sat on the edge of counters as if they were suicidal maniacs.

It felt like I had tripped and landed on a tab of acid.

It was obvious this was where Luna's brain went every night.

It was like seeing the most beautiful creature on earth's cage at the zoo.

"I want to show you something," she said, stepping over a book that was on the floor.

"Okay," I responded, sitting down uncomfortably on the couch.

She went into her bedroom and then appeared with an orange and white floral embroidered, hardcover journal.

She handed it to me.

"What am I supposed to do with this?" I asked, holding it in my hands like it was shards of glass.

"Open it."

"What?"

"Just open it."

I opened the damn thing. And on the very inside it read,

Luna Elrod's Journal.

She was smiling. "My real name is Luna."

Dumbfounded, I whispered, "Luna Elrod," mostly to myself.

"I don't tell people my actual name," she said, "so that day... when I introduced myself to you and I told you my real name, I sort of shocked myself."

"Why do you not tell people your real name?" I asked.

She shrugged. "Protection purposes."

Still entirely unsure what that meant, I asked, "so, Jane? Your name at your work, where did you come up with that?"

She smirked.

I rolled my eyes. "Let me guess, another one of Sands characters?"

"His mother. Jane M. Sands in the book, *Broad in Daylight.* His worst enemy but his most vital muse. His best work is about her."

"You are insane."

"I think so," she said, beaming.

I paused and looked at her. "Why did you tell *me* your real name?"

She shrugged. "I guess that's what I'm still trying to figure out."

Luna Elrod Journal Entry
Date: November 14th, 2016

Some people simply won't get out of the ocean, even when they are warned about riptides.

Chapter Nineteen: risotto
Date: December 2016

Unlike most parents, my mother never shied away from answering inappropriate questions asked by a child at the breakfast table. "Mom, why did I hear yells for so long last night?" "Mom, why was there a naked man walking around with a guitar?" "Mom, why did that man sing for so long into your eyes like that?"

"I was making love, honey-love," she would respond bluntly, drinking a mimosa.

"How do you do that?" I would ask.

"Honey," she would say, "making love is like making risotto. It's an adored dish, but it can come off intimidating and complicated at first."

"How so?"

"Well honey, because it's long and extraneous, and if you don't stick with the process, you don't always get the outcome you'd originally been hoping for."

"What's the process?" I'd sit on the edge of my chair with a sippy cup and wait desperately to hear the words that came out of my mother's mouth.

"Well… first, you must warm the broth. Now, you can do this in various ways. One of them, for example, is singing into mommy's eyes for a very long time. Next, you must add the broth to the rice. Now this is where things can get intimidating because you can add all sorts of things! Caramelized onions, napa cabbage, or perhaps even wild mushrooms! You can make the risotto as wild or as bland as you wish, seeing as everyone who is dining agrees to the added ingredients."

"Wow," I would say, completely mesmerized.

She would hold a finger up. "But, if you add these ingredients, you absolutely cannot get distracted and forget to keep stirring. The stirring is the most important part, honey-love. It's how you reach the end goal."

"What's the end goal?"

"A lovely meal," she'd say, holding up her mimosa.

--

Luna and I spent most of December making risotto.

She'd come over uninvited. Banging on the door. Asking to cook more risotto.

Sometimes it would be two, three in the morning and I'd hear her banging.

I'd look at myself in the mirror and think, *what have I done?*

I have created a risotto addict.

I'd come home from work, and she would be on the kitchen counter, ready to cook.

I'd think, *what have I done?*

One time she came bursting in wearing nothing but a pink curtain from her bedroom.

"Is that your bedroom curtain?" I asked, holding a pan, cooking a grilled cheese.

"I thought it looked better as a dress than a drape."

What have I done?

But I did absolutely nothing to stop it.

In fact, I started leaving my door unlocked.

Luna had no limitations with her risotto either. She wanted it anywhere. And everywhere. Even places that didn't have kitchens. Like the library.

"Tell Susan you're taking a five-minute break, and meet me in the bathroom," Luna would say, sitting in my library cart.

"That sounds ill-advised," I'd respond.

And then I would meet her in the bathroom.

The whole thing was quite frankly out of control and entirely inappropriate.

But even Jim seemed to be encouraging this misconduct.

"Can you please teach me how to warm broth," he begged me one evening when we were getting dinner before our AA holiday party.

"No." I said, taking a bite from my steak. "I need somebody to take the broth away from me."

"Ugh man, you're the last person that deserves having those skills. You don't even appreciate them."

"Jim." I said, with deep concern in my voice, "this is not okay. My life is out of control."

He rolled his eyes. "Loosen up man. If having (risotto) with a woman you're in love with is 'out of control,' then I'd suggest you just start drinking again. You were way more fun back then."

I took another bite. "Then why does it feel so wrong?"

"Because you have never cooked it with somebody you actually care about before."

I narrowed my eyes. "Wow Jim. That might just be the truest thing you've said all day."

Jim pointed his fork at me. "That's false. I also commented on Susan's lovely bosom."

I threw my napkin at him. "What's wrong with you?"

AA hosted a Secret Santa holiday party every year and it was about as much fun as an AA holiday party sounds.

I had Max this year as my Secret Santa, and I used it as my time to shine my niche and brilliant sense of humor that nobody in the group ever understood. In my ingenious attempts to get the crowd to laugh, I got Max a self-tanning kit. I wrapped it up in newspaper and was ready to hear the laughter from around the sadly decorated room.

It was tradition that everyone came in a Santa hat, well, everyone except me. Even Jim would squeeze a Santa hat onto his huge head every year. One year Cindy had to tape it to the side of his face because it kept falling off.

But this year, I also wore a hat.

"Nathan with Christmas cheer? Who got Ebenezer Scrooge in the spirit this year?" Max said when I walked in.

"His girl," Jim said, fixing his hat that was already slipping off.

"I'm going to pin that hat to your head using thumb tacks next time," I countered to Jim.

"Hope you guys like sugar cookies with green and red frosting!" Elizabeth exclaimed, walking into the room holding onto a plastic snowman tray. "Jeez! Nathan! Warn somebody before you become happy." Her tray almost went flying when she saw me.

Jim walked over to her plate with an outstretched hand. Elizabeth smacked it away. "Not before everyone gets to look at them Jim!"

"I am not happy," I said to Elizabeth taking a cookie, "just a little less depressed."

"Yeah, still the same old Nathan," Sofia retorted.

Landon clapped his hands together in the way that he always did to get us to stop communicating with each other without his control. "Alright my people, let's get this party started!"

The rules were that we spun an empty beer bottle to see who's turn it was (this was Max's idea. I'll give him credit for this one).

The bottle landed on me first.

Landon handed me the gift that had my name on it. The manner in which it was wrapped I knew Jim had to have been my Secret Santa.

"Jim." I said before opening it.

"Bastard!" He cried, "how'd you know it was me?"

I held up the gift wrapping that was falling apart at the edges. "Your hands are way too big to properly wrap anything."

Jim sighed. "I knew I should have let Cindy help me."

"Open the fucking present!" Sofia called out, "I'm on the edge of my seat!"

I rolled my eyes and peeled off the flaking wrapping paper.

It was a gray hardcover journal.

"Open it," he said.

"Why do people keep telling me to open journals?" I mumbled to myself.

"What?"

"Nothing." I said and opened it.

"From a Sober Santa."

I was never good at saying how I felt, so I just didn't.

I nodded at him.

He nodded back.

And then the bottle spun and landed on Max.

"What is it?" he asked, holding it in his hands as if I had just offended him deeply.

"It's self-tanner," I said, a tad too exuberant.

"So, Nathan had you, *obviously*," Sofia said, rolling her eyes, "this game isn't very fun."

"Why would you get me this?" Max asked.

I pointed at him, chuckling. "Because you like to fake tan?"

Max looked at me with a straight face. "Would you have said something like that to Kurt Cobain? No, probably not. Imagine how you'd feel if I end up like him-"

"Max, please," Landon said, "it's just a gift."

I looked at Jim and shrugged. He was trying not to laugh.

And then the group started bickering with each other about game rules and presents and in an anxious attempt to get everyone to calm down, Landon started spinning the bottle again.

I clutched onto my journal.

I did not want to drop something so special.

Chapter Twenty: Sober Santa
Date: Childhood Decembers

Christmas as a kid always started out good.

My mom used to get three or four Christmas trees, putting one in every corner.

She strung lights from room to room, we hung ornaments, made gingerbread houses, and listened to Elvis' Christmas Album.

One year she got a snow machine. She turned her records on, and we danced in the faux falling snowflakes until our entire apartment was a snow hill. Afterwards, we had to sweep the fake snow off the terrace. I remember laughing until my chest hurt as people walked by, looking up frantically as paper snow was dumped on their heads.

"Merry Christmas!" she shouted, "it's snowing in Northern California!"

Christmas as a kid always ended badly though.

She liked her hot chocolate and Baileys this time of the year. By the time I was opening my gifts, she'd already be pouring her second mug at eight am.

I never knew how my mother got her money, or where the never-ending supply came from, but every year, I got more and more gifts to try and make up for her ruining Christmas the previous year.

It was just me and her. Every year. But when I look back on those days, it was really just me.

She'd try to distract me with a new G.I. Joe doll as she was crying in the corner over some guy named Joe or show me a book that I'd get lost in so I wouldn't notice her passed out on the green sofa.

I'd check her pulse, in between chapters.

The best gift she ever got me was a gray hardcover journal. I remember feeling the thick, dense spine, thinking it was so cool. I remember thinking that someone like Hemingway probably started writing in journals like that one.

Hours after I unwrapped the journal, she passed out. She was lying on the couch in a Santa hat and a red dress that had white puffs sewed on the sleeves.

Watching her, I wrote my first story.

"The Drunk Santa."

It was about how Santa couldn't get to all the kids' houses on Christmas Day because he would get too drunk and wouldn't be able to drive the sleigh anymore. Santa would end up crashing on the roof of a different kids house every year and pass out in the sleigh.

So instead of wanting gifts from Santa, the kids started hoping that he would get too drunk and spend the night on their roof, so they could go out and spend time with him and the reindeer.

In the story, the kids began leaving hot chocolate and Baileys instead of cookies. They started stuffing their own stockings with booze, in hopes that Santa wouldn't be able to resist. They started wishing for Santa's drunken presence rather than toys.

The kids didn't care how drunk he was, or if he had brought them any gifts, all the kids wanted was a Christmas Day spent with Santa.

--

So, when Jim got me that journal, I only wished I knew how to respond.

Chapter Twenty-One: Christmas Eve
Date: December 2016

Christmas Eve, just the two of us in my apartment. Luna was sitting by the fireplace, reading aloud, *A Christmas Carol*, in red pajamas she had sewn herself.

I was also in red pajamas Luna had sewn.

But the strangest part of the holiday season thus far was not the fact I had worn a Santa hat to AA, or the fact that I was wearing festive, hand-made pajamas, it was that Luna, and I, were with each other, on a holiday typically spent with family.

Granted, this was not strange for me, considering I had no family, other than Jim (where I typically spent all my holidays bringing over store-bought mashed potatoes that I pretended to home cook), but it did make me all the more curious of Luna.

"Luna-" I started to ask.

"Wait, Nathan. I'm just getting to The Second of the Three Spirits. This is the best part."

"Why aren't you with your family?" I asked, unable to pause my interest.

She sighed, loudly. And then closed the book.

When she didn't answer, I asked again. "Why aren't you with your family?"

She shrugged. "Because I left them."

I looked at her uneasy. "What do you mean you left them?"

"I left them." She said again, as if she was reading off the ingredients to a pot-roast.

"Can you clarify?"

"I left them in Breathitt County, Kentucky. Where I'm from."

"I meant can you clarify why you left them- wait, you're from Kentucky?!"

She sighed. "Okay picture this," she put her hands up as if she was generating a movie screen out of thin air, "a couple of uneducated teens have sex in the back of a beat down Ford Truck and make a baby. And better yet, they keep the baby! And then they try to raise it in their parents' house with no idea what to do with the 'looney blonde,' other than cry and call the pastor."

"Looney blonde?"

She nodded. "That's what all 12,953 people in my County called me."

"So, you ran away?"

"It was better that I left. They didn't want me there anyway."

Luna Elrod Journal Entry
Date: December 24th, 2016

As far as entertainment went as a kid, well, there were the rusty nails in the backyard I used to pierce all the girls' ears in my 5th grade class with. Tetanus was a warm welcome party into the 6th grade. That got me my first slapping from my father.

I spent most of my childhood in timeout or in the principal's office. I was often told that I was unmanageable and arduous. I looked up the definition of arduous in the school library and cried until I passed out.

I overheard my mother crying to the priest once, begging him to perform an exorcism on me. She said she was convinced I had a demon living inside my soul. After that I tried to hurt myself with the barbwire that was in the backyard. Maybe I could bleed the demon out myself.

I was not only afraid of myself, but I was starting to believe everything my town was saying about me. Maybe I was a sinner and a liar.

Maybe I was crazy for climbing a Hickory tree and refusing to come down for two days until I caught a Goldfinch. The sound of my mother's cries, nor the smell of my grandmother's chicken pot pie couldn't get me down. Only the force of the fire department could stop me from catching my bird.

Maybe I was lying about the way soft jazz made me feel, or how fanatical the color yellow was. Those things made me so lively that I climbed a yellow gas station with a radio and tried to get the entire town to dance along with me.

"What's wrong with you?" the kids in my class would ask.

"Do you not feel that too?" I would ask through tears, wondering why nobody felt the kind of pain or joy I did.

We lived with my grandparents. They had all kinds of junk in their basement. Old flags, tools, cassette tapes, typewriters... I made do with all of it. But what I was most interested in, were the dusty books.

I used to go down and pick a new book every night before bed and then I'd stay up all night with a flashlight reading them. I either never slept, or I slept for days.

One night I dusted off a book called *In the Vein of Feeling Something*. It was written by a man named Cutty B. Sands.

It was the first time I ever felt understood.

It was the first time I had ever felt like I didn't need to rid of the demon in me.

Maybe someone did feel pain and joy like I did.

Maybe there was a world somewhere, out there, that understood me?

My town called me the "looney blonde."

But Cutty B. Sands seemed to write about women like me.

He seemed to have experience with the "looney blondes" of the world.

I started staying after school every day in the library. I read every single book he wrote.

Every novel. Every poem. Every stanza ever written.

He was cold. And bitter. He didn't trust the world.

But that didn't matter to me, because I knew in his presence, I'd be safe.

I'd be safe from the outside world that didn't understand me.

Feared me.

Whereas he had studied minds like mine. Knew minds like mine.

When I read *In the Vein of Feeling Something* for the first time, my life revealed itself.

"Can the whole world be one person?" He asked.

I wanted a world where I was normal.

I wanted a world where my mind was admired.

Nobody knew who Cutty B. Sands was. He wrote under an alias and never disclosed himself. The only information I could find on him was that he once resided in Sacramento.

I planned to leave for California the day I turned 18.

Because I wanted to know, can the whole world be one person?

A world for my mind to belong.

That night, on Christmas Eve, I woke up to a call from Jim. It was three in the morning. Luna was asleep aside me.

"Is everything okay?" I asked, half-asleep into the landline.

"Yeah- uh, sorry to wake you, but I was just wondering if, if you maybe wanted to go for pie?"

He didn't have to say anything else before I said I'd meet him at a diner in fifteen.

Sometimes when people have a craving for brown sugar and granny apples, you just agree.

We sat at the diner across from each other in silence, poking at the apples coated in lemon juice and cinnamon, yet to take a bite.

It was 3:35 am.

"Thanks for the journal," I finally said.

Jim nodded.

I breathed heavily out of my nose. I didn't know how to continue.

Neither did he.

I took a bite of my pie and then angled my fork at him. "Mmmm, just how you like it, Jim."

"Really?"

I nodded.

He took a bite.

More silence.

"This whole herbage thing really blows this time of the year, huh?" I asked.

Jim swallowed. "Especially the big fucking green ones that perch in your living room."

I gritted my teeth together. "Yeah. That's the worst kind."

"With the damn ornaments?"

"And the giant star? I mean what drugs was the person doing who first thought to put a gold star on top of a wholesale pine tree?"

"And what about the lights? I mean what's with the fucking lights?!"

"You just wrap and wrap and wrap that shit around a tree and people expect you to be normal about it?"

Jim laughed until he was crying.

I nodded.

And then we sat there until sunrise. Eating our pies. Not saying a word.

Sometimes when people have a craving for brown sugar and granny apples, you just agree.

Luna Elrod Journal Entry
Date: December 24th, 2016

One year, on Christmas Eve, I think I was around eleven or twelve, I wanted to see Santa Clause for myself.

I was being bullied at school for still believing in him. For still believing in the Polar Express and the flying reindeer and the little elves. I was being bullied for believing in magic, like always.

So, I was going to capture a photo of him and prove it. Prove to everyone, that magic *was* real.

I had a plan. I was going to stay up all night and wait for him at the top of the stairs. Once his plump belly was bending over, reaching into his red bag and pulling out my gifts, I was going to capture it with my grandmother's vintage Polaroid camera.

After dinner, when everyone was gathered around the television watching *It's a Wonderful Life,* I snuck into my father's medicine cabinet and found his Ritalin. He always had some kind of pill in his medicine cabinet that he got from random men at diners and street fairs. And I was always curious enough to try each one.

Once my father passed out on the couch, my grandparents had gone to bed, and my mother finished her night tea, I tip toed out of bed, took the pill, and changed into an all-black outfit.

I crept to the top of the stairs and then I waited, clutching onto the vintage camera.

An hour later, shaking from the Ritalin and my eyes sore because I refused to blink, I heard somebody walking to the living room.

"This is it," I whispered, smiling ear to ear, getting the camera ready to capture the enchantment.

The Christmas tree sparkled in the carpeted room. The ornaments hung loosely from the pine needles, shining in the light from the television. The house perfectly awaited the company of delicately wrapped presents.

And then I saw my grandpa.

I saw him walk into the room carrying a handful of wrapped gifts. I saw his plump belly bend over and place them under the tree. I saw him walk over to the cookies I hand-decorated and eat a few of them. And then I saw him put a blanket over my father.

And in that moment, I realized, *I* was the freak.

There was no magic.

Everything everyone had said about me was true.

The way my mind saw things wasn't real.

My wings were cut.

I was drowning.

What happened next is a blur, but I remember screaming bloody murder, gifts being thrown into the fire, and my once asleep father holding me back as I threw cookies at my grandpa.

My mother was crying on the phone with the priest, as he prayed with her.

My grandmother held a cold towel to my forehead.

The water dripped down my face. Pulling me under.

I was drowning.

And then my father slapped me.

And I passed out onto the couch.

Chapter Twenty-Two: Christmas Day
Date: December 2016

Christmas 2016.

It was the first time since my mother's passing that there was a Christmas tree in my living area. It wasn't the most traditionally attractive tree, granted Luna had cut it down herself in a mini skirt and dragged it over refusing assistance from numerous helping hands. By the time she got back, the tree, and the mini skirt, could have used some supplementary material. But Luna took care of that as well.

Pine, roast beef, and non-alcoholic eggnog came together for the holidays to fill my apartment with quite *powerful* scents. It certainly overpowered the usual smell of black coffee and Luna sure heard my opinion on the matter. My complaints went unheard.

"This'll do." She said.

And that was that.

I was jolted awake not long after I had gotten home from pie with Jim to the sound of bells in my ear. Luna demanded I come to the living room immediately and served me with eggnog and a slab of roast beef. But when she didn't like my sulking, she chased me around the apartment ringing the bell until I cracked a smile. And when I immediately frowned afterwards, she did it again.

I caved, and we opened presents, watched multiple holiday films, played Christmas Carols, and I even agreed to make homemade hot chocolate. But I drew the line when Luna said, "let's take our clothes off and play in the snow."

"Luna?" I said, knowing she was being serious, "what snow?"

"Let's go find some!"

"Where?"

"Big Bear!"

"Luna? That's an eight-hour drive! And besides! Nobody plays in the snow *naked*."

"Nathan, it's like skinny dipping but seasonal!"

"It's already two o'clock!" I exclaimed, "by the time we get there it will be nightfall!"

"Nathan, nobody says *nightfall*."

Before the clock struck 2:05, I was driving her eight-hours to Big Bear Lake.

The dark had already settled in the underbelly of the mountains and black slush became a fast lover with my tires. Luna had her head sticking out the passenger seat window.

"It's so beautiful," she kept saying.

"You can't even see anything," I grumbled, "and can you roll the window up? It's freezing."

"That might be your cold heart," she responded.

"Or the frost bite you've invited into the car."

"I've also invited him to dinner tonight."

When we finally reached what seemed like a destination in a landscape of unspecified bitter cold, Luna stripped down and got out of the car.

"You meant the naked part too?" I asked as I watched her run into the madness.

I sat in my car, wondering why it was I didn't feel exhausted. I had only gotten a few hours of sleep before Luna woke me and then was coerced into driving eight hours in the dark.

Luna kept yelling from the abyss. "Come on!"

I shook my head as if she could see me.

There was no way I was going to join her out there in the frigid obscurity. *Especially* without my clothes.

But nature is more powerful than man. And sometimes a moon's gravitational pull causes the ocean to create a tide, pulling dead carcasses into the unknown territory of the sea.

And so, I found myself in the falling snow.

I covered up my bits and parts I wasn't used to exposing in bitter cold public areas.

And we danced.

"I don't know how," I whispered.

"You don't know how to what?" she asked.

I clenched my fists and closed my eyes. "I don't know how to tell you that I think the whole world can be one person."

It was some time before I opened them, but when I did, she smiled and said, "you just did."

Luna Elrod Journal Entry
Date: December 25th, 2016

I have a sneaking suspicion I fell in love with him before I even met him.

Chapter Twenty-Three: New Year's Nightmare
Date: January 2017

A few years back I went to see a hypnotist. I was willing to try anything to get sober. I had recently relapsed and was struggling to think about anything else besides the inside of a Jack Daniels bottle. The only issue was, this wasn't my first attempt.

When I arrived, I was uncommonly greeted by a photo of myself. But with a pair of woman's sunglasses on and the words NEW YEARS NIGHTMARE in bright red across the picture.

The woman sitting behind the counter looked up, saw me, and screamed until the cops showed up.

Supposedly, I had gotten black out drunk on New Year's Eve, wanted to poke around at sobriety as a resolution, and went to see a hypnotist for a quick fix. But things took a turn when she wanted to do a proper job.

"I meant just hard liquor you hussy!" I shouted, "beer, wine and rum drinks on vacation don't count!"

And when she wouldn't listen, I stole her sunglasses, jewelry, and anything else laying around that was up for grabs.

I paid her back for the debts and spent the night incarcerated. But clearly, she still held a grudge.

But who can blame her. I *was* a New Year's nightmare.

Luna hadn't been over in a few days, and knowing how she operated, I suspected it was because she had big plans brewing for the holiday.

I called her when I woke up. No answer.

I texted her. And then I watched as the message sat alone. Waiting for a response.

I shrugged and began my usual morning routine, but it kept getting thrown off due to my lack of willpower to stop checking my phone.

Had I become a teenage girl waiting by the landline for the radio station to announce the winner of underground boy band tickets? What was wrong with me?

Why did I just keep hovering over the device as if I was waiting for it to wake up and insult me?

I called her again. No answer.

I paced.

I looked.

I paced.

I checked.

I paced.

I called again.

"LUNA!" I screamed at no one, "ANSWER!"

I sat down on the couch. *Breathe Nathan. You are majorly overreacting. She has a life. Let her call you when she gets the chance.*

I breathed.

I looked.

I breathed.

I checked.

I breathed.

I called again.

I got up and started taking down the Christmas decorations.

I breathed.

I looked.

I breathed.

I checked.

I breathed.

I called again.

But when she didn't answer the next call, I picked up the giant piece of herbage that was decorated with ornaments in the middle of my living room and threw it out the window.

And then the phone rang.

When I saw her name as the caller ID, I laughed out loud at myself.

See Nathan?

"Hi!" I answered.

"Nathan?" her voice sounded raspy, like she had just woken up.

"Are you just waking up? I'm sorry- I hope I didn't wake you."

"I was sleeping."

"I'm sorry, I just wanted to ask what plans-"

"No plans."

"What?"

Silence.

"Luna? Is everything okay?"

"I can't tonight, sorry Nathan. I have to go."

"Luna?"

She hung up.

Fuck.

No plans? How was I supposed to avoid becoming the New Year's nightmare without her?

I called Jim.

But he and Cindy were going to a hotel in Malibu. He had "found the recipe for risotto!"

Great timing, Jim.

I called Susan.

Apparently, the library isn't open after 1pm on the holiday. I asked if she needed any janitor work done around the place. No. She said. Go have fun, Nathan. She said.

Go have fun? Facepalm.

The only fun I would be having is forcing Luna to hang out with me. An hour later I arrived at her doorstep with a bouquet of white daisies, donuts, and root beer.

"Luna," I said, fumbling with the door handle, "let me in."

No answer.

"Luna? Your door is locked, not sure if that was a mistake but can you come and let me in." I knocked again.

No answer.

"Luna! I have daises and donuts. Your favorites!"

I pulled out my phone and texted her.

Nothing.

So, I called her.

I heard her phone ringing from inside the apartment.

"Luna! I can hear your phone! I know you're in there!" I called out.

I knocked louder.

"Luna?!"

"Go away Nathan!"

"What?"

"Go away!"

I nearly dropped the contents in my hand on the ground in shock. "Luna? I'm confused," I said, leaning up against the door, "did I do something to upset you?"

"Leave!"

"Luna, can you at least explain to me what I did?" I said to the doorframe, "please let me in, can we talk about this?!"

Silence seeped through the cracks of the door.

"Luna. Please."

My hands turned weak and in attempt to overcompensate for the infirmity, I thrusted the root beer cans into the door. "I'm not leaving!" I shouted, and then I rammed the donut box into the door. The crumbling insides hit the ground, becoming no longer a Luna savor nor edible.

"Luna? Why are you doing this?"

I propelled myself into the door, which then sent me crumbling to the ground.

The shouting and the tears that followed the confusion continued for far too long became a strain of silence that was far too deafening.

My mind couldn't make out how we could have just gone from the best Christmas of my life, to… this.

A neighbor came out yelling, threatening to call the police.

"Fine!" I shouted, throwing the flowers (the last saving grace) on the ground. "You women don't make any sense!"

I got in my car and drove off.

Leaving a mess all over her front porch.

And an even bigger one in my chest.

Luna Elrod Journal Entry
Date: December 31st, 2017

My ocean mind has entirely consumed me.

I can't breathe underwater.

I can't swim either.

The waves are too strong.

A piece of algae has wrapped itself around my foot and is pulling me under.

I let it sink me, I don't have the strength to fight it.

Nature is more powerful than the human force.

No one can save me.

I belong to the sea now.

Chapter Twenty-four: new year, old me
Date: January 2017

The grounds of logic do not apply to an addict who must be soothed.

Which is why there is no explanation for why I found myself on Third Street.

I slammed my car door shut and within seconds was yelling at the hipsters and the herbage to "get the fuck out of my way!"

I entered the mishmash that was the *Canterbury Tales*. If I couldn't be with Luna tonight, I wanted to be somewhere that reminded me of her.

I had no intention of drinking, of course. I just wanted to feel close to her.

But foreplay has a way of turning me on.

Luna Elrod Journal Entry
Date: January 1st, 2017

You can scream for help all you want when you're underwater.

But no one can hear you.

Jane. Was the only word I could properly slur.

Jane.

Jane.

Jane.

Where are you, Jane?

Why did you hurt me, Jane?

Come and find me, Jane.

"Jane."

I paid the bathroom bouncer fifty bucks.

Jane.

This time, when I entered, I grabbed every flute of champagne that was offered to me.

"Yes. Thank you."

"Yes. Thank you."

"Yes. Thank you."

"Yes. Thank you."

I sat in the back of the audience, and watched the women dance on stage. A martini placed in between my feet and a cigar in-between my lips. The women all clumped together like dried mascara. The dancing. The lingerie. The hats. The chairs. The red and gold paint in the room. It was all depleting me of oxygen. Glamorous sinister hands gripped around my neck and choked me until the only gold remaining in my life was the jewelry my mother left behind.

I found my way to the bathroom.

I leaned against the sink, rubbing my eyes, and reached into my pocket to pull out another cigar.

But before I could even light it, a guy I couldn't quite see through my blurred eyes said, "hey man, there's no smoking in here," and pointed to a *No Smoking* sign.

"I was just smoking out there," I said, motioning out the door.

"Bathroom is a no smoking zone," he replied.

My eyes focused and I got the visual of who this totalitarian was, telling me I wasn't allowed a buzz in the privacy of my own bowel movements. He was wearing a black suit and tie, his hair was slicked with what looked like recent semen, and his name tag said "MANAGER."

I narrowed my eyes at him.

He seemed to move on from my now burning cigar after he caught a glimpse of himself in the mirror.

"Are you the manager?" I asked, taking a puff.

He flicked at the name tag. "Yep."

I nodded, hunched over, still gripping onto the sink.

He looked me up and down, noticing my lit cigar. "I said no smoking in here."

"Who's Jane?" I asked.

"There are many Janes in the world," he responded.

"How about the *Jane* you know."

He smirked. "I know a few."

"How about the one you named the password after?"

"It's just a password, it means nothing."

"Yeah right."

He held his hands up, laughing. "Okay fine. Caught me."

Jane.

I attempted to stand all the way up. "Why?"

"Why what?" he asked, unamused by anything other than his reflection in the mirror.

"Why is she the fucking password?"

The smirk grew anew on his face.

I clutched the sink harder. Ash from the cigar burning my fingertips.

That snicker was going to be the very thing that killed me.

"Well," he fastened his tie, "persistence is key, right?"

I stood up.

He fixed his hair.

"Are you fucking her?" I asked.

"Not yet," he waved his tyrant finger, "but I will be. She can't say 'no' forever."

We held each other's gaze.

"Besides," he started again, "if that bitch misses one more shift, I have one more thing to hold over her head. Who else is going to hire that unmanageable slut? And hey, I told you to put that out!"

I took one more hit of the cigar before I woke up in jail.

Luna Elrod Journal Entry
Date: January 1st, 2017

I've had three cups of coffee, two red bulls, a sprite, a root beer, and I still can't get myself out of bed. I can feel my heart beating out of my chest, begging to be released, begging to be set free, but I've chained it up inside me.

I've clamped my heart to my head, in hopes that it'll resuscitate my mind.

I can feel my arm dangle over the side of my bed, but I don't recognize it as my own. I don't know who's arm it is. I wiggle my fingers, waiting for my brain receptors to acknowledge that it's in charge of those movements. But I don't know those body parts.

So, I lie in my bed, and I watch as someone else's hand writes this, I watch as someone else's arm moves the pages of my journal. I watch as someone else's fingers hold a pen.

I can't seem to remember anything. I can't remember what I did a month ago when I was out in the world. I can't remember the things that I did, the things that made me leave this bed.

I can hardly remember the face of the person I'm in love with.

My bed is slightly damp. I think I wet it last night, I probably couldn't get myself to the bathroom. There won't be any way I can get myself into the shower today either, so I will have to come up with a way to wiggle off the sheets and sleep on just the mattress for the rest of the day.

Chapter Twenty-Five: a rude awakening
Date: January 2017

My cuffed hands cradled my head as my hangover tried to pound its way out.

"Can I at least bum a cigarette off you man?"

The cop that had the unfortunate duty of working the morning shift of the holding cell New Year's Day looked at me with a vacant expression.

"Some chew? Anything? Come on!" I begged. "This headache is killing me."

Silence.

"Great. You're a real hoot and a half," I said, rolling my eyes and turning my body to face the other direction.

I sulked in the corner to try and prove a point, but I couldn't keep my ego muzzled. "So, what exactly happened again?" I asked.

"You assaulted the manager of a luxury club."

I smiled, chuckling to myself. "Bastard deserved it."

The same vacant expression came as a reply.

"Don't tell me you wouldn't have done the same," I said, instigating.

"No."

"Not even a slap?"

"No."

"A kick?"

"No."

"A purple nurple?"

"OH, SHUT THE FUCK UP ALREADY, WOULD YOU?"

Me and the officer both looked over at my crackhead cellmate who obviously had enough of my quips and was repositioning himself to face the other wall.

Now we were both sulking in the corner to try and prove a point.

"What's your deal?" I puffed at him.

"You won't shut up," he sneered through yellow teeth, "and I'm trying to have a conversation with Jonathon."

I looked around, confused, being it was only me and him in the cell. "Who's Jonathon?"

"My friend?" he pointed at the wall.

"Oh," I said, nodding exceedingly, "your *friend*."

"Yeah, and I can't hear him over your babbling." He turned and started talking to the wall named Jonathon again.

"Okay." I said, holding both my hands up in surrender.

Who was I to judge him anyway?

What felt like lifetimes later, the cop opened my cell. "You get three calls."

"I thought it was only one?" I asked.

"That's Hollywood."

He walked me over to the metal phone booth and handed me the phone.

In attempts to phone Jim, my finger slipped, and I ended up dialing Luna's number instead.

"No answer," I told the cop, despondency being the only thing we shared.

"Two more."

No answer.

"One more."

No answer.

I looked at him again, seeing only a reflection of my own pity in his eyes.

"Alright, listen," he said, "I'll give you one more. But that's it. And only because I want you out of here. You seem to piss off the other guy and it's annoying me."

I nodded, thanking him silently.

"And call a different number this time for Pete's sake."

I stood there for a moment, thinking.

Then I dialed the number and listened as it rang.

"Hello?"

"Hi," I said.

"Nathan?"

"Yeah, it's me."

"Why are you calling me from a jail landline?" she asked.

"Susan," I exhaled, "I won't be coming into work today."

"Nathan?! What's going on?"

I hung up.

Sometimes you just aren't hungry for brown sugar and granny apples.

My ocean is so

S

T

R

O

N

G

My waves are pulling me

U

N

D

E

R

Chapter Twenty-Six: "Write (work)* Drunk, Edit Sober" - Peter De Vries

Date: January 2017

"Are you drunk?" Susan asked me the next day as I sipped black coffee laced with tequila (vicious combination. Highly recommend if you're considering some light self-sabotage).

"No?" I responded, hiding behind a thick pair of black sunglasses.

"Is there tequila in that drink?"

"No?"

"Nathan, I can smell the tequila in that drink!"

"No?"

"My office now."

I sat, sprawled out in Susan's office. My eyes unopen behind the sunglasses.

"Nathan. Why did you call me from jail yesterday? And why are you drunk right now? What is going on?"

I shrugged, then pulled the sunglasses down the brim of my nose. "Just having some fun. Not like you'd know anything about that."

She looked like I gut punched her.

"Sorry," I said.

"What's gotten into you?" she asked, bewildered, and then softened her tone. "You know you can always talk to me."

I nodded.

She waited for my divulgence as we sat in silence.

And then I eventually said, "herbage."

She nodded, as if she understood. "Go home. Come back tomorrow. Cleaned up."

"Okay," I said.

The next morning, the sting of freezing bathwater woke me up. An empty bottle of tequila floated by my pruned wrists.

Fuck.

I was late for work.

I managed to slide my naked and disoriented body out of the tub, into the kitchen where my breakfast consisted of black coffee and Casamigos Blanco, and then to the library.

But my drunkenness was just about as blatant as Susan's sexuality.

"Why are you wet?" she asked, gripping onto her brooch.

"It's raining... outside..."

She took one glance out the window and saw the clear day's sky.

I shrugged. "You told me to get cleaned up."

She walked away.

Susan and I were never very good at using extraneous details when it came to discussing difficult topics.

After I failed to do any of my tasks the coming week, it was clear as the non-raining sky, that I had been fired.

Susan left a note on my desk in the office that said,

"You're fired."

Fuck.

Once Jim got home from Malibu and he noticed I wasn't going to AA, he was pounding on my door faster than one could say, "Look! Cream pie!"

I jumped out of my apartment window.

And then proceeded to run.

I just wasn't hungry for any god damn pie.

I threw my phone away in a trashcan outside a liquor store so he couldn't reach me either. It was unusable anyway, given the number of times he was calling me.

I ran down the highway with a handle of Tito's. Not that I preferred Tito's, it was just the first thing I saw in the store, and I knew Jim would already be looking in all my favorite spots.

And then I booked myself a motel room off I-80 for a couple weeks.

It was a quick progression from fired to failure.

But not long after,
I found her.

It was a dive bar near my motel named *Dive Bar*.

The place was moon made.

Bringing in only what the ocean tides had dragged up.

Half the walls were blue, the other half hardly painted. As if they had started the job and not completed it.

Newspaper clippings were pasted around the walls with shiny lipstick marks kissing them into place. Books being used as coasters.

And dead daises hung from the ceiling.

But most notably, the outside sign was a mermaid.

My fear of swimming in an oddly shaped oasis was only curable by someone who belonged to the sea.

Was she luring me in again? She had control over me even when she wasn't there.

"You fucker," I whispered to no one in particular, standing outside the bar, smoking a cigarette.

The wind was blowing the smoke directly into my eyes, but I didn't care.

I was drowning. I needed her to save me.

Even though I had so many hands reaching to pull me up, there was only one that I wanted to grab onto. And it was the one holding me under.

I walked inside.

Right into the siren infested waters.

"What brings you here tonight?" the man with a shaved head behind the counter asked.

"I know the girl on your sign," I responded, sitting down at a bar top.

"Who? The mermaid?"

I nodded.

He laughed at first, and then when he saw I was serious, his demeanor changed. "How many mermaids do you know?" he asked.

"One too many."

The man reluctantly served me for the next few hours while I silently inhaled water.

I am unclear as to why sadness and pain make such a delectable combo, but it sure is one hell of a customizable cocktail.

Why is it as humans, we believe so fervently that our sadness deserves pain?

As if something so innately natural is so nefarious we must be punished for it.

Or maybe our minds just don't want to suffer alone.

So, they bring our bodies down with it.

Maybe it's because a more tangible type of pain is easier to digest.

There was a man sitting next to me about the size of Strong Jim. It was a mystery how he was able to wrangle those muscles through the front door.

"Hey," I said.

He looked over at me and raised his drink in cheers.

"Hey asshole," I said again.

He looked at me confused. "Excuse me?"

I clenched my fist.

I woke up in the hospital. A black eye and a bruised rib cage. I laughed, madly, as I spit up blood.

Did you know that the ocean influences the Earth's climate? They say it
functions as the world's 'heart.'
If I'm the ocean.
And he's the world.
That means I control his heart.

Chapter Twenty-Seven: how not to detox
Date: January 2017

I was detoxing.

The fluids from the IV were failing to overcompensate for the pain that I was in, so I threw my legs over the side of the bed, and I grabbed the IV pole. There was no way I was staying here. Especially because I knew the nurses would start asking me questions about my "mental state" and that was not something I was going to indulge anyone with.

I hobbled out of the hospital bed and peeked out from behind the curtain that was housing me. No one was in sight. I could feel a breeze sliding up between the cut in the back of the hospital gown I was wearing, but I was short on time and couldn't afford to search for my clothes, let alone stumble around to try and get them on. So, I strolled out, swiftly, and breezily.

The hospital must've been either short on staff or short on giving a damn this day, because I made it out of the hospital without being stopped. Ass out. No shoes. IV pole intact.

Either way, you can't blame the establishment.

I shuffled into the first gas station I came across. It took me awhile to get my IV pole up the step, but I managed to wiggle it, along with myself in. The siren sounds of the beer swimming in the cooler were stronger than the inconvenience of my transportation.

The beer, cold with condensation. Me, hot with anticipation.

I had my eye on one thing.

"Hey man, you can't be barefoot with your ass out in here," the cashier called out to me.

I grabbed a beer out of the cooler and cracked it open. "Okay," I took a swig, "I'll go get some shoes."

"Come on man," he said.

"I'll take this case of beer," I threw a $20 on the table, "keep the change."

"That case is $25!" he called after me, but I was already headed elsewhere.

Luna Elrod Journal Entry
Date: January 10th, 2017

I woke up to my wings yanking me upwards to the sky.

Pulling me out of the water.

Wet and damaged.

But once again,

I am flying.

High.

High.

Over my sea.

My eyes are the sunshine that will dry up the tsunami damage around me.

McKinley Park.

That's where I was, clutching onto the IV pole with my bare ass on the park bench.

I cracked open another beer and poured it into the IV bag.

Straight to the point.

I sat in peace until a woman in lululemon noticed me.

"Oh my god an escapee!" She shouted.

I looked around. "Who?"

"You!" She shrieked, pointing a finger directly at me.

"Me?" I asked, opening another beer.

"How did you even manage to escape the psych ward?"

"Hey lady, it's not politically correct to use that terminology anymore. And I wasn't in the psych ward. *Obviously*, I'm an alcoholic."

"I'm calling the police!"

"You wouldn't happen to have any cigarettes on you, would you?"

She scoffed. "You think *I* would smoke cigarettes?"

"You definitely need one."

"You need help."

I tapped the IV injection port. "I'm in the process of getting it."

And then the woman kept shouting and I kept asking for a cigarette until she pulled out her pepper spray and sprayed it right into my eyes.

"Oh, fuck!" I clutched onto my face.

"I've always wanted to do that." She said, satisfied.

"Well, consider your bucket list complete!" I shouted and grabbed another beer, pouring it all over my face, and when that didn't help, I ripped grass out of the ground and rubbed it into my eyes.

"Nathan?"

"What?!" I screamed, unable to see or process that somebody here knew my name.

"Oh my god-"

"Who is that?" I yelled, hitting my fists on the park bench, grass and beer coming out of my red and inflamed eye-sockets.

"I'm calling Jim."

That's when I recognized her frail and panic-stricken voice. "Elizabeth?" I looked in the direction her voice was coming from.

I could hear her calling Jim.

"Elizabeth, stop!" I blindly lunged after her, trying to grab her phone.

"Get off me Nathan!" she screeched, "you smell terrible!"

"Give me that!"

"Why are you so sticky! Get off me! Your butt's touching me!"

"Hang up, Elizabeth!"

We continued to wrestle, and as my naked body became increasingly more exposed, more women gathered around us, shrieking in horror, watching a half-nude grown man connected to an IV pole, covered in beer, attack a strange, yelping woman.

"Help her!"

"No, it's fine!" Elizabeth called out, "I know him!"

"She has Stockholm syndrome!"

"Call the police!"

"Stop him!"

"Ew… was that his butt?"

I flailed around blindly, trying to hang up Elizabeth's phone, when I heard a truck pull up and come to an abrupt stop.

Before I knew it, I was being punched right in the face.

I crashed ass first to the ground.

Chapter Twenty-Eight: 3.14159
Date: January 2017

Incense and wild berry. They say that your sense of smell is the strongest. Which is how I knew exactly where I was when I woke up.

Landon's house was jarringly out of tune with reality. Every variation of a carpet you could fathom smothered the room like someone had just robbed Simas Floor & Design Company and needed a place to crash for the night before they took off on Aladdin's magic carpet.

And that wasn't even the worst of it.

Buddhist prayer bowls situated themselves in every corner, conch shells cluttered his kitchen table and prayer flags hung from every doorway. But nothing was quite as potent as his incense sticks that burned throughout the day and into the night.

You think a hangover headache is bad? Try getting pepper sprayed, punched in the face, waking up in this sector *and* being hungover.

Landon, Jim, and Elizabeth stood in front of me, all three of them with their hands on their hips. I rubbed innocently at my puffy eyes. "Hey guys... what's up?"

"Shut it." Strong Jim said.

Landon shook his head.

"What's wrong with you!" Elizabeth shouted, "you embarrassed me in front of my friends!"

I sat up, feeling my ribs ache, I had forgotten about *that* ailment. "Those were your friends?"

"I'll be lucky if I can still call them that!"

I waved her off. "You don't want to be friends with those uptight girls anyway."

"Those 'uptight girls' were trying to do Pilates in the park before they went into downward dog and saw your disgruntled naked angst!"

"Who the hell is trying to do Pilates in the park during January anyways?!"

"I'll go make some lemon tea," Landon said, softly.

"Could I also have a mint in that?" I asked, but after seeing all three of their eyebrows raise, I added, "please?"

"Really?" Jim asked, "you think now is a good time to be taking requests?"

I tried to crack a smile, but my jaw hurt too bad. "Mint settles my stomach." I shrugged.

"There won't be much settling this!" Jim roared, holding a fist in the air.

"I think Landon could use a hand," Elizabeth said, and then ran after him to the kitchen.

I looked down at my lap, wishing one of Landon's magic carpets could whisk me away. "I'm sorry, Jim." I said.

He looked at his feet.

We remained in a deeply sensitive silence.

"Why?" Jim finally asked, lucidly.

I shrugged. "Herbage."

He finally laughed.

I chuckled dimly, feeling it in my ribs.

"For the record," Jim said, "I should probably punch you in the face more often."

"Agreed."

Landon and Elizabeth came back in the room bearing tea.

"You two made up then?" Landon asked.

We both shrugged.

Landon handed me my tea and then sat down cross-legged on the floor. "Do you want to talk about it?" he asked.

I shook my head.

He nodded, knowing that would be my answer. "Okay then. But we do have to talk about rehab, Nathan."

I nodded. "I know."

We all sat in silence, sipping herbal tea, wishing that the lemon beverage was the thing that most profoundly bonded us.

"Are you okay?" Elizabeth finally asked, wiping away her tears. "I've never seen you like that before."

I moved my hand to hers, grabbing it. "I will be now," I nodded, "thank you, Elizabeth."

Landon wanted to take me to rehab right away, but I was able to convince him to give me one night at home under the surveillance of Jim.

"Are you sure you will be okay until then?" Landon asked, as Jim and I were on our way out, "you can sleep here if you need."

As appetizing as Aladdin's Lamp seemed, I shook my head. "I think I can manage," I said, and then pointed to Jim, "besides, I have my bodyguard to watch me."

He patted my back and lead Jim, Elizabeth, and I out the door, the smell of incense following not far behind us.

After dropping Elizabeth off and embracing in a very long and very endearing hug, we arrived back at my apartment. I was opening the door as Jim was reminding me for the eighth time to be packed and ready by seven am. "I know Jim, for the thousandth time-" I was saying, rolling my eyes, when I opened the door all the way.

She was standing in a blue dress, in the middle of my living room.

"Luna?"

Jim's face was a pop-up toy that had just sprung open. "That's Luna?"

"Hi! You must be Jim!" she cheered.

"Luna? What are you doing here?" I asked.

Jim's face was still stuck. "That's Luna?" he asked again.

"Uh," Luna commenced, "I got a call from jail?"

Jim looked over at me. "Jail?"

"I, I- uh, I'll explain that later," I said waving it off, "Luna, that was like, a couple weeks ago?"

"I didn't check my messages until today," she said.

"Jail?" Jim asked again, his face agape.

"Is everything okay?" her face fell, "what's going on?"

I ran my hands through my hair searching for a logical response. "How did you get in?" I landed on.

"It was unlocked," she said.

"Ah," I nodded. Typical drunk move.

"Nathan- are- are you okay?" she asked.

"He relapsed," Jim chimed in.

"Thanks Jim," I whispered.

"What?" She looked as if I had just taken the color blue from the universe.

"I- I'll explain later," I said again, "I need to go to bed. I have rehab tomorrow."

"Why?!" she said, trying to put this all together.

"Because Luna. That's how you detox. And get clean."

"He's an alcoholic," Jim said, nodding.

I looked at Jim with nothing but contempt. "Your comments have been very helpful, thank you Jim."

He nodded, expressing his gratitude towards my sarcasm.

"I'll do it." Luna said.

"Do what?"

"Help you detox."

"What?" Jim and I exclaimed at the same time.

"I'll help you detox," she said again, as if she had just decided that she was going to summer camp. "I'll stay here with you until you're done."

"Luna?" I laughed, "it doesn't really work like that."

The space filled with strange silence as we all stood awkwardly trying to figure out who the crazy one in the room was.

"I mean, I guess that could work." Jim eventually said.

"What?" I looked at him with distressing concern.

"She could supervise a detox as long as you go to your outpatient appointments daily." He shrugged.

"Jim that is horrible advice!" I refuted.

He shrugged. "I never said it was good."

"I can be here 24/7!" Luna said, far too excitedly.

"You can't do that Luna," I said, "you have a job. And besides, someone your size couldn't stop me from wanting vodka no matter how hard you tried."

"No, I don't," she shook her head, "I got fired. And I have pepper-spray. I could stop you."

"Oh god, not more pepper-spray!" I nearly fell to my knees in agony at all these ideas being thrown around like loose change, "wait what, you got fired?"

She nodded. "Yes. I missed too many shifts."

"Luna-"

"I can do it."

I shook my head. "No," I said.

"Yes," Luna said.

"Yes," Jim said.

"No?" I said again, looking at Jim in rage this time.

"Yes," Luna said.

"Yes," Jim said.

I hit Jim in the shoulder. "What the hell is going on here?"

He shrugged. "What's the worst that could happen? I'll supervise the situation. It could be fun."

"This is not summer camp!" I shouted.

Jim grabbed me by the shoulders and pulled me out of Luna's ear shot. "Listen," he said, "you already relapsed, and we don't have anything fun in our lives anymore. Why can't we just see if we can all do this together? Like a sort of trauma camp. Please. It'll help distract both of us. And if we fail, off to rehab you go."

I looked over at Luna who had both hands folded over. She was smiling and begging, "let me do this, please."

How could this be? The very thing that ruined me could not possibly be the very thing that heals me. I felt the impeding boomerang of this moment hit me hard in the back.

The very thing that ruined me could not possibly be the very thing that healed me.

But nature is more powerful than man. And sometimes a moon's gravitational pull causes the ocean to create a tide, pulling dead carcasses into the unknown territory of the sea.

I sighed. "I cannot believe I am going to say this right now, but you actually make a point."

Jim's smile was so big. I couldn't remember the last time I had seen it.

And for some reason that I can't explain, I said, "okay."

"Yay!" Both Luna and Jim jumped up and down and embraced each other as if they were now suddenly life-long best friends and hadn't just met within the last five minutes.

"But this isn't like learning how to fucking crochet!" I said, "so don't get so fucking giddy."

Luna smiled and squeezed Jim's hands into hers. "I won't" she said, in a way that meant she will.

"I won't either," said Jim, in a way that meant he most definitely will.

"Okay." I said, and then shuffled down the hall to my bed. "Your shifts start at seven am tomorrow."

Luna Elrod Journal Entry
Date: January 27th, 2017

People love to witness chaos, but they fear to live in it.

I've been a lone bird my whole life.

The other birdies fly away from me.

They watch me.

But only from afar.

For fear of getting too close.

I normally fly solo over my ravenous ocean.

But for the first time ever,

I'm not flying alone.

Chapter Twenty-Nine: makeshift rehab
Date: January & February 2017

The next morning, Luna was asleep on the couch and Jim was asleep on the living room floor, three pillows supporting his wide neck.

I rolled my eyes. This was an insane plan.

I started the coffee pot and leaned against the kitchen sink, watching them both breathe slowly, their heads resting on bright pink decorative pillows Luna had left at my apartment.

One human too small for the couch.

One too big for the floor.

I suppose love can come in all shapes and sizes.

Not that I'd know anything about that though.

Luna must've heard the low rumble of the coffee pot because she rubbed her eyes and sat up. She smiled and looked at me sleepily, "good morning."

"There is nothing good about this morning," I responded.

She laughed, that insane laugh. "Looks like you're back to normal."

Jim heard the morning chatter and stretched his arms out. "Good morning!!"

"See!" Luna said with joy, "it is a good morning!"

I rolled my eyes, poured my coffee, and walked back to my room.

The hell show would be starting soon.

--

You underestimate how unflattering detoxing is until there is a beautiful woman sitting next to you holding a towel to the back of your neck as you throw up all the contents in your body and sweat through every article of clothing you own.

The last thing I needed amid this note-worthy experience was to feel self-conscious about it.

Not to mention, I was in this situation in the first place because I couldn't handle this beautiful woman sitting next to me.

So, *why* was I allowing her to be in my life again, let alone *bring* me to life again?

It was poetry, really.

The turbulence of this journey, however, was often more distracting than the discomfort of my insecurities.

Symptoms came pouring in hotter and heavier than my daily cup(s) of coffee.

Day one.

I sent a mug crashing to the ground, spilling searing liquids all over the kitchen floor and spreading glass shards like AIDS in the 80s.

"Everything okay?" Jim asked.

"Yeah sorry," I grabbed the counter, "hand tremors."

Luna picked up all the broken pieces and made a ceramic gardenia flower out of them.

Day two.

I shattered a lamp, a plate, and two more mugs.

Luna made ceramic vases out of them, which served as objects for me to throw up in.

Day three.

A rapid heartbeat convinced a spiraling Luna and Jim that I was in immediate need for medical attention. Jim picked me up by the legs, reluctantly, I might add, threw me over his shoulder and tossed me into the car.

Luna drove. One of her skinny arms clutched to my chest, the other hardly on the wheel. Jim shrieked, cramped in the backseat as she flew through multiple red lights.

"Eyes on the road Luna!" I yelled.

"But what if you die?"

"With your driving it seems we all will!"

Day four.

Luna set a tent up in the living room for Jim to sleep in. He was tired of waking up to the sunlight that crept through the curtainless windows.

"You know you have a house, with an actual room. And a bed. And a wife." I said, as I watched him gleefully set up his tent with pillows and blankets.

"Oh, that's a great idea!" he responded, "I'll have Cindy bring over an air mattress!"

"Jim, I meant doesn't Cindy want you in your own bed with her? You've been gone almost a week."

Jim looked at me reflectively. "That's a great idea! I'll have her come too!"

Day five.

New member on board. Cindy. Who was a much better candidate for doing laundry than Luna, who had started hand washing my puke-soaked, sweat-stained clothes in the sink.

"Luna, I have a washer and dryer?" I implied, "why are you hand washing my clothes?"

"I like to watch the birds from the window and blow them bubbles with the dish soap," she responded.

"What are you Snow White?"

She smiled. "That's a great idea! I'll make seven ceramic dwarfs!"

"And I'll get more detergent," Cindy replied.

"Everyone seems to have great ideas except for me," I groaned.

Day six.

Luna taught Jim the lyrics to all the showtunes from *Chicago.*

I had fleeting breaths that left me nearly speechless, but between each exhausting exhale I still found the irritated energy to tell them to 'please stop singing while I lie afraid and sickly on the couch like one of the poor husbands in the musical waiting to be slaughtered.'

They'd supposedly be "cooking" white rice and chicken, but I wasn't too convinced, considering all I'd hear is poor vocals to *Funny Honey* and never the beeping of a pre-heated oven.

"This is purgatory! Not Broadway!" I'd yell.

They didn't seem to ever hear me though.

Day seven.

They sang *and* crafted.

I would be puking in the bathroom calling out for a towel and glass of water, but they would be unable to get up because their hands were wet from saturated newspaper.

"This is eternal damnation! Not Hobby Lobby!" I'd yell.

They didn't seem to ever hear me though.

Cindy would come through with my necessities. "Don't worry," she'd wink, "there's only three more songs left on the soundtrack."

The days going forward were spent on the floor of my shower with water violently hitting the top of my head, tripping over Jim's tent or Luna's art, sweating through every piece of clothing I owned, and cooling myself with my silent tears when nobody was watching.

Although Luna moved far too slow to ever be considered for any position in a hospital, Jim always seemed to be in the way and one song lyric behind, and Cindy would disappear whenever I seemed to need her the most, I couldn't help but appreciate their company.

This would have been a lot harder in a room full of people that didn't love me as deeply.

They all cooked, held cold towels to my head, took me to my out-patient appointments and helped with anything I could have possibly needed. And trust me, I needed a lot.

But for a couple like Jim and Cindy, helping someone else with their pain can often distract from your own.

And Luna could plant forehead kisses on my sweaty head when she knew I was too tired to complain about it.

You don't get that in rehab.

Besides, Luna had a way of making the world feel as if there was a possibility for purity. Much like a child often did.

One that may have been taken from Jim too soon.

So, after a while, I stopped commenting on their maddening antics.

Chapter Thirty: rehabilitation art gallery
Date: January & February 2017

My apartment had turned into an artisanship workspace against my will. Jim and Luna could not stop crafting and singing to save their damn lives. Let alone, save my damn life that was very much on the line.

One afternoon, after my out-patient appointment, as Jim was helping me out of the car, his smile was so wide I could have fit a six-pack of Coors Light in it.

"What could possibly be so funny about this?" I asked, annoyed, "am I amusing you?"

"Can't a guy be in a good mood?" he asked, unable again, to wipe the giddy look off his face.

I rolled my eyes. I couldn't find it in me to further interrogate.

Jim helped me up the stairs and unlocked my apartment door.

"Rehabilitation Art Gallery"

A hand painted sign hung from the beams in my hall.

The lights were dimmed. Luna's daisies flooded the apartment like a sea of white, alongside intricate groupings of citrus candles that swam on the outskirts of the floorplan, away from the flammable dangers of the flowers.

Mysterious dishes sat (impatiently awaiting Jim's presence) on the counter and flutes overflowing with sparkling water on the table-top comedically taunted this entire affair.

And just as I was convinced all my senses were entirely satisfied, my ears lit up to the sound of *The 13th Floor Elevators* playing softly on my record player.

The two nitwits' crafts were displayed everywhere. Old books transformed into instruments on bookshelves, butterfly wings created from keys suspended from the ceiling, clay tea kettles perched on coffee tables, papier-mâché bowls held grub, and mason jar windchimes cooed in the windowsill.

Amongst my sicken state, they had robbed me and turned all my household possessions into art projects. But just as I was about to scold them, I noticed the canvases that hung all over my walls.

"Earth Shaker - Luna Elrod"

"A gyro with Euros - Luna Elrod"

"A hippie from way back - Luna Elrod"

"Love as a brain enhancer – Luna Elrod"

"Nathan and Strong Jim sitting in a tree, D.R.I.N.K.I.N.G - Luna Elrod"

And a portrait of me,

"the whole world - Luna Elrod"

I was often at a loss for words, but it was very rarely I was at a loss of irritability.

This was one of those moments.

"Surprise!"

My hand slipped off the hallway table.

Elizabeth, Mateo, Daniel, Sofia, Max, Xavier, Landon, Cindy, and Luna all jumped out from behind the kitchen island.

"What-" I stuttered, falling backwards, "how did you all fit back there? What is going on?"

"Welcome to your rehabilitation art gallery!" Luna cheered, holding a flute of water.

"And snacks!" Jim exclaimed, not waiting any longer to dive right in.

I couldn't speak.

"I brought cream pie," Elizabeth said.

"You hate cream pie?" I questioned.

"I know," she said, winking.

"Alright everyone! Wander around! The raffle will begin in twenty minutes!" Luna exclaimed.

"What raffle?" I asked, still unaware of what was going on.

After everyone decided that my confusion was no longer cute, they started to mingle and enjoy the party. Luna came and wrapped her arms around me.

That was all I needed to allow whatever was going to happen to happen.

Once she had decided that everyone had done their appropriate amount of wandering (which was much longer than twenty minutes, for the record), Luna demanded we all gather for the auction.

She was auctioning off the canvas she painted of Strong Jim and I relapsing in a tree. Tasteful.

Jim's smile finally disappeared. "I hope you win," he whispered to me.

"I hope you win," I whispered back.

"And the winner is…" she reached into a jar with all our names, "drum roll please."

We tried our best. Some more than others. But I wasn't too convinced anyone was overly excited for this prize.

"Jim wins! Yay for Strong Jim!"

Jim looked at me distressed. "Cindy is going to just *love* this."

I returned his look of concern.

"Yay!" Cindy shouted, embracing Luna with a sweeping hug, "I love it!"

Jim and I swapped looks.

"Is she okay?" I asked.

"I'm not sure… she's been overly excited about the smallest things lately…"

I chuckled. "I suppose that would be from the risotto."

His smile made a quick return.

--

Luna was talking to Landon in the kitchen, Jim and Cindy were admiring their new artwork, discussing where about in the house to hang it, Mateo and Elizabeth passionately argued about pastries in the kitchen while taste-testing all the food, and Daniel, Sofia, Xavier, and Max were sitting on the couch listening to Max's new single on his phone.

I leaned against the wall, watching her.

Watching my entire world.

Once she was alone, I approached her with one question. "Why?"

She shrugged. "Because."

She had become acquainted with interpreting my one-word questions.

And I had become acquainted with interpreting her aloof answers.

I nodded. "My landlord won't be too happy about all the nails in the walls," I said.

Luna smiled.

And then I sauntered off to bed.

I could hear her laughter from down the hall.

Luna Elrod Journal Entry

Date: February 16th, 2017

I either feel like a God or a fool.

Nathan is like a portal to the in-between.

Chapter Thirty-One: everything in between
Date: March 2017

When my symptoms started to fade, Luna found it safe to begin attempting to revive the couch from my sweat stains with a steamer and a bottle of water.

"Luna."

"Yeah?"

"Why are you doing this?" I asked.

"It gets the stains out," she said.

"No, I mean, why are you doing all... this?"

"Because Nathan, I don't necessarily enjoy snuggling up on the couch next to yellow sweat stains."

"No," I said again, "I mean..." I waved my arms around in hopes they would communicate for me.

"Oh," she said, deciphering my message, "because."

I sighed. "I'm serious though, you shouldn't be spending your twenties like this, you need to go out in the world and be... be yourself."

"I am myself here!" she said, slightly defensive and mostly frantic.

"Luna, I didn't mean it like that-"

Her eyes got wide, as if terror himself had stretched them out. "I want to be here," she said, "I want to be here." She held the steamer in an anxious manner, as if she was worried that it might also try and tell her to go out and have fun.

I nodded, calmly. "Okay."

She sat back once she realized I wouldn't bring it up again. "Okay."

And that was the end of that conversation.

Luna Elrod Journal Entry
Date: March 4th, 2017

I finally got to stay at shore and throw somebody else a life vest for once.
It was the first time in my life I got to feel like something besides a burden.
When I'm with him, I try to exist in the same realm as him.

His presence is so grounding.

If anyone can make me feel at peace, it *has* to be him.

He cautions me from the taxing mind games my ocean plays on me.

I can see the world through his lens.

Nathan will be the thing that finally allows me to lead a normal life, keep a
job, start a family, be a mother.

Stay in one place.

We will have a house on the water, white picket fence.

We will have an Airedale Terrier that runs around gently protecting our baby
as she crawls through the grass. I will rest my head on his shoulder as we
watch our child walk for the first time, breathing in the tender wind.

I will feel nothing but calmness.

And when I'm in a relentless sadness, Nathan will come and lay with me, he
will pick me up from the bed and carry me to our pool, he will throw me in
as he yells, "see Luna, you can fly!"

And I will fly over my whole world.

And when I feel so high that I can jump from a skyscraper, he will take me
back down to earth and ground me. He will remind me that the true joy is in
our little family, sitting in the grass in the backyard, not up on the Eiffel
Tower. He will hold my hand and say, "let's go float."

And I will float and not drown.

Nathan is my gray area. He is my ground.

He is my everything in-between.

"Nathan." Luna said one morning when she could tell I was starting to feel better.

"Yes?"

She put her book down, deciding how to ask. "Why?"

I guess it was her turn to start asking the questions.

I didn't know how to answer this. I didn't want to make it seem as if her disappearing from my life was enough to send me down such an intense spiral. But it was. Which is why it was complicated to explain. How does one spell out that they aren't stable enough in their sobriety to be with the only person they want more than their own wellness?

"I mean, I suppose it all kind of started when you broke up with me." (I *suppose* that's how).

She looked at me confused. "What are you talking about?"

I looked at her confused.

"I never broke up with you?" she said.

"What are *you* talking about?"

This conversation was not off to a great start.

She looked at me waiting for my bewilderment to turn into a recap of events. Apparently, it must have worked because she then fell completely devasted. "Are you talking about the day that you came banging on my door?"

I nodded uncomfortably.

She bit her nails. This wasn't something Luna did often. She wasn't generally at a loss for words so when she was, her mannerisms weren't well at hiding it.

We sat in silence.

"I wasn't breaking up with you." She eventually said.

"Oh," I said, trying to hide my confusion. "So that's just typical dating behavior for you?"

"No." she said.

"I'm confused, Luna. Did I do something wrong then, that you were upset with?"

"No." she said again.

"Then?"

"I don't really know Nathan."

"What do you mean you don't know, Luna? Do you understand how strange of behavior that is?"

She stood up. "Do you understand how strange of behavior what you did is?"

I had touché written all over my face.

She sat back down.

"I know," I said.

She nodded.

Silence.

"Can you at least try and explain what happened?"

"If I do, will you?"

"Deal."

"Okay," she said, sitting quietly, pondering. "Sometimes, it feels as if my mind is a wave that crashes over the rest of my body, pulling me under so deep that I can't physically process the outside world because I am being drowned by my own thoughts."

At the time, I thought I understood. "And that was just one of those days?" I asked.

"Yes."

"And so, you *weren't* breaking up with me?"

She nodded. "Your turn."

"Okay," I said, taking a deep, serious breath. "Sometimes baby needs bottle."

She threw her book at me. "You dick."

Looking back on it, I should have known. I should have seen it.

But I was far too hung up on the delighted fact that she hadn't ended it with me.

Luna Elrod Journal Entry
Date: March 5th, 2017

I shouldn't let vulnerable swimmers tread my tides.

But I'm far too hung up on the fact they keep trying.

Chapter Thirty-Two: dumpster fried chicken
Date: March 2017

My symptoms subsiding miraculously coincided with Luna's jovial mind finding the next adventure to obsess over. But this time, Luna ripping away the logistics of how one lives in a functional society gave me a buzz that felt fresh after a long stretch of unrelieved agony. I felt a new bender on the horizon that could fulfil me more than any substance: *Luna*.

"Have you ever crawled inside a dumpster and eaten the food you've found in it?" Luna asked.

"Luna, I really hope you have never done that."

"You've never been dumpster diving!?"

"No Luna, and I never ever will-"

But before I could finish the sentence, I was driving her to the dumpster behind the cafe that she loved.

It was a quarter past ten and the only shed of light was a broken lamp that hung over the 'canteen' dumpster. The metal rust ached as it creaked in the wind, hardly swinging enough to cause a ruckus but enough to let you know it was suffering. The shades of green and stains on the outside of the tin-can teased the absurd time inside that Luna hoped to join.

"You are not really going to go in there," I said.

"No," she said, grinning, "we both are."

"Luna, you are out of your mind."

"Always have been."

But like a knight in shining armor, a master lock gleamed under the broken light. I exhaled a breath of gratefulness.

"It's locked, Luna," I allayed, "guess neither of us are."

"Said the man with no imagination."

"Said the man with logic."

She ignored me, pulled out a bobby pin from her hair and opened the car door.

"Luna, what are you going to do with that thing? What if we get caught?" I yelled after her.

"Weren't you just in jail? What do you care?"

She flipped her hair back, got out of the car and danced over to the lock, slowly and provokingly, swaying her hips and arms as if she was going to seduce the thing open.

She was, in her entirety, equally as glamorous as she was insane.

How was it so natural for a girl in pearls and a silk gown to crawl inside a dumpster and eat conspicuous nosh? I watched as she picked the lock with her bobby pin in an ultimately worrisome way (If women unite on a simultaneously good hair day, it may be over for us).

She opened the lid and jumped in without hesitation.

Fuck.

She was out of sight for a couple moments, causing me to worry that she might've hit her head on common sense, but then she jumped up with a cinnamon bagel in her hand. "Nathan! Come on! The waters warm!"

"You know I hate oddly shaped oases!"

There was absolutely no way I was going to join her in that unfamiliar food court.

Minutes later I was sitting on a black garbage bag inside the dumpster. Luna was showing me the assortment of pastries, bagels and panini sandwiches that were still wrapped in sheet paper.

"Every night, cafes like this one, have to throw out all the food that wasn't sold, even if it's still good," she was saying, "you wouldn't let all this good food go to waste now, would you?"

"Yes, I would," I said.

She frowned. "Come on! Just try one thing."

"Or how about we go out to dinner instead."

"Nathan! We already are out to dinner."

"Luna, just a week ago I could barely stomach white rice and now you want me to eat food out of a dumpster?"

She hit the side of my knee.

"Fine. Give me the god-damn chicken panini."

Her eyebrows flinched, questioning my choice. "Are you sure?"

"Do you want me to try it or not?"

"One chicken panini coming right up!" She handed me the wrapped sandwich that was still uncomfortably warm. I examined the sourdough and tomato that stuck to the sides of the dumpster fried chicken.

Was I insane? Or was I in love? (Is there a major difference?)

I took a bite.

Luna couldn't have been more pleased with herself.

I rolled my eyes.

"Thoughts?" she asked, elated.

"It's terrible," I groaned.

She smiled. "I knew you would like it."

We sat in silence on top of the garbage bags.

"I'm like a dumpster snack," Luna eventually said.

"What?"

"Yeah." She nodded. "Thrown away from society. But still pleasantly delectable once discovered."

"You're delectable alright."

Luna Elrod Journal Entry
Date: March 7th, 2017

Please ocean.

Please.

Don't make any riptides.

Please.

Stay very calm.

Exactly as you are now.

Chapter Thirty-Three: how she met my mother
Date: March 2017

"Where's your family?" Luna finally asked me.

I flinched.

She was eating fruit out of a strainer on my kitchen floor.

"Why are you sitting on the floor?" I asked.

"Where's your family?" she asked again.

"You're getting water all over the floor," I said.

"Where's your family?"

"Luna."

"Where is your family?"

Fuck.

I shrugged.

"You don't know?"

I nodded.

(To be fair, I *didn't* know. My father was an enigma. I had slept through my mother's funeral, so I wasn't entirely aware of her whereabouts. My grandparents were dead, and my mother had no siblings. So, I wasn't entirely wrong).

"Nathan."

"Ugh."

I drove her to the graveyard.

I looked at her with fitful eyes when we arrived. "Only one thing," I said, "I don't know where she is."

"Like… metaphorically?" she asked.

"No. Metaphorically I am extremely certain where she is. I am talking about *literally*."

Her eyes spasmodically wandered my face, waiting for my sense of humor to reveal itself. "Nathan? You must be joking? You've never been to your mother's tombstone?"

I shook my head. "Didn't even make it to her funeral."

She gasped.

I shrugged.

"How come you have never told me about her?"

I shrugged.

"Well, do you want to go find her?"

I nodded.

"Alright," Luna said, "come on."

The commonality of the name Catherine doesn't strike you until you've searched a graveyard for two hours looking for your mother. Luna was becomingly increasingly concerned for my sanity, and I was becoming decreasingly nervous for her to meet my mother, considering the odds of that happening were lowering every minute.

"Are you sure she's here?" Luna asked.

"No, not sure at all. Like I said earlier, she's definitely in…" I looked around and then pointed to the ground, *"the inferno,"* I whispered.

Luna stopped walking, she had taken her shoes off and was carrying them in her hands. "Nathan."

I shrugged. "I swear they said she was here!"

"Who's they?"

"The people!"

"What people?" She was looking at me like I had said my mother went out and buried herself.

"The people who do the dead people shit!"

"The coroners?"

"Yeah them!"

"Are you sure? I mean… you did say you weren't even at the funeral… maybe they buried her somewhere else."

"Never mind," I said, "let's just go back."

"No." Luna said.

"We can't find her!" I exclaimed, ready to call this quits and fabricate a story about being raised an orphan.

"Then," Luna looked around, "there."

"She can be your mother for the day," Luna said, pointing to the tombstone.

"My mother would never have a bible verse on her tombstone."

"Hi Cathy," Luna sat down next to my fake mother. Daises were growing out of the nearby dirt patch. She picked them out of the ground and laid them gently in front of her. "It's so good to finally meet you."

I can't say I was pleased with this situation, but for some, unexplainable reason, gravity felt more in line to follow along with my heart rather than my mind. I sat down on the ground next to her.

"Hi mom," I said, wincing.

We sat in silence.

Luna put her hand on mine. "Anything you want to tell her?"

"Nothing that she needs to know," I said.

Luna's eyes cut daggers into mine.

I scratched my throat. "What I meant was, mom… I want you to meet my girlfriend, Luna."

She nodded with appease.

I gave her a displeased smile in return.

"Does she like me?" Luna asked.

I gave her a vexed look at first, but then it dawned upon me that in all my life I was never able to show my mother something I was proud of, and for her to see it sober. And in that moment, I realized that was finally occurring.

"Yeah, actually," I responded, "she does."

Luna smiled her earth-shattering smile.

"I knew it," she whispered to herself.

Silence.

"What was her favorite color?"

A moment as heavy as this one was hoisted from the gravesite as Luna's tenderness warmed the landscaping. I laughed. "Out of everything you could ask, that's where you start?"

"A favorite color says a lot about a person."

"It was green."

"Beautiful. Green symbolizes harmony and new beginnings."

"It also symbolizes fertility in the Middle East."

"I'm sure she would've been very happy to be fertile in the Middle East."

"What are you doing at my mom's grave?!"

Luna and I both looked up at the middle-aged man who hovered above us with a bouquet of roses in one hand and a bible in the other. "And who's fertile?"

"Oh, uh-" I struggled to get up, wiping dirt off myself. And just as I was about to politely explain the situation and the mix up- Luna started shouting.

"Run!"

Before I could even finish my sentence, Luna was racing barefoot through the cemetery shouting at me to flee from a very confused, feeble man.

"Don't come back!" the old chap yelled, watching Luna run.

She turned around. "Your mom's hot!"

"Oh," I said, "I suppose this would be a good time for me to start running."

"Shame on you," the man said, waving his bible in my face.

Despite the lack of similarities running and alcoholism share, I made it back to my car in one piece. Luna was sitting on the roof the car, laughing.

"What's wrong with you?" I asked, panting.

"A lot."

--

Not that it's any of your business, but that was one of the best dishes of risotto we ever made.

Chapter Thirty-Four: pie, herbage, & rock n roll
Date: March 2017

Jim had taken his tent out of my living room and left on the hierarchy that he could no longer stay at a place that held a permanent stint of puke and an ambience of unfavorable energy.

"Nobody was forcing you to stay here," I said, as he packed his stuff up.

"I would seriously consider hiring a cleaning service, man, I mean this place is really tragic."

"This was your idea!"

"See you tonight for dinner," he said, pinching his nose and slamming the door.

"Bye Jim! See you tonight!" Luna said.

Cindy invited us over for dinner as a "congratulations on detoxing," celebration, but really, I think it was to get us all out of my apartment and into a home that wouldn't completely obliterate your appetite.

And it was a welcomed invitation, and we had a splendid night, but one homecooked meal in an unaffected atmosphere turned into Luna discovering her 'true calling' for the culinary arts.

"I really liked that pistachio-crusted halibut Cindy made," Luna said on the car ride home, "I think I'm going to try and recreate it. I had a vision of one of the fish's sisters' named Dijon wanting to be honored in honey mustard sauce. It might be my true calling."

"My true calling is eating that fish named Dijon." I responded.

The first week commenced as an innocent gesture and I can't pretend I didn't have fun dabbling in the domestic lifestyle with a pretty woman and a ribeye, but the simplicity of a homely fate faded very quickly as Luna's cooking tendencies turned malignant. As one's typically does.

The second week, Luna never came to bed. She blended, and beat, and baked until sunrise. I woke up the next morning to a thanksgiving feast that could have knocked The Pilgrims on their sorry asses.

"Since when did you learn how to cook like this?" I asked the next morning, dipping my finger in whipped feta.

"I figured it out last night," she said, swatting my finger away, "it's an art Nathan, you wouldn't understand."

The next night she was up until sunrise again. Clanking pots and pans, setting the fire alarm off and spilling sugar everywhere.

"Luna, come on, come to bed," I called from my room.

She didn't seem to hear me though.

I put a pillow over my ears and grunted into the mattress.

But as the broiling and boiling nights rolled on, her ruckus in the kitchen forced itself into my REM zone and swiftly began having the same drowsy effects as melatonin, or a lullaby.

I was able to fall asleep at the drop of a pan.

And her new culinary skills seemed nothing but a charming attempt to make the people she loved happy.

Over the course of the next three nights, Luna came to bed one time, and it was to have me try her zucchini enchilada roll ups. At three in the morning.

"Jim said he's trying to cut back on carbs, what do you think of this? I found this recipe in one of your moms' old cookbooks-"

"Luna, why are you not sleeping?" I asked, rolling over to face her. She held her fork up and the smell of salsa roja filled the room. "On second note, let me try that."

Luna had more energy after five nights of not sleeping than I did after a refreshing nine hours under the covers.

"Are you feeling, okay?" I asked one morning when I woke up to six different pies on the kitchen table, an artist statement next to each one, "even Jim can't eat this much food."

Pumpkin Pie – Luna's sweet pumpkin sensation surrounded by a firm crust that supports the malleable insides of an unpredictable slice after a knife.

Apple Pie – Luna's granny smith commotion of a lifetime, get in line before mine! (for mine will eat it all)

Pecan Pie – Luna's controversial paradox. A nut made unhealthy! What a ball. Come for the nuts but stay for the cream.

Key Lime Pie – Luna's American sweetheart, Key. Take a bite into her lime filled heavenly soul. It's the first time in pageant history a contestant has been made edible! And out of limes!

Cherry Pie – Luna's double cherry pie made with the intent to give you double d's! Or perhaps the other d…. (diabetes).

Lemon Meringue Pie – Luna's lemon goddess pie made from the very lemons Vincent Van Gogh painted. Guess Gogh isn't the only tortured artist around here, don't eat my art too fast or I might shoot my ear off into the next one!

TBD… Luna's (ear)ie haunted and honey pie (;

She kissed me on the mouth as I was mid-sentence. "Never better."

Luna Elrod Journal Entry
Date: March 12th, 2017

My fingertips harbor so much creative energy.

Vigor and zest fly out of my hands as if they are entities of their

own.

They want to create, love, touch, and perform.

I must go now.

I have people to feed.

Despite having spent years studying the English language, I never figured out how to speak it. So, I decided to try and thank Jim another way: cream pie. And I will admit, Elizabeth's claims of it being an 'uncomplicated' choice of dessert may have persuaded my decision in tackling this confection alongside my beloved sous chef.

I'm not sure what crack Elizabeth was smoking, because a cream pie was anything but simple.

It didn't help that Luna talked at the speed of light the entire time we were baking. I feared she was constantly on the verge of passing out from lack of oxygen and I'd be stuck figuring out the cream pie on my lonesome.

But there weren't many things I enjoyed more than the sound of her voice. So, I didn't stop her.

Luna had a way of making the impossible, possible. So, nonetheless, the pie was created from the hands of a nonachiever by the instructions of a genius.

When I arrived at Jim's to give him the 'thank you,' he was occupied doing what seemed to be unessential weeding in his front yard.

"Did you just discover landscaping?" I called from my car.

"Cindy told me to go make a mess outside," he said, bending over, out of breath.

"Given the state of her tulips, it looks you've done the job." I got out of the car with the pie.

"Is that cream pie?" he asked, stopping mid herbage throw, the gloves on his hands hardly fitting over his fingers.

"Jim!" I said seeing the damage up close, "what the hell are you trying to do? Contribute to soil erosion?"

Jim crept up to the product of *my* damage. "You got a fork?"

"Oh shit," I said, "no."

"That's fine," he said, and then shoveled a piece of pie into his mouth with the hand rake he was holding.

"Jim?!"

"What?" he asked, going in for another slice.

I handed him the pie and we both sat down while Jim single-handily consumed the entire pie with his make-shift fork.

We sat in silence. The only sounds coming from either of us was the moans of Jim's satisfaction and the scraping noise of his rake against the tin.

"Luna makes a good cream pie," he eventually said, taking a breath.

"Hey!" I hit him in the shoulder, "I made this one."

He chuckled.

"What's so funny?"

"Nothing," he said.

I rolled my eyes.

Jim kept laughing.

"Seriously, what is it."

"I'm just picturing you with your bloated fingers trying to make something so meticulous."

"What? I don't have bloated fingers. You have bloated fingers, look at you! They barely fit in those gardening gloves of yours."

"They're Cindy's," he said.

"Whatever."

He punched me in the arm. "Hey, by the way. You're welcome." He held the pie up.

I knew he would appreciate my 'thank you'.

"Want to help me weed?"

I looked over at the dismantled, viridescent vegetation that was lying in a pile like defeated soldiers.

"Something about being able to take control of the herbage feels nice," he continued, making a choking gesture with his hands.

"Sure," I said.

We got off the porch and got to work.

When you've spent most of your life searching for the meaning of it in a bottle that was designed to make you forget what you were looking for, digging in the dirt with another grown man who seems to believe the essence of our existence is buried somewhere deep in his wife's flower beds, felt like a reasonable way to spend an afternoon.

Two best friends ripping up herbage in a tactless frenzy screaming, "fuck it!"

As if this was what we were supposed to have been doing all along.

"What the hell is going on?" Cindy called from the front porch.

Jim and I turned around, our shirts stained with sweat and dirt. "Uh, weeding?" we both said.

"My tulips?!"

"…the weeds?"

"Jim, I told you to make a mess! Not ruin my garden!"

"Isn't that sort of the same thing-" Jim started to say but couldn't finish his sentence because Cindy was now chasing after him with her yellow kitchen towel raised in the air, ready to attack. "You idiots!"

"We were helping get rid of the pests!" I tried to offer up, shrugging.

"You two are the only pests!" Cindy said, now running after me.

"Hey! I was just a witness!" I yelled.

"Tell that to my tulips on your shirt!"

Jim was moving slower than me, so she turned at an angle and started to go after him again.

I ditched my car and ran as fast as I could in the other direction from the yellow towel.

"See you at the meeting tomorrow morning!" Jim called out.

"If you're still alive by then!" I turned back and exclaimed, "let me know when it's safe to come back and get my car!"

The entire run home, I clutched my heart, laughing.

Pie and herbage, I suppose, are not always that dismal.

Luna Elrod Journal Entry
Date: March 17th, 2017

Nathan sleeps so peacefully at night.

I watch over him.

Admiring him.

He scratches his nose in his sleep and then unconsciously reaches for me.

I hold his hand and pretend to soar off with him.

I wonder if he dreams of me.

If he dreams of all the places that we fly to.

Chapter Thirty-Five: Nirvana or eternal damnation?
Date: April 2017

Once I was no longer in need of constant assistance, Luna said there was "business" she had to attend too. Business in which required "a chainsaw and a mini dress." She said it would take a few days and not to worry, she would be back.

There were some things better left un-answered.

So, who am I to ask?

And besides, this time, I knew that she would come back.

I was momentarily excited because I figured this would be an exemplary opportunity for me to get my routine back on track. With Luna around it was nearly impossible to lead a life of pattern. And while she was a distraction from the alcohol, I still believed it was important to remain a solid routine.

But my apartment had never been more at a loss of harmony. So, I was unsure where to begin.

After she left, I sat down on the couch, feeling a relentless itch to get my life on course and an excited drive to do something utterly mundane and boring.

But the quietness had never felt so vicious.

I turned my album on, but even the record at full volume felt muted compared to the ferocity that was Luna's presence.

Why was my routine falling off like the needle on the vinyl?

I got up. Brushed my teeth. Ate toast. Then brushed my teeth again. But as I stared at myself in the mirror, I felt as if there was something very imbecilic about the whole ordeal. I threw the toothbrush in the sink and went into the living room.

I picked up my phone to call Susan. I was about to ask her if there was a shift I could pick up, but right as I dialed her number, I was embraced with the regretful remembrance.

"Fuck," I threw my phone down.

The words echoed at a maddening volume.

I sat on the couch some more. Shifted around. Fixed the pillows. Shifted around some more.

I called Jim, but he was making risotto to apologize for the garden mishap.

"You know, you really didn't have to answer!" I remarked.

I called Landon. Pilates.

I called Elizabeth. Creative writing class.

Mateo, Sofia, Daniel, and Xavier. All busy.

Think Nathan.

Luna's paintings were still hanging on the walls. I walked up to the self-portrait of me.

"the whole world."

What would Luna do? I thought.

I sighed.

And then, begrudgingly, I called Max.

And of course,

Of fucking course,

He was free.

Luna Elrod Journal Entry
Date: April 3rd, 2017

If a riptide does come rushing through, what do I have to be afraid of?

If a piece of algae wraps itself around me, what do I have to be afraid of?

If a shark comes veering its sharp teeth, what do I have to be afraid of?

I now have a dock I can crawl onto.

I now have a life vest.

I now have a raft.

I now have safety from drowning in my ocean.

A garage band concert. In the middle of the day.

Is where I found myself.

I have to say, watching men in their thirties strive for Steven Tyler's range while fingering a keyboard was not necessarily how I intended on spending my sobriety. But at least there were free snacks.

"How do you stay sober at these?" I asked, with four sandwiches wedged between my lips.

Max's oversized *Nirvana* tee blended in with the musky garage dust that was dimming the place. The scent of sadness lingered in-between the sturdy smell of grime. He head-banged and waved his middle finger in the air as if his outraged phalange could save the planet from suffering.

"This is a completely spiritual experience," he said, "no drugs or alcohol needed to feel a buzz."

"This is what you consider spiritual?"

"Yeah man, it's the most punk rock shit ever."

"Sure… but how does that make it *spiritual*?"

Max turned and looked me dead in the eyes. "Finding Nirvana doesn't have to entail all that hippie dippie Landon shit with ginger tea and incense. It's whatever you want it to be. Sometimes finding Nirvana can literally just be listening to Nirvana."

That was the most profound thing I had ever heard Max say.

Max dropped me off after the show.

"Thanks," I said.

"Anytime man."

I nodded at him in appreciation. Regardless of how awful the experience was, Luna had a point about this whole 'people' thing.

"Hey! Maybe you and I can form our own rock band sometime? How would you like jamming out with me?" he asked, as I got out of the car.

"No."

Chapter Thirty-Six: meant for grazing
Date: April 2017

Typically, one would not consider a door made from wood problematic. If anything at all, a prospective interior designer could describe a door made from wood as a fashionable ornamentation, somewhat of a luxury if you will.

That is, unless, you have Luna Elrod as your girlfriend.

In which case, a front door made from wood is something to be concerned about.

My jaw dropped at the sight of a large gaping hole cut through the front of my door.

A hole not quite big enough for me to squeeze into, but big enough for a large dog.

Or a small woman.

I suppose this was what the chainsaw and the mini dress were for.

I pushed open the door, at a clear loss for how, exactly, to react (what is the appropriate reaction for when your girlfriend takes a power tool and cuts a hole through your front door?).

I braced myself for what awaited me beyond the hole.

My (previously) gray walls were glimmering with a sour, damp, odor due to the fact they had been painted yellow. An infestation of plants took over the kitchen window, making their presence wildly known from across the room, teasing me, like they knew there was potential for us to get along. The old gray rug that once lacked life on my floor had been replaced with an orange throw carpet. A tapestry so animated, you feared it might start talking back.

But what caught my attention the most were the daises that hung from yarn along the crown molding. All over my entire apartment.

Daises everywhere.

"Why couldn't I have just been robbed?" I pleaded.

Only one wall was left gray.

Where the yellow lacked, long green limbs grew. Purple petals blossomed from wet paint, rendering the depiction of an alfalfa plant.

I met its gaze.

We held eye contact.

She consumed the wall.

She consumed my mind.

Her arms reached out.

Trying to grab ahold of me.

It stroked the daunting silence of my Luna-less apartment away.

the words *"meant for grazing"* were written under the mural.

Luna Elrod Journal Entry
Date: April 4th, 2017

I am being dragged around by a snaggletooth shark.

My dress is caught in its mouth.

It won't stop whipping me around the sea of impulse.

I am desperately fighting for my dock, my hands are out, wailing to try and

grab onto it.

Grab onto something steady.

So that I can be freed from this agitated shark.

I tentatively approached the herbage that was in my kitchen.

Not one, but *eleven* succulents lined the windowsill.

A pressing attempt at kick-starting my green thumb.

I grimaced before noticing that each plant had a nametag.

Elizabeth.

Mateo.

Daniel.

Sofia.

Max.

Xavier.

Jim.

Landon.

Cathy.

Susan.

Luna.

And in the sink, (with not to mention, the water still running), there was a large Devil's ivy.

> *"To watch the one's you love grow with you, and around you.*
> *Because beauty should **always** be in your way."*

Luna had dismantled my front door with power tools even though she had a key. Painted my walls without my landlord's consent, swallowing me into a color I never had interest in, placed herbaceous vegetation in my way, including the painted one on my wall, and most notably, almost flooded the place by leaving the sink on.

So, *why*, was I *so...*

Elated?

Luna Elrod Journal Entry
Date: April 5th, 2017

My dress ripped from the shark's mouth

I have no fight left in me

I am sinking

Deep

Down

Into

The

Familiar dark bits of the ocean.

Chapter Thirty-Seven: an addict
Date: April 2017

My apartment was too small for a world like Luna's mind. She needed a vast landscape to purge her creative floods.

I formulated a plan. And I made it happen.

It took three days.

I was so excited to show her what I did, I forgot to put shoes on.

I drove at full speed to her apartment, barefoot.

Her door, as usual, was unlocked.

"Luna!" I called, as I came through the door.

No answer.

"Luna! I have to show you something."

No answer.

I went into her bedroom. All her lights were out. I flipped them on.

She was under the blankets.

"Luna?"

I pulled the blankets off her. Cigarette ashes lined the mattress. Holes blistered through her blankets from left over buds.

"Luna? What are you doing?" I asked, taken aback, "how could you be so thoughtless and let cigarettes burn on your bed? You could have started a fire!"

She didn't answer me, instead, she turned to the other side of the bed.

"Luna. I'll ignore your irresponsibility for now. I need to show you something."

No response.

I was on such an exhilarated high, that her current state of desperation was nothing but a hindrance for me. I figured the lack of sleep from last week's cooking mania had finally caught up with her. As soon as she saw my surprise, she would come out if it and become her ferocious self again.

She just needed some air under her wings.

"Luna, I know you're exhausted because you didn't sleep much last week but trust me, you're going to feel full of energy soon enough."

I picked her up and carried her out to my car. She tried a few times to shove me off her, muttering a few things about putting her back, but she was too tired to fully convince me to put her down and leave her be. Her complaints bounced off me like irritating kids on a trampoline.

She was going to be wide awake soon enough.

I drove twenty minutes west. Luna sat in the passenger seat, silent and still. I couldn't tell if her eyes were even open. I reached over and squeezed her hand, but she didn't squeeze back.

She would be her brilliant, beautiful self again. Soon.

I pulled into the parking lot.

Silence.

"Luna," I said, "follow me."

She didn't move.

"Don't make me carry you again."

Nothing.

My heart was thudding louder than any sound of sorrow, so I got out of the car, opened the passenger door, and grabbed her.

"Alright, I guess this is how it's going to have to be," I said, throwing her over my shoulder.

She was limp, rarely moving as I carried her to the entrance of a red brick building.

Sacramento Art Studio's for Rent

I couldn't contain my joy.

But complete quietude radiated from the other end of me.

In blind jubilation, I carried her in.

Vibrant white paint stifled my heavy breathing as an array of sculptures lead us down the hallway. Eclectic paintings from the strokes of contrasting geniuses lined the walls, telling a different tale with every trail.

Rooms passed and art remained until we stood in front of room 112.

"Luna Elrod"

I put her down.

"What is this?" she finally asked, a fleeting moment of curiosity that seemed to leave within the moments it departed her mouth.

I smiled. "Just open the door."

She listened, finally.

Paints, brushes, materials, clay, fabrics, charcoal, acrylics, and canvases: the tsunami that came pouring out when she opened the door.

And in the middle of the raging tidal wave were daises that glowed under a heat lamp in the center of the room.

The sun that dried up the water.

"This is your new studio, Luna," I said, "I figured it might be best to paint here and not inside people's apartments. You'd be less likely to get in trouble that way."

No response.

I waited. For her to wake up.

For her bright, brilliant self again.

I waited.

"I signed a twelve-month lease," I said after I couldn't wait anymore.

Nothing.

So, I waited again.

"Oh! How could I forget," I reached into my pocket and placed a gold key into the palm of her hand. "You can come here whenever you want, Luna. It's open 24/7. You just need this key to get in."

Silence.

"Maybe this is where your mind can come to explode."

She looked at me, tears streaming down her cheeks. "Why would you want to see my mind explode?"

"Luna… obviously I didn't mean literally-"

"Why would you want to see my mind explode?" She asked again, "even metaphorically?"

"Because Luna! It's beautiful. And brilliant."

She was apprehensive. Her eyes bloodshot. "Take me home," she said.

"Luna-"

"Take me home."

Luna Elrod Journal Entry

Date: April 6th, 2017

I wanted him to calm my ocean

Not come begging for a fucking tsunami

I drove Luna back to her apartment. The tears I couldn't hold back hid between streetlamps and passing cars.

At her place, she climbed back into bed as if we had never left.

I watched her sleep.

Her inactivity hypocritically plucked at my rage.

A sticky substance regurgitated itself in the back of my throat.

The teasing whispers of all the reasons I deserved *one* hit.

But this time, the hankering in my throat, the aggressive desires, and the teasing whispers weren't about alcohol. They were about…

Luna.

Provoke her.

Wake her up.

Get her to say something irrational and insane.

Find something that will set her off.

Push her to her limit.

                Get her out of that fucking bed.

Cravings. Desires. Whispers.

Just one hit.

Cravings. Desires. Whispers.

Just one hit.

"Luna," I said, after nearly five hours of deep, agonizing, torture.

And when she didn't answer, I pulled a lighter out of my pocket.

Set it next to her.

And wrote her a note.

"If you really loved me, you'd set my pain on fire and rebuild your wings from the ashes."

Luna Elrod Journal Entry
Date: April 7th, 2017

Not only is he knowingly caught in my riptides, but he is swimming further away from shore.

Chapter Thirty-Eight: pyromaniac
Date: April 2017

One week passed.

I was able to maintain a buzz from her art in my apartment.

But I was still consistently fighting off the teasing whispers and the thirst in the back of my throat.

And then I woke up to the throbbing pandemonium of my landline.

It was Susan.

I could hear her spit hitting the other end of the phoneline.

Unaware of what was causing the wrath, my buzz started turning into a high.

"What happened?" I asked, calmy.

She wailed.

"I understand the implication, but I would love to know what I did this time," I said.

"You know what. Nathan."

I paused, pondering everything that she could have potentially been upset about (and there was a lot). "No really, Susan. I don't know."

"The entire non-fiction department! It's gone up in flames!"

"What?" I asked, beyond stunned.

"Set on fire!"

Silence filled my end of the call.

"It's been completely destroyed Nathan!"

"The non-fiction department sucked anyway!" I said, in attempt to offer condolence, "but what does this have to do with me? You fired me!"

"Oh, I'll tell you what this has to do with you. They found black knee-high boots outside the scene," Susan huffed into the phone, "the fire department said whoever started the fire most likely had to take those heels *off* and run, due to the rapid nature of the flames."

The teasing whispers stopped.

The relapsing foreplay had come to fruition.

I had been quenched.

"Okay," I said, trying to hide my smile so the landline wouldn't snitch on me.

"And don't you know it, I will be pressing chargers and opening an investigation."

"Okay," I said again.

Susan hung up.

I slowly put the phone back down.

She really loved me.

Luna Elrod Journal Entry
Date: April 15th, 2017

As humans we can't control anything.

Not the weather.

Not our family.

Not the stars that float above us.

When I was a little girl, I had a teacher tell me that the only control we have

as humans is how we react to the things we can't control.

So why is it, I can't even control that?

Maybe my town was right.

Maybe I am selfish.

Maybe I am a vexed witch.

Maybe there is a demon rooting away in my thalamus.

Maybe I do need to pry open my brain, grab tweezers, and pluck out all the

parasites that eat away at my control.

If you don't have control of yourself, what do you have?

The ocean drowns me.

The ocean drags me around.

The ocean sends me high up on a wave.

I can fly.

I soar.

My wings break and I fall from the sky.

I fall into the ocean and drown.

Sunbathe and repeat.

I ran to her apartment. Barefoot *again*.

The sun, the breeze, the leaves, the smell of spring leaves.

I didn't care if the entire planet caught on fire.

Because my world was only one person.

As I ran, the sun hit my face in what felt like the first time in forever.

My heart was running ahead of me. I was struggling to keep up.

Nature is more powerful than man.

Sometimes a moon's gravitational pull causes the ocean to create a

tide.

Pulling dead carcasses into the unknown territory of the sea.

I realized then that the sun had been missing from my entire life.

And it was now hurtling down, large, and bright, right-on top of me.

It was apologizing for all the times it had left me in the dark.

My arms were spread out, ready to forgive it.

Luna's door was unlocked.

She was sitting on the kitchen counter in a blue dress.

She had a daisy behind her ear.

My heart was still pounding as I burst through the door.

I could feel hers too. Reaching out towards mine.

She was so beautiful.

"I picked this daisy in the garden," she said.

"The one you planted?" I asked.

She smiled. "And burned."

We didn't leave her apartment for three days. The sunshine stayed with us the entire time.

Regrowing her daises.

And soaking up my sorrow.

Luna Elrod Journal Entry
Date: April 18th, 2017

you never run out of places to explore when you get the whole wide world to yourself.

Chapter Thirty-Nine: North Bimini
Date: April 2017

An aggressive knock on the door jolted me awake. Luna's dilated pupils looked at me for answers, "who is it?" she asked.

"I have no idea-" I responded, lethargic, rubbing my eyes.

The combative sound came surging through her door again.

"I'll get it," I said and swung my legs over the side of the bed.

Luna grabbed the covers of the bed to hide herself, "make it stop," she said, looking around frantically.

"Hello?" I said, opening the door, my eyes not yet fully functioning.

"Deputy Chris," the man in uniform said, holding up a badge, "is Iris Moore here?"

I looked at him, confused, before I burst out laughing.

"Sir?"

"Sorry-" I did my best to contain myself, "Iris Moore is *not* here."

He raised an eyebrow. "Do you mind if I take a look around?"

"Why would you need to do that?" I refuted, now suspicious of the inquiry.

He held up a legal document. "The lease on this apartment says that Iris Moore resides here."

I nodded, registering what this was all about. "Ah, yes, well," I stuttered, trying to think quick on my feet, "she did... yes... but now I live here... I am subleasing from her." (*Technically*, I had been paying her rent since she had lost her job... so this wasn't a *total* lie).

He looked me up and down. "Do you have the paperwork for that?"

"Uh, well, it was kind of an *under the table* deal," I said, squinting my eyes, "if you know what I mean."

"Mhm," he observed me for a moment longer, "sir, the person whose name is on this lease is the main suspect in an arson charge. You wouldn't happen to know anything about her whereabouts, would you?"

I shook my head. "No sir."

"Do you understand that the woman who you are subleasing from is potentially a very dangerous person?"

"Yes, sir. *Very* dangerous indeed."

He eyed me again. "So, you did an under the table sublease with a missing person who is now the lead suspect in an arson charge, and you're not worried?" The Deputy pried.

"Sir, forgive me for my bluntness, but I'm an alcoholic. There are way too many things I need to worry about before I get to that."

He gave me an unsettled glance. "Alright," he said, "I'll leave you be for the time being, but don't go anywhere. I'll be back for some further questions regarding this investigation once I get more information. You understand? And find me that 'sub-lease' with Ms. Iris Moore."

I nodded. "I understand, officer. I'll see what I can do."

He raised his eyebrow again before turning around and leaving.

"Rude," I muttered as I watched him head back down the hall.

I shut the door and turned around just as Luna shoved a bag at my chest. "We have to go," she said, already packing herself a suitcase.

"Go where?"

"Just pack Nathan!"

This was so much more exciting than booze.

Luna Elrod Journal Entry
Date: April 19th, 2017

I finally have someone to fly with.

Even when the world is trying to drown me.

Five hours later we were on a one-way flight to North Bimini in the Bahamas.

"Now I get why you have so many aliases," I said, looking up and down the flight at the others who seemed to juxtapose our nervous energy with their relaxed get-away mood.

Luna filled the airplane seat with her pale-brown brimmed beach hat, pink satin mini dress, and high-bridge sunglasses. She hesitantly chomped on a stick of bubblegum, while consistently pulling her sunglasses down the edge of her nose and letting her eyes take inventory of the plane. "Where are we going again?" she asked.

I laughed out loud. "You're joking right? Luna, you picked it."

"Oh," she said, "right."

I held up the ticket. "North Bimini."

She nodded. "I knew that."

I shifted in my seat, trying to gauge Luna's demeanor. "Are you okay?"

She pulled her sunglasses off. "Let's never go back."

"What?"

"Let's never go back. Let's stay in the Bahamas forever. And have babies there. And be together forever."

"Luna-"

"Okay?!"

I smiled and squeezed her hand. "Okay."

I was more than okay with that.

Once the plane reached a cruising altitude, the flight attendants started coming down the aisle with drink menus. The last flight I was on I breathed in and out over two-hundred times, tapped my foot nearly two thousand times, walked up and down the aisle twice, and got caught trying to smoke a cigarette in the bathroom.

But this time, I just looked over at Luna.

No need for breathing, or foot tapping.

Just pure calmness

Surrounded me.

Chapter Forty: surviving sunset
Date: May 2017

It was just Luna, the sun, the sand, the water, and me.

In fact, Luna's beauty intermixed with the universes. Her rosy cheeks blended in with the pink and orange sunrays. Her blue eyes and the Atlantic Ocean melted together amongst the hazy sky. And it was often hard to tell the difference between Luna's hair and the sand.

She was equally as beautiful as the universe.

She was my universe.

Two weeks with her felt like two seconds but simultaneously two lifetimes.

Two lifetimes in two seconds.

I could not survive without her.

There wasn't a world without her.

I was not going to give her up.

I had her in the morning.

I had her in the afternoon.

I had her at night.

And when I woke up the next morning, a headache would creep its way into my cerebrum and a thirst would surface, a longing that wasn't fulfilled until I had her.

She was all I could think about. Even when she was in my hands.

Even after she had been ingested.

My body rejected her at first. It didn't know how to metabolize her. She made me sloppy. She me nauseous and inarticulate. She made me rebellious. She was a potent toxin.

But I was so wrong.

She's all pleasure.

She's euphoria.

She's my beautiful little ritual.

It can't get any better than this.

Luna Elrod Journal Entry
Date: May 1st, 2017

I'm soaring high above my ocean.

High above my entire world.

My wings are here to stay.

And if they are ever cut.

I shall not survive.

We had been living on the island for a few weeks and had already become accustomed to the people, places, and things of the land around us. It didn't take long to acclimate considering we were both running on fugitive energy, and we had gladly familiarized ourselves with the way of life here.

Wake up. Run barefoot to the beach. Eat fruit. Drink from pure coconuts. Swim in the water. Mingle with the locals. Read. There wasn't much I wouldn't have done to keep these rituals a regime.

Until one morning, Luna and I were at the street market eating mangos and pineapples with tajin seasoning, when a cluster of loud and obnoxiously dressed persons piled into the marketplace. It was a startling contrast between the normal crowd at the market in North Bimini mid-day.

"What's going on?" Luna asked, barefoot with fruit juices running down her hands.

I looked around to gather evidence. "There," I pointed.

"What?"

"It's an assemblage of loud tourists walking a thin line between excitement and cultural appropriation."

"What?" Luna asked again.

"It's a cruise."

Docked a short distance away, a colossal ship boasted its flamboyant colors and large stern. The last few tourists wiggled their way off and the captains and crew followed behind in the distance.

"Wow," Luna said, "it's beautiful."

"Not really," I said, grabbing some fruit from her and biting into it.

She pointed at the ship and looked at me, wide-eyed.

"What?" I asked.

"Fries."

"What?"

"Fries," she said again.

"What about them?"

"Those French fries probably have American salt. And American ketchup."

"Luna, if you want fries, we can just go get some from the pub down the street-"

"Nathan!" she said, fruit juice now all over her bare feet, "I want *those* fries."

"And how do you plan on getting-"

She didn't seem to hear me though. Considering she was already a yard ahead of me, marching toward the ship.

"This fucking woman."

When I caught up to her, she was already talking to the man guarding the ship from rogue women on a mission for saturated fats.

"Our daughter!" she was shouting.

"What's going on here?" I asked, out of breath from running after her.

"Oh, here he is," she grabbed my arm, "honey, I was just telling this kind man about how our daughter has our passes in her backpack but she is currently held up in the market bathroom with the unplanned events of her first period and she won't stop crying and there's blood everywhere and tampons here are sold few and far in-between and the ones you *can* find are the size of a walnut with no outer shell to insert itself with. You have to force it up there yourself!"

I side-eyed the man in horror. "What does this have to do with this poor man, *honey*?" I asked.

"He won't let me back on the ship to grab a tampon from our room! So now our poor daughter has to either hurtle an unserviceable tampon up her unexplored uterus or bleed to death!"

I side-eyed the man again. Wondering who was going to break the palpable silence first.

Thankfully, he did.

"Is this your wife, sir?" he asked.

"Uh-"

"Yes, I'm his wife!" Luna shouted.

"I don't see any rings," he said.

"We don't wear our rings on vacation! They are too expensive to risk losing! Any other interrogations sir?! Our daughter is dying!"

"She's dying? I thought you said she was on her period?" The man asked.

"What's the damn difference?!"

The man looked over at me, took a couple glances at our bare feet, and sighed, so loud, the entire island could've felt the vibrations.

"They don't pay me enough for this," he said, before scanning his badge, and moving over to let us on the boat.

I think he would've preferred getting fired over listening to Luna's imaginary rampage for one second longer. I looked at him in shock before Luna grabbed my arm and forced me aboard.

"That's the method you went with?" I whispered once we got in, "you couldn't have just settled for 'we lost our fucking tickets'?"

She shrugged. "Nothing scares a man more than the anatomy of a woman."

I shook my head. "All that for a couple of fries."

The ship was an ostentatious nightmare lacking parental guidance and dietary restrictions. Children ran rogue as if it was their societal duty to misbehave and parents were taking more of a mental vacation than what appeared to be a physical exploration. Water slides wrapped around the entire place, neon lights flooded the judgment of guests, and food stands lurked around every inch of the ship just to ease the vacationers' fear of never being too far from a giant hotdog. It was as if God asked a five-year-old to describe heaven.

It didn't take long before Luna found the fries and was waving me over to buy her four plates. "Satisfied?" I asked.

"Are you satisfied now?" I asked again, as she was draining my wallet at the ice-cream stand.

"How about now?" I asked as she dragged me into the rave room and forced me to dance in the fluorescent lights.

"Now?" I asked, as I got pulled into the movie theater and found myself watching Forrest Gump.

"Now?" I asked as we got massages, and played pickleball, and swam in each pool on every level.

"How about now? Luna?" I asked, as we stood on the back of the boat and watched as the dock slowly disappeared from our eyesight.

"Maybe we should've been a little more cautious of time," she said, watching as our current homeland was shrinking in our line of vision.

"Maybe," I responded.

"What do we do?" Luna asked.

I rubbed the back of my head. "I guess we just have to wait until the ship docks next, and then find a boat or a plane to take us back to North Bimini."

Luna nodded.

"The real question is, where are we going to sleep tonight?"

"Sleep? Nathan are you serious?" Luna exclaimed, "there is far too much to do here, there is no time for sleep!"

"Luna, I'm exhausted, why don't you go and if you need me, I'll be right here."

Luna's blue eyes blended in the with the sea behind her, the luminescent yellow and pink from the sunset intermixed with her rosy cheeks. She was restless with the rest of the world around her, but I needed my sleep so I could keep indulging in her.

Luna ran off before I could say more, and I found myself dozing off on a beach chair while the sun set.

All her beauty had settled into the depth of the ocean for the night.

And so, I fell asleep fast.

--

"Nathan! Nathan!"

My eyes shot open. "What? What?" I was still laying on the beach chair that I had fallen asleep in. The sun was rising, it couldn't have been later than five am. Discombobulated, I searched for where the sound of my name was coming from.

"Nathan! Nathan!"

Luna was straddling the railing of the ship, clutching onto the handle. She was staring at something in the water.

"Nathan, the fish! We have to save it!"

"What?" I asked again, rubbing my eyes in puzzlement trying to force myself to fully wake up.

"The fish!"

My eyes adjusted to the tears streaming down Luna's face, her mascara staining her linen blue dress. "The fish, Nathan! We have to save it!" she said again.

I threw myself out of the chair and ran over to grab onto her waist. "Luna! Why are you sitting on the railing like this? You could fall!"

"The fish!" she said again.

"What fish?"

Luna pointed down to the water.

My eyes followed her finger to a small dogfish floating at the surface of the water.

I exhaled. "Luna, love- that fish is dead."

She turned to me sobbing. "Nathan, we have to help it!"

I looked at her perplexed. "Luna? How do you plan on saving a dead fish?"

She didn't seem to hear me though, because she had escaped my grip and thrown herself overboard, into the uncalm waters below us.

"Luna!" I shrieked, trying to grab her arm, but she was already falling from the second story of the boat into the ruffling waters. I watched as her sun-kissed body plopped into the ocean like a grain of salt in a pot of boiling water.

I turned around and screamed for help.

All I could think to do was scream.

The wandering staff came running towards me.

"SHE'S IN THE WATER!" Is all I could manage to plead.

I grabbed the railing and watched as Luna's head popped up from the water. She was swimming towards the dogfish.

Once the blonde hair was spotted, everyone started shouting and talking into their radios.

And before I could watch Luna swim in the ocean by herself any longer, I was climbing the railing and throwing myself overboard after her.

"SIR!?!" I heard echo behind me.

As I fell into the water, the wings on my back finally grew.

"Luna!" I screamed, swimming toward her.

"Nathan!" she called, holding onto the dogfish.

"Luna, are you fucking crazy?" salt water gargled in my mouth.

"It's dead, Nathan," tears continued to stream down her face, her mascara staining the blue ocean black, "it's dead."

I nodded and wrapped my cold body around hers. "I'm sorry, Luna."

She held the fish to her chest as she cried into my neck. I kicked hard enough to keep all three of us afloat.

And for what felt like forever, we embraced in the cold ocean over a dead fish.

Two emergency boats came down the side of the ship.

Luna's big eyes looked at me as they drove towards us. "Thank you," she said.

"For what?" I asked.

"For jumping in with me."

I shrugged. "I guess I'm not too scared of oddly shaped oases anymore."

She hid her smile behind the dogfish.

The first raft tried to pull Luna into the boat, but she wouldn't surrender until they agreed to take the dogfish too. The second raft grabbed me and helped me in while Luna still resisted.

But because they didn't have the time or bandwidth to argue with a rogue woman who had thrown herself overboard to save a dead fish, they let her bring the tiny shark.

And then the three of us were sent up the side of the cruise ship in two yellow safety boats. Drenched, reeking of dead fish, and more alive than ever.

I watched as Luna stroked the dogfish in the boat next to mine, her hair stuck to the side of her face, her makeup washed off from the ocean.

She was the universe.

And nobody loved the universe like she loved the universe.

And that's what made her equally as beautiful.

Luna Elrod Journal Entry
Date: May 6th, 2017

When creatures die in your body of water, no matter the circumstances, you can't help but feel responsible.

Chapter Forty-One: Cutty the damn dogfish
Date: May 2017

Once the crew discovered we were not passengers aboard, rather, inconvenient trespassers, we were quickly removed, dropped at the next dock with a ragged towel, the dead fish, and told to seek psychological help.

Management toyed at pressing charges, but after Luna threatened to expose how weak their security was and their 'frail' railings, they changed their minds quickly.

"Bye!" Luna waved the ship off genuinely.

The people watching on the boat shook their heads.

I flipped the finger.

"Nathan?!" Luna hit me, "they were nothing but wonderful people."

"They threated to sue us?"

"As they should have!"

"Mhm."

"Well, what now?" She asked.

"We have to find our way back to North Bimini," I responded, "we can start by finding a boat service."

It's amazing how money motivates people. We were only on this random island for less than three hours with not much strenuous effort needed other than flashing a couple of American dollars and Luna's phenomenal smile.

We were back on North Bimini before sunset.

But because Luna insisted the dead dogfish's needs were more imperative than our hygiene, she demanded we have a burial for it immediately.

"You don't jump in after a fish to then not give it a proper send-off," Luna said, "we need to do this right."

Who was I to argue?

Luna walked us to a little street market where an older, small, Bahamian woman was selling scarves and colorful straw baskets.

"Hi Cordelia," Luna said, smiling softly at her.

"What is that?" The woman asked, pointing at the fish.

"You two know each other?" I asked, perplexed about when this relationship could have been formed.

"I don't know that damn fish!" Cordelia responded.

"Cordelia sells flowers on the street at midnight. We chat about life and love when you're sleeping."

"What?" I asked, again.

"Her name means heart," Luna said, "which means she knows a lot about love."

"It means I know little about logic," Cordelia responded, "and I know very little about what this situation is." She waved her arms around in Luna's direction.

"This is Cutty," Luna held the fish up, "and he needs a hat and a scarf."

"What?" Cordelia and I both asked at the same time.

"I said, he needs a hat and a scarf."

"Why does he need a hat?" Cordelia asked.

"Why did you name it Cutty?" I asked.

"You kill that fish?" Cordelia asked.

Luna lowered the fish to her stomach. "Oh. I hope not."

I looked back and forth between the two of them. "What are you talking about? No, she didn't kill that damn fish. She tried to save it actually."

Cordelia and Luna both looked relived.

"And why the hell does it need a hat and a scarf?" I asked.

Luna held Cutty up to show his naked body. "He needs a proper burial, and I'd hate for him to go out in poor fashion."

Cordelia nodded like it all made sense now. "Well, in that case, you came to the right place."

"It's a fish, Luna?" I said, still not on the same page as the two women in front of me.

"How would you like to be buried, Nathan? Naked?!" Luna asked, baffled.

"Actually, I'd prefer to be cremated."

"I just knitted a new scarf today and as a matter of fact, I think it's perfect for the occasion. I'll be right back." Cordelia got up and shuffled to the back of her little store and then came back with a cobalt blue scarf and a white hat.

She handed the scarf to Luna. "To match your eyes."

She handed the hat to me. "To match your pale skin."

"Oh, thank you!" Luna exclaimed.

"Thanks," I muttered.

"Now go bury that fish!" Cordelia exclaimed.

"How much do we owe you?" I asked, "I have to run back to our hotel, we sort of-"

But before I could finish explaining why I had tattered, empty pockets, Cordelia shook her finger at me. "I don't want your money," she said, pointing at Luna, "she makes me happier than any money could buy."

I suppose Cordelia did know a thing or two about love.

The beach. That was where she wanted to bury him.

I did most of the digging. Luna sat cross-legged, holding onto Cutty who was now in a white hat and blue scarf. The wind blowing her hair and his hat.

We didn't speak. Despite the amount that could have been addressed.

Luna placed Cutty in the hole.

"Bye, Cutty," she said, "you are the whole world now."

We covered him in sand.

And then she placed seashells over him in the shape of a heart.

We sat in silence on the beach for the rest of the night.

The ocean crashed mournfully at the shore.

And when the sun set, and darkness consumed the entire sky,

I watched as the lines between the universe and Luna blurred.

Yet again.

Luna Elrod Journal Entry
Date: May 7th, 2017

If Cutty couldn't survive my ocean, who can?

Chapter Forty-Two: Bahamas pt. 2
Date: May 2017

May 8th, Luna Elrod did not get out of bed.

She said she needed a day to mourn the loss of Cutty. So, I stayed in bed with her. I suppose letting yourself grieve isn't an entirely perpetually bad thing.

May 9th, Luna Elrod did not get out of bed.

So, I stayed in bed with her. Grieving isn't a task that is usually accomplished in one day.

May 10th, Luna Elrod did not get out of bed. But my body could no longer negotiate with the hands of emotion. I ripped the covers off her. "Luna, you can't mourn forever, let's go run to the beach! Or go get lunch! Anything you want! Let's just have a day. You and me."

She grabbed the covers from me and put them back over her head.

"Luna, come on, we can't do this forever," I said.

Silence.

My thoughts raced with seductive exposition. Teasing me.

Get her up.

Wake her.

She just needs something to revive her.

Get her out of this trance.

I paced the bedroom, trying to brainstorm how to cheer her up. I called room service and ordered everything on the menu. She didn't eat a single thing. I tried physically to get her out of bed, but she cried until I put her back.

None of it worked.

She was resistant.

Her sadness was contagious and the longer I spent around it, the sicker I got. The more intense the sensual dialogue became.

I walked out of the room.

Down the hall.

Into the elevator.

And out the hotel.

I walked to the beach. Down the entire beach. And back again.

I walked until the sun set.

The next morning, Luna Elrod didn't get out of bed, again.

And when her beauty didn't intermix with the sunrise and light up my ecosystem, my body became imbalanced.

And I couldn't handle it.

I couldn't handle not having my *beautiful little ritual*.

Luna Elrod Journal Entry
Date: May 10th, 2017

People die in my ocean.

An eclectic Spanish man with a gold tooth and rose tattoo approached me at the bar, holding up a dime-bag.

"100 US Dollar," he said.

"What?" I lifted my head off the table. "No," I waved him off.

He didn't budge. "This is good stuff. 100 US Dollar."

"Nah man, leave me alone," I put my head back down on the table.

"This right here," he pointed to the dime-bag again, "this will get you up."

I shot my head back up. "I said leave me-" *Wait a minute. Did he just say?* "Get me up?" I asked.

"Sí," he nodded.

"I'll take it."

I gave him the cash and he handed over the bag.

I got up to leave when the bartender approached me. "Hi Sir, sorry for the wait, what can I get you to drink?"

"Nothing anymore," I said.

I hadn't had a drink yet. But I didn't need one anymore.

Luna Elrod Journal Entry

Date: May 11th, 2017

She was curled in a ball. Her head under the pillow.

"Luna," I nudged her, "are you still this upset about Cutty?"

She shook her head.

I put my hand on her head. "What is it then?"

And for the first time in three days, she looked at me. Dried tears crusted her flooded eyes. "I'm drowning, Nathan."

She was sinking.

And I was going through withdrawal.

I *needed* to fix this.

She put her head back under the pillow.

"Have you eaten anything?" I asked.

She didn't answer.

"Luna, you need to eat."

She didn't answer.

I felt the dime-bag in my pocket.

She needs to eat. I told myself.

She needs to get out of bed. I told myself.

She needs to feel like herself again. I told myself.

She needs to intermix with the universe again. I told myself.

She can't live like this, I told myself, *it's for her own good.*

I can't live like this.

It's for *our* own good.

"I think I have something that might make you feel better," I said.

Luna Elrod Journal Entry

Date: May 12th, 2017

He is my whole world. He *can* protect me from my unpromising sea.

Chapter Forty-Three: intermixing beauty

Date: May 2017

An addict must be soothed.

Luna was snorting cocaine every day now. It was the only thing that got her out of bed. And kept her out of bed.

I watched in silence for the first week.

Watching her do drugs was more comforting than watching her melt between the bedsheets.

At least she was eating. And living.

That to me, was less depressing than the way I watched her previously dissolve.

We woke up.

I smoked a cigarette.

Luna did a line.

I smoked another cigarette.

Luna did another line.

And then the day would unveil before us.

Luna intermixing with the colors of the universe, once again.

So yeah, I stayed quiet.

Luna Elrod Journal Entry
Date: May 19th, 2017

A BOY AND A LINE.

THE WHOLE WIDE WORLD IS FUCKING MINE.

May 23rd

May Twenty-Third was the best day of my life.

I was sitting on the beach, smoking a cigarette, drinking a black coffee.

Luna was collecting seashells, and I was pretending the leftover powder under her nose was from the sand.

I watched her in peace.

My raison d'etre.

I was hazy in her presence, blurry-eyed as she ran up to me, a handful of seashells.

"Let's get married," she said.

It was a sensation that could never be duplicated.

A feeling you could spend your entire life chasing.

I was put into a bottle and sent on a long-winded adventure through the ocean.

And then one day I washed up on shore and was found by a rugged handsome sailor.

The sailor opened the bottle.

And then he let me out and gave me a world to reside in.

Chapter Forty-Four: the wedding
Date: May 2017

Our pastor was a non-denominational minister named Erris. A tall, brown man with woolly-bear caterpillars for eyebrows. I feared they might crawl off his face and we would spend our wedding day chasing after them. And his white linen suit was rather tight, it wouldn't have hurt if he had gone up a size. Or two. The long sleeves wrapped tensely around his rather wide arms, the button enclosures about to burst.

His presence, however, was soft. A welcome counterpoint to my intensity.

I was under an Arbor on the beach, waiting for Luna. Erris was standing slightly too close for comfort. I worried that he would feel the heat coming off my sweaty palms or feel the condensation from my tears. There wasn't anything I wanted more than to spend the rest of my life with this woman. So much so that my body was having a physical reaction in her absence as I awaited her arrival down the aisle. I couldn't stand the seconds in between the moment that held the possibility for this to not actually happen.

Time held my sanity in its hands like a careless child.

The beach was embellished with a curated seashell runway and blue taper candles. The arbor was wrapped attentively with daises. It was undeniably sensational and yet my mind could look nowhere else except down the aisle.

To honor the legalities of our marriage license, we needed two witnesses. Cordelia was more than excited to help us out with that and brought along five of her cohorts. Each one found their joyous way down the aisle with a bouquet of hand wrapped laced daises stitched by Cordelia herself.

And then *she* started walking towards The Arbor.

She was barefoot. Her long white beach dress dragged along the sand. Gold hoops and bracelets jingled on her, performing a lullaby, and a daisy crown sat atop her curled blonde hair.

My linen-suit a mere touch of reality amongst a backdrop of beautiful intoxication.

She held a bouquet in one hand and Cordelia, who was guiding her down the aisle, with the other.

"Wow," I said.

"Wow," Erris said.

It can't get any better than this.
She will be my beautiful, little, ritual.
Forever.

"Hi," she said, her thumb brushed my tears out of the way.

"Hi."

"Hi," Cordelia said.

"Hi," Erris said.

The four of us stood still in what felt like a pandemic of emotional paralysis.

"Cordelia did my makeup," Luna finally said.

"She didn't need it anyway," Cordelia responded.

"Alright, I-I guess we should start this?" Erris said.

I nodded.

Cordelia patted Luna's arm and went to stand with her girlfriends.

Erris began his spiel. But nobody listened.

"Hi," Luna said again, her thumb brushed my tears out of the way.

"Hi."

"Hello?" Erris said.

"Oh, uh, sorry, what?" I asked, finally taking my eyes off her.

"Nathan," Pastor Erris said, "repeat after me."

I repeated his words. "I, Nathan, take you, Luna, to be my wife. I promise to be faithful to you, in good times and in bad, in sickness and in health, to love you and to honor you all the days of my life."

"Luna," Erris said, "repeat after me."

"I, Luna," she said, "take you, Nathan, to be my husband. I promise to be faithful to you, in good times and in bad, in sickness and in health, to love you and to honor you all the days of my life."

We used stems from the daises for the ring exchange.

"In the sight of God and these witnesses," Pastor Erris nodded to Cordelia and her friends, "I now pronounce you husband and wife. You may now kiss the bride."

May 23rd

May Twenty-Third was the best day of my life.

And it soon became the worst.

Chapter Forty-Five: the reception
Date: May 2017

I had almost forgotten about her little morning routine that had now seeped its way into the afternoon, evening, and night. And now our wedding ceremony.

A routine I had introduced into her life.

We were standing around at a bar near the beach, Cordelia and her friends were taking tequila shots, Erris was trying to flirt with Cordelia, her friends were trying to flirt with Erris, and Luna was over the moon on white powder inviting everyone to move in with us. They all agreed feverishly, and I had to smile and keep my impulsive responses to myself.

She came running to me and jumped into my arms.

"Let's go dancing!" She shouted to everyone.

"Yes!" was the consensus. She hung onto me, while I hung onto *no*.

"Luna, I think maybe you should take it easy on the-" I started to say.

But she didn't seem to hear me.

Stereo Nightclub.

It was a dance floor with a straw-hut roof. Disco balls and neon lights hung from the hay and the music was so loud it pounded your head for you. It gave me déjà vu to my mother's old apartment as if her trinkets were the musings for this hotspot.

Cordelia had become privy to Erris's toying's after her fifth tequila shot and was now canoodling with him on the dance floor amorously. Luna was dancing with Cordelia's friends, and I needed a buzz before I could find the courage to move my uncoordinated body in the strobe lights, so I sat down in the sand and watched her.

I dragged on a tobacco filled paper-roll while I watched what was really giving me the buzz gyrate with five little old ladies.

As she danced, and spun, and became blurred in my vision, I watched her pull out another dime-bag from her purse and dip her fingernail in it.

I watched, silently.

And then she did it again.

I watched, once again, silent.

Another.

I watched.

And another.

Silence.

She was becoming more alive with every dip. The world around her increasingly more insignificant with every sniff.

And just as I was peaking, feeling the buzz build up inside me, a gust of wind came through the crowd, sweeping its way to Luna. Her dress, falling victim to the strong Bahamian winds, flew all the way up and around her neck, covering her head.

She was entirely nude underneath.

I waited for her to quickly grab at her dress and pull it off her face, considering, one, she was completely naked in front of a crowd of strangers, and two, the dress was wrapped around her face, preventing her from seeing and breathing.

But instead, she just kept dancing.

She just kept throwing her arms up in the air. Blind and naked. As if she hadn't even noticed her vision was absent and her body was exposed.

My cigarette hung loosely at my lips.

My buzz impaired.

I stood up, threw the dart in the sand, and walked over to Luna who was still throwing herself around the floor. I pulled her dress down myself. "Luna," I said, "your dress."

"What about it?"

"It was up and around your head?!"

"Oh," she said, laughing, "I hadn't even noticed."

I grabbed the dime-bag out of her purse and marched to the ocean. She ran after me, screaming.

"Give it back Nathan!"

This time I didn't seem to hear.

She was gaining on me, so I started running.

"I'll fucking kill you, Nathan! Give it back!"

Right as I made it to the inky waters, she caught up to me. I emptied the contents of the bag into the shoreline as quickly as I could. She fell to her knees. "WHY!?"

Tears streamed into the dark water, blending her pain with the universe's blackness. "WHY DID YOU DO THAT TO ME?" She started digging in the sand, trying to scoop up any remnants of the drug.

"Because Luna!" I shouted, "I should have never given it to you in the first place! I just wanted you to get out of bed!"

She was on her knees sobbing. I got down next to her. "I feel everything through you," I said, "and I don't feel good about this."

She hit and slapped my chest, her tears and anger spitting at me. The ocean crashed over us, trying to pull us out to sea, grabbing onto our white wedding clothes as if our matrimony was part of the ecosystem.

And then I held her until she couldn't physically afford to keep sobbing.

The sun set and black water melted over us. Her tears, a salty concoction that begged for her constant affection, retired from their desires.

"I'll drown without it," she said, gripping onto me as if something was trying to hold her under.

"No, Luna," I said, "no you won't."

Tears rolled down my arm. But they weren't Luna's this time.

"I'll protect you," I said.

"But my waves are too strong."

I carried her back to our room.

It was the first time she slept in days.

It was the first time I hadn't.

Chapter Forty-Six: flight from hell
Date: May 2017

The next morning, I had a crucial decision to make. There have been very limited times in my life where I have made the right decision. And on this day, how *badly* did I still want to pick what was wrong.

But, even amid my unforgivable desires and careless previous choices, I thought I was picking what was right. For once.

--

I packed up all our stuff. Luna didn't have the wherewithal to argue with me. Strong cravings for her to get out of bed and throw things at me consumed my ego while I crammed everything into our luggage. I would've taken any kind of rage or retaliation. Anything over her quietude. That's how hooked on her I was. I would've preferred domestic violence over her perpetual silence.

I really thought I was making the right decision.

I really thought I was fighting off my pining thirst.

We got on a flight back to Sacramento.

Luna sat looking out the window of the plane, refusing to speak to me. I was hopeless in the face of her anger. She didn't understand my motives and all I wanted was to take her back home and make things right.

"This is for your own good, Luna," I said, "*our* own good."

She ignored me, pulled out her journal and scribbled down a few things.

"I don't understand Luna," I said, begging for a response, "is this about Cutty still? He was dead before you jumped in... there was nothing you could have done to save him-"

"Some people don't grow wings until after they've died," she said, finally looking at me.

"What?"

"I need to go to the bathroom," she stood up and pushed past my knees, "excuse me."

I put my head on the tray. It felt like I was detoxing. A headache scratched at my temples, body aches ran up and down my arms and legs, chills, nausea (lions, and tigers, and bears, oh my!) I grabbed a paper straw to itch myself with, although, it was ineffective considering it was failing to rip open my skin and itch directly at the bone marrow. I was in untreatable discomfort with no relief in sight.

"Excuse me," I said to the flight attendant passing by, "can I get a Coke?"

She nodded.

A few minutes later she arrived with my Coke and I unironically realized it had been about ten minutes since Luna had gone to the bathroom. I looked back to see a few people had started forming a line, but Luna was not in sight. Unless she had managed to accumulate a new bag of cocaine between last night and when we got on this plane, the chances she was doing it in the bathroom were slim to very likely.

I shrugged it off, because the other character trait that girl had was taking her time to do just about anything. A bathroom break for Luna could last anywhere between one minute to one hour.

The flight attended came back around and I signaled her towards me. "Hey, can I get another one?" I pointed towards my empty plastic cup.

She nodded and left again.

I shifted around in my seat until the flight attend came back, but this time she was empty-handed. She leaned down towards me and whispered, "sir, does your girlfriend have any medical issues we need to be concerned about? She's been in the bathroom for about twenty minutes now and we just want to make sure she's okay."

"What?" I said, "no, no, she's fine, she just has no concept of time, she's fine." I waved her off.

"Sir?"

I shrugged on Luna's behalf.

The flight attendant's anxieties did not appear to be relived. "We have reason to believe that there might be a need for assistance. Are you sure she doesn't have any medical history we should know about?"

"Okay, hang on," I tried to get out of my seat, but I couldn't, "what the fuck?"

"Sir, you're still seat-belted in," the flight attendant, named Dory, noted.

I looked down. "Shit." I unbuckled my seatbelt and shoved myself into the aisle and down towards the bathroom. At this point I was growing concerned that she *actually* had found more cocaine and was doing it in the bathroom.

I hated that a part of me felt excited about that.

I shuffled past a line of people to get to the door. "Hey!" They all shouted.

"I'm here to help, people!" I recoiled. "Luna, what's going on?" I tapped on the door, "there's people waiting to use the bathroom, is everything okay in there?"

No answer.

The passengers in line looked at me with daggers in their eyes as if I was the one responsible for putting the knives in their optics.

I tapped on the door again, "did you fall in, Luna?" I asked, trying to lighten up the situation.

I looked over at Dory who was unamused.

"Okay," I held my hands up, "sorry."

"Sir. We need you to get your girlfriend out. She may be having a health problem or possibly doing something illicit."

"She's my wife first of all, and second of all," I lowered my octave, "it's definitely the ladder option."

"My mistake, I don't see a ring..." she said eyeing my hand with a judgy undertone, "and excuse me?"

I made a face back. "What's everyone's concern with a ring these days?"

"It's normal protocol for a wedded couple."

"Excuse me if we aren't entirely normal."

"That just sounds cheap."

"Can someone please help her or get her out?" a passenger from the line called out.

I sighed. "Okay, listen, Luna," I said to the bathroom door, "if you don't respond in three seconds, I'm going to come through this door, got it?"

When there was still no response, I counted, "one, two, three," and then glanced over at Dory for her silent permission to take the door down. She gave me a shrug and then a nod, giving me the go ahead to bust through the door.

I don't know if it was denial or the adrenaline from the situation, but when I thrusted my shoulder into the folding door, whatever I had in mind that would be on the other side, I assumed, would cure my intolerable symptoms.

Not make them worse.

Luna was sitting on the floor, her head on the toilet bowl, her eyes closed.

"Luna?" I knelt beside her and shook her, her eyes rolled to the back of her head. "Luna!" I grabbed her shoulders and jolted her. "Wake up!"

Gasps came from across the plane. "Oh my god," Dory heaved, "you said that she didn't have any medical issues, what happened?!"

"She doesn't!" I shouted.

"Then what's going on?!" Dory responded, in a state of shock.

"Just get her some fucking help!" I yelled.

Dory ran down the aisle, shoving past the line that was increasing quickly in size. Another flight attendant ran up with a towel. People were calling out for doctors or nurses, asking if there was anyone that could help.

"Wake her up!" I yelled, to nobody.

Luna's arm rolled off the toilet. Tears streamed down my face landing on the white sockets of her eyes that I was forcing open. My brain itched this time. With a force no paper straw could scratch at.

Dory called over the interphone system, "is there a doctor on this flight!?"

I grabbed Luna's wrist like I used to do for my mother. The same panic that I felt when I didn't feel my mother's washed over me. There was no pulse.

I yearned to slip into my peaceful and ignorant domain of substance abuse.

And then an empty Advil bottle fell out from Luna's skirt and rolled to my knees.

There was an emergency landing.

There were people who ripped her out of my arms.

There was somebody who shoved me into an ambulance.

There was a stretcher.

There were gasps and cries.

There were protocols.

But really, there wasn't anything at all.

Luna Elrod Journal Entry

Date: May 31st, 2017

I've fallen into my ocean.

And there's no saving a butterfly with wet wings.

Chapter Forty-Seven: Texas.
Date: June 2017

"You can go see her now," a nurse in blue scrubs said, "she's awake."

"Is she asking for me?" I asked.

The nurse looked sympathetic. "She's being sort of… difficult."

Thank God, I thought.

I got up and followed the nurse.

"She's right in here."

I nodded.

My eyes hadn't fully adjusted from the brain fog that was protecting me from perceiving my reality, but when I entered the room, I gained a little more clarity to the scene happening before me. Luna was sitting on the hospital bed, trying to pull an IV out of her arm, yelling at the nurse taking care of her.

"Ma'am," the nurse was holding down the other end of the needle, "you can't pull that out!"

"Just let me suffer and then let me leave!" Luna shouted.

I stood awkwardly in the doorway, waiting to be addressed.

Luna stopped trying to wiggle out the tube. "What is he doing here?" she asked, pointing at me.

I held up an awkward hand. "Hello."

"Hello sir," the nurse said, exhausted, "are you the husband in question?" he raised an eyebrow.

I nodded.

"Tell him to leave," Luna said, crossing her arms.

"Good luck," the nurse said nodding at me and leaving as fast as possible.

Luna shuffled her body to face the opposite direction of me. "Nathan. Please leave."

"Luna-"

"I said, 'please!' Nathan!"

"Luna!" I said again, startling even myself with my deafening diction, "are you aware of what you did?!"

She sat cross-armed facing the wall.

"How could you do that?!" My voice boomeranged around the room, "how could you do that?!"

She didn't speak.

"How could you do that?" I asked again, quieting my tone.

Silence.

I put my head in my hands, whispering the same thing over and over.

I ached in the wake of her silence until she finally turned to me.

"Nathan," she said, "I think there's something wrong with me."

I shook my head. "No, Luna, there is nothing wrong with you. It's me. I'm just no good for you. I should have NEVER given you those drugs."

"No, Nathan, there is actually something wrong with me," she said again.

"No, Luna, there is nothing wrong with you-"

"NATHAN!" she hit the hospital bed with both her fists.

I picked my head up from between my hands and looked at her.

We stared at each other in silence. It was the silence that used to penetrate the air before we even knew each other's names. A silence infused with frightful curiosity. And a suffering passion.

It was a very rigid, very unnerving silence.

She sunk into her bed. "The doctors did an evaluation on me."

"So what? Who cares what the doctors say?"

"Listen god-dammit!"

I let the silence pursue painfully anew.

She started again, "the doctors, they said-" she put her head in her hands as if what she was about to say next was going to physically hurt her, "…I don't want to live like this anymore."

"Luna?"

Desperation surged out of her eyes, calling for someone to listen and understand. "I don't think it's normal to feel this much."

I put my face in my hands again.

"The doctor said there's a place for me."

My head shot up. "What do you mean *a place*?"

She shrugged. "A place. To help me."

"What the fuck kind of place?" I asked, my voice boomeranging again, "and what do you mean to *help you*?"

"The doctor said it's a place I can go to learn about myself, and possibly get medicated… if need be."

Now there was desperation in my eyes. Anger filtering through my nervous system. "Where the fuck even are we?!" I shouted.

"Texas."

I turned to the doorway. A doctor holding a clipboard was standing in it. "We are in Dallas, Texas." She said again.

"Dallas?"

"That's where your plane had to take an emergency landing." She invited herself into the room and stood by Luna, marking a few things down on her clipboard.

"God-fucking, dammit," I ripped the hair out of my skull, "so my wife needs to go to some *'place'*, and we are in Texas?"

"Is there a problem, sir?" The doctor asked.

"Yeah, there's a problem! There're two problems actually!"

"Nathan?!" Luna exclaimed.

"And what seems to be the problem?" the doctor's lipstick was so red I almost asked if she had come in here seeking more blood.

"Well, for starters, we are in Texas."

"Nathan!"

"Okay, sir," lipstick was now sitting on the chair closest to Luna, "let's be adults here."

"Where are you taking my wife? Let's start there."

"We aren't *taking* her anywhere," lipstick responded, "but it is highly recommended she gets a proper diagnosis. And I know a great place she can receive the help she needs where you guys live in California."

"What do you mean a diagnosis?!"

"She needs-"

But before I could let any more words break through my survival mode, I was standing up, throwing my pointer finger around. Lipstick stood up right after, also throwing her pointer finger around, threatening to call security. Luna put her hands over her ears, shouting at both of us to be quiet.

"Nathan would you just listen to her!"

"You aren't going on any medication! There is nothing wrong with you!"

"Sir!"

The noises mixed like frozen fruit in a blender. Lipstick was shouting, Luna was crying, I was spinning. Nurses ran in and out, security was called. Pillows were thrown. Insults were shot.

And then.

I was running.

Down the hall.

Through the hospital.

And out the door.

Luna Elrod Journal Entry
Date: June 1st, 2017

The doctor said that I'm not the only oddly shaped oases out there.

Chapter Forty-Eight: pie.
Date: June 2017

The joint was called Pioneer Tap House. The place was empty considering it was a bar a couple blocks away from a hospital. I don't think the vibes are necessarily that high in this part of town. But then again, brilliant idea for the hardcore kids. A stomach pump just a block away. And even more ingenious for those in need of a quick fix after some bad news. In reconsideration, I am shocked at how empty the place was.

Johnny was the hero behind the bar. I remember his name vividly because he had a name tag that said, "Hi, my name's Johnny!" That kind of thing is helpful for the plastered drunk who can't remember their own name.

"Hey Johnny!" I said in full derision, "mind throwing me a menu?"

"Sure thing," he said, sliding it across the bar top.

Johnny was one of those guys that probably treated his hair better than he treated women. His coiffed hair flowed out of his hat like beer from the taps and he wore a tight white shirt in the sort of way only guys who had zero percent body fat could wear. Each one of his eight abs could've had a name tag of their own.

Guys like Johnny could work at a Tap House a couple blocks away from a hospital and still be considered cool. Like it was edgy of him to serve tequila shots a couple feet away from death. Guys like Johnny could spend more time looking in the mirror than in their lovers' eyes and women would still want to sleep with them.

I sneered at him.

"What can I get you this afternoon, sir?" Johnny asked.

"Please," I held up a hand, "must you be so blatant about the hour of the day?"

"I think the sunshine is doing a good enough job of that on its own."

I lifted an eyebrow at him and then glanced at the menu. "I'll take a Horse's Cock," I said.

"What?" Johnny said in full bafflement.

I looked back down at the menu. "Oh *sorry*, I mean Horse's Neck. Common misconception."

Johnny grabbed at his neck. "Really?"

"Oh Johnny," I said, rubbing my face, "oh, beautiful Johnny. One can dream."

Bourbon, house made ginger syrup and angostura bitters, topped with soda and a lemon peel garnish. Served on the rocks. Horse's Neck.

"One Horse's Neck," Johnny said, putting intense emphasis on the word *neck*.

"Ah, that's the stuff," I said, watching him place it in front of me.

"Anything bringing you here so early?" He asked.

"Again, must you be so blatant about the hour of the day? And besides, you need a therapist's license before you go about digging into one's personal dirt in a boneyard like this."

"Or a gun license."

I gave him a look. "Jesus, Johnny."

He shrugged. "Not everyone wants to talk around here."

"I'd be one of those folks."

"Nah," Johnny said, "the folks who don't want to talk don't order Horse's Necks. A drink like that is always a conversation starter."

I side eyed him. "What made you decide to become a bar tender?"

"I was too good-looking to model and too smart to be a doctor. So, I ended up somewhere in between."

I chuckled. "Touché, my friend."

He poured himself a whiskey. "Cheers."

I raised my glass. "Cheers."

If Luna was going to get medicated. So was I.

Luna Elrod Journal Entry
Date: June 2nd, 2017

I'm not mad at him anymore. I don't think I can be.

Nathan is my world.

I am the ocean.

The ocean covers seventy percent of the world. The earth relies on the ocean.

He is grieving the loss of his riptides.

If Amphitrite told Poseidon that she was taking away the sea
and Poseidon, with his large three-pronged spear, no longer had the power to
create storms, earthquakes or sink ships anymore…

What is he to do?

I woke up on a park bench. A half-eaten burrito scattered on my chest, a bag under my head, and a fork with a broken leg in my hand.

There was only one thing to do.

I called Jim and told him I was finally craving pie.

Chapter Forty-Nine: real life rehab
Date: June 2017

Jim took the first flight out to Dallas. I went back to the hospital to try and find Luna, but I knew it was hopeless. She was gone.

Jim met me at the hospital. I was sitting on a bench outside of the room Luna had been in. He didn't say a word. Just grabbed the back of my neck, helped me up, and lead me out of the hospital.

We drove in silence to the airport.

Took the next flight back to Sacramento.

Got a slice of pie at a diner.

And then he brought me to rehab.

All without saying a word.

*The paperwork below is a photocopy of an evaluation found in Luna's journal

Doctor Notes:

Doctor: Dr. Kennedy   **Hospital:** Sacramento
Camellia Mental Health Institution
Patient: Luna Elrod

REASON FOR VISIT:

Transferred from Medical City Dallas Hospital by recommendation of Dr. Hoffmann, M.D.

SYMPTOMS:

Client's symptoms include periods of feeling elated, energized, racing thoughts, impulsive behavior, grandiose plans, speaks fast in a manner that does not make sense to others, high sex drive, decreased need for sleep. Client also experiences periods of feeling hopeless, poor concentration, trouble getting out of bed, deep sadness, thoughts of death or suicide, feelings of low self-worth and guilt. Client experiences extreme mood shifts, manic episodes, and depressive episodes. Client has attempted acts of self-harm and suicide.

DOCTORS COMMENTS:

Bipolar Disorder.

The first week in rehab I spent getting stabilized. The second week I spent mostly in silence. The third week I spent glued to a chair watching the daisies grow outside a window. And the fourth week I met Aiyden.

He intruded on my sulking. "Are you always this cryptic?" an unfamiliar voice asked behind me.

I turned to see a very theatrical little man. His Prada pool slides, and deep-pink acrylic nails took up more space than that of his body. His eyes failed to hide that he couldn't wait a moment more to hear what my story was. I recognized him from meetings.

"None of your business," I answered, turning back around.

"What are you looking at?" he asked, prying again.

"None of your business," I responded, again.

"You're in rehab sir," he said, "everything here is everyone's business."

"If that's the case then why'd you get your nails done for rehab?" I jabbed back.

He sat down next to me. "I didn't expect to get taken from the nail salon and thrown into this junkie yard now, did I?" he responded, waving his nails in my face, "otherwise I would have had them re-do this tacky shade. Most people don't *plan* their rehab visit."

I gave him an unfriendly look.

"Your turn," he said, "what's happening out these windows that has had you so adhered to this chair for the last week?"

"Nothing."

"Mhm," he sighed, "well you won't talk in meetings. Figured maybe you would one on one."

I glared at him, hoping he would get the memo and move onto the next sufferer. But when he didn't leave, I said, "I prefer to ache independently."

"You don't say," he said with an eyebrow raise.

I sat up straighter, putting my elbows back. "I'm only here to detox safely and then I'll be on my way."

He only got more comfortable in his chair. "Okay."

I gave him a displeasing look once again before asking, "what's your name?"

"Aiyden," he said, crossing his knees, "and you're Nathan."

I furrowed my eyebrows. "How do you know my name?"

"Because everyone around here talks about you."

"Oh really? And what do they say."

"They say you're the handsome, angry, mystery, who probably has a deeply sad backstory that's made you this way and most of the girls and gays want to fix you."

"Jesus, don't they have anything better to talk about?"

"No. We're in rehab with no access to the outside world."

"No offense," I said, "but I don't think anyone in *here* should be trying to fix anyone."

"Touché." Aiyden responded.

We sat in silence.

"So, is that why you're bothering me with investigative questions?" I eventually asked after giving up on trying to get him to leave.

He nodded. "Karen bet me her lunch roll that I wouldn't be able to get anything out of you."

I laughed. "Well, it looks like Karen's getting to keep her lunch roll today."

Aiyden exhaled. "Ugh, and it's saffron rolls today, my favorite."

I eyed him. "You could have used the extra roll too."

The next day he infringed upon my solitude again. The roll of the day was a croissant au fromage and he had French dreams plastered all over his buttery complexion.

"Kiss your crescent shaped fantasies goodbye," I said before turning to look at him, "I'm not talking."

"Come on!" he said, "me and you both know I need those French calories more than Karen."

"Start making smarter bets then," I retorted.

"You know, if you don't start talking soon, Tabitha might not be inclined to recommend you leave at your suggested end date." (Tabitha was rehabs version of Landon. Just shorter and darker and existed more on *this* planet).

"Nobody's going to stop me from just signing myself out."

"Karen might if she eats anymore of those rolls."

The next week he just sat, ate, and watched me. I sat in silence, watching the daises grow. Hardly giving him anything to find amusing. It didn't matter however, because the rolls of the week kept getting more and more intriguing.

"You see this sesame seed challah roll?" he held it up in front of my face, "I could have two of these if you just tell me one tiny bit of information about yourself."

I didn't speak.

The begging, the curiosity, the bread fixation, and the intrusion continued until the fifth week when Aiyden sat down next to me with one bite left of his rosemary focaccia.

"We could share the next one," he said.

I looked over at him. "Do you like herbage?"

"As in plants?" he asked.

I nodded.

"*Herbage* is a very strange way of just saying plants."

"It's Early Medieval Latin," I said, "it's the proper way to describe natural pasture distinct from the land itself."

This time Aiyden gave me an irritated look. "No wonder you never talk. You're extremely unrelatable."

I laughed. "Potentially. Except for the insufferable fact we have one very relatable trait in common that landed us both here."

"Well, the answer is yes. I do like plants."

I nodded. "And there we go again. Not relating."

"Why do you ask?"

I pondered my answer for a moment before responding. "Every time herbage enters my life, I end up killing it."

"Well, are you watering it?" he asked.

I nodded. "Of course."

He shrugged. "Well then... are you suffocating it?"

I looked at him with a blank expression.

"Too much water can also kill a plant you know."

And after that, I started talking in meetings.

Flying.

And sinking.

Turns out there is an entire community of drowning birds.

Flying.

And sinking.

Chapter Fifty: Tabitha
Date: July 2017

The first time I talked in a meeting I listed off all the ingredients to rhubarb pie. Tabitha just crossed her legs and asked, "why rhubarb?"

I shrugged. "I think it's interesting a seasonal vegetable can make a sweet dessert."

She nodded. "Do you often eat pie?"

"Only when it's necessary."

Tabitha wore rings as large as her knuckles and she'd twist them whenever she was intently listening. The first few times I spoke, I thought she was going to twist the jewels right off. So, in a thoughtful concern for her gemstones, I tried to say the least amount as possible.

The next time I talked, I briefly mentioned my disdain for herbage.

"If you don't allow yourself the trouble of taking care of plants, how do you expect to have any beauty around you?" Tabitha asked.

"Who's to say everyone is deserving of beauty."

"Do you think that you aren't?"

"How can I be deserving of something I can't keep alive?"

"But you've been able to keep yourself alive through addiction and suffering. Does that not count for something beautiful?"

"My life has been at the expense of much greater beauty."

"Well then, maybe you should start watering yourself so that you too, can become beautiful." Tabitha held direct eye-contact with me as she turned her emerald stone.

And then the third time I talked; I told her everything.

"So, your wife, she's in the hospital right now?" Tabitha asked.

I nodded.

Tabitha sat back and let it register before she curated a response. That was the uncomfortable thing about Tabitha, she didn't just speak to fill silence, and she had no problem dragging on awkward stillness. I sat in petrified quietude, regretting not sharing the recipe to coconut custard pie instead.

Aiyden looked over at Karen, "does this mean I get your roll today?"

Karen snapped back. "No! You didn't get that information out of him, Tabitha did!"

Aiyden groaned. "But he didn't start talking until I provoked him!"

Tabitha leaned forward, ready to speak, silencing everyone with just her commanding presence. "You said your wife was there for you when you needed her? When you detoxed right?"

I nodded.

"But you couldn't be there for her? When she needed you?"

I shook my head in denial. "This, this is different."

"How so?" she asked.

"Because!" I shouted unexpectedly peeved, "she doesn't belong in a place like that! There isn't anything wrong with her!" I clenched my fists.

Tabitha tilted her head. "Nathan… It sounds like your wife *does* need help."

I jetted out of my chair in rapid disappointment with the way this conversation was proceeding. "How can you say that? You don't even know her."

"Nathan, how many people do you know experience highs and lows in such extremes like your wife does?"

I was still standing, looking for the words to prove her wrong. "None. But that's what makes her so remarkable. People don't see the world how she does. They can't take the beauty from her too." I wiped the tears from my cheeks.

"Or do you mean they can't take that from *you*."

I unclenched my fist.

Tabitha held my gaze.

"What do you mean?"

"How much do you love her?"

I stared into her unfiltered brown eyes before sitting back into my seat. "With my whole life."

She held a bejeweled finger up. "It sounds like your wife doesn't want to live like this anymore, Nathan. Sometimes love isn't just about what *we* want."

I clenched my fist again, held it in a ball for a good minute. Counted to two, twice. And then I let it go.

"Okay," I said.

Luna Elrod Journal Entry
Date: July 2nd, 2017

Could I ever really fly?
Or were my wings a figment of my imagination?

Dr. Kennedy told me I'm a victim to my own brain chemistry. I leaped out of the chair and threw my journal at him. He told me he'd seen worse than a flying notebook.

I cried and yelled and screamed and called him a liar. But instead of hitting me, like my father used too, and instead of swimming in my riptide like Nathan used too, he walked across the room and picked up my journal. He handed it back to me and told me to listen to the other patients talk and write down what they say.

And why would I ever do a thing like that? I asked.
Because last I checked those things are meant for writing, not flying. Much like yourself. He responded.
Real clever, Dr. Kennedy. But I will do no such thing.

(I did such a thing).

Birdie #1:

After a manic episode, I typically have left myself amongst a colorful assortment of odd and dangerous situations. Nobody trusts me, especially not myself. I lack autonomy over my own mind, my own pride, and my own soul.

Mania might feel euphoric, but hell, it's one way to rip the joy out of the rest of your life.

Birdie #2:

I used to love the creative and divine energy mania would bring to my life. I was a sculptor. I created endless fabrications of life.

But with every high comes a low.

And the more intense the high, the more intense the low.

So eventually when I was creating art with my hands and my mind, it always led to creating devastation.

So, I no longer wanted to make art.

…Because every time I felt myself touching the sun, I always knew… that eventually… there would soon come a day, where I wouldn't see anything but darkness.

Birdie #3:

I could make you feel like the best drug you've ever done. But the second it was over; I was all alone again.

My comedown is always more intense than the ride up.

That's why I mourn mania.

Because the friendships and the love I receive during a high are never strong enough to last through the suffering that comes after.

Mania is like a portal to hell.

It's like going through heaven to get to hell.

So now I mourn heaven. Because I know what comes next.

The coffee was at its warmest every morning at exactly 7:03 am. If I was out of bed by 6:56, I could make it down the hall without any disruption and wait exactly two minutes for the coffee to finalize its strength and pour myself a hot cup of joe. Then I had exactly one hour and six minutes before the bathroom was freshly cleaned, to then later, dispose of said coffee.

After coffee and coffee removal, I walked the hall twenty-two times. Next, I would do two sets of twenty-two jumping jacks, a twenty second plank, and twenty pushups. Then I laid out by the pool until meetings began. Twenty-nine minutes on my stomach. Twenty-one minutes on my back.

My back was my most valuable angle. According to Aiyden.

I was laying out by the pool one day when Aiyden came wandering out in a bathing suit that was more flamboyant than his pink nails. "Wow," he said.

"What."

"You're laying by a pool with lemon water," he sat on the chair next to mine, "how could your fists possibly be clenched?"

"Because we are still in rehab."

He pulled out a green tube and started squeezing it all over his face. "At least we are rich in rehab."

"What on god's green earth is that green stuff doing on your face and not the ground?"

"It's called a face mask."

"A what?"

"You put it on your skin for replenishing effects."

"Why?"

"Because Nathan, it's good for your skin."

"Oh."

"Jeez," Aiyden said, "has anyone ever told you how uptight you are?"

"No," I responded.

"You'd think after everything you've been through; you'd learn to let go of control a little," he smeared more of the gunk on his face, rubbing it into his temples.

"That doesn't make any sense," I said.

"Sure, it does," he replied, "you think you'd eventually learn that your clenched fists and uptight ways don't exactly do jack shit from stopping shit."

"And what makes you so wise, genius?" I asked, dramatically clenching my fist in his face.

He shrugged. "Just saying. You rue the day. I replenish with face masks. And we still both ended up addicts."

"And your point?"

"I'd much rather be an addict who replenishes with face masks."

Luna Elrod Journal Entry
Date: July 4th, 2017

They started me on medication today.

Dr. Kennedy said I can still be a creative ecosystem, but I can do it without flying and I can certainly do it without drowning.

He said my mental illness isn't what supplies my beauty, it's my heart.

I asked him what gives him the nerve. He said his diploma.

I had seven days left and I tried to find ways to make it seven more. Every other time I'd been in rehab I couldn't wait to get the hell out because the only thing that awaited me in the outside world was Jim with a slice of pie and my mundane desolation.

But this time what awaited me was scarier than what sent me.

I was out by the pool with Aiyden, drinking lemon water. This time we both had green mud on our faces because despite my disputes, my skin needed to be replenished.

"I can't leave," I said.

Aiyden side-eyed me. "Is that a joke? Nathan, we aren't *actually* on vacation."

I shook my head. "It's a perfect simulation that keeps us sober and safe."

"Well, what are you going to do? Buy the place?"

I sat up straight. "Now there's a thought."

"Nathan, you've got to be kidding. This place is so fucking boring."

"I love boring."

Aiyden laughed. "If that was the case, you wouldn't have married that wife of yours."

I looked at him in consensus. "Touché."

"You'll be fine," Aiyden responded, "you just have some serious apologizing to do."

"But I don't know how."

"You have no choice but to figure it out."

I nodded. "Okay."

I was dragging my hand along the wall to get my last cup of coffee, in complete denial I was going to have to be ripped from these very barriers that were protecting me, when Tabitha caught up with me.

"Nathan!" she said, "it's your last day, isn't it?"

"Tabitha!" I said, refusing to slow down because hot coffee was on the line, "yes, indeed, it is."

She turned awkwardly attempting to keep up with my stride. "What's the first thing you're going to do when you get out of here? Get a burger?" she asked, teasing me.

"Wow," I said, "you make it sound like it's prison in here."

We were both now trekking down the hall like two old ladies on a speed walk.

She shrugged. "It's sort of like a mental prison."

"If you want to look deep into it, it's also like a sanctuary for safety."

Tabitha chuckled.

"What's so funny?"

"Nothing, nothing." She waved me off.

We arrived at the coffee, I reached for the pot. "No, seriously, tell me."

"Nathan," she laughed again, "you look too deep into everything."

"Well," I mumbled, "I don't know how you could possibly say such a thing-"

"I mean you have actually thought so long and hard about life you were able to create your own manual on how *not* to exist."

"The main issue is I pick and choose when to use that manual," I responded.

Tabitha laughed.

I thought about what she said a moment before responding, realizing she was right. "In my defense, not everything is black and white. Some things need to be examined."

She smiled. "Yes, but similarly, not everything is in-between. There are some things that have clear answers. Some things that you don't need to look so deep into."

"As in?"

She turned to leave. "You'll figure it out."

I watched her walk down the hall, her rings taking up more space than her. *God*, I thought, these AA therapists and their vague, eerie metaphors. Maybe she was more like Landon than I had originally thought.

"Oh, and Nathan," Tabitha turned around, "it was nice working with you. I'm glad you finally opened up."

I nodded and raised my coffee. "You're good at your job."

She flashed me a peace sign and waved me off.

If only that harmony could have remained with me.

Luna Elrod Journal Entry

Date: July 7th, 2017

I've explored the universe vigorously and I've fallen in love with the world
madly.

But I've never taken the time to tour my own mind. Or fall deeply in love
with myself.

Until now.

Chapter Fifty-One: too much water
Date: July 2017

There was a whole world out there and I wasn't convinced it was better with me in it. A lot more herbage would be able to grow without my footsteps.

I looked out the window, watching the daises.

Too much water can also kill a plant you know.

"Good luck," Aiyden said, appearing out of nowhere per usual. He handed me something in a brown bag.

I nodded. "What's in the bag?"

"Something special," he winked.

"Oh," I said, "I got you something too."

"What is it?!" He asked with glee.

I bent down and grabbed a plastic bag filled with each of the rolls from last week.

Aiyden covered his mouth. "You didn't."

I laughed. "Relax. You could use the carbs more than me."

He patted me on the back. "Screw Karen, she can keep her *pain au chocolat*."

I looked back out the window at the flowers. "I don't know if I can go out there."

"Well good thing it's not up to you."

"I could still buy the place and keep everyone on my payroll."

"Look," Aiyden said, "you owe it to your wife to apologize. And the only thing scarier than going back out there and trying to say sorry is dying in here a coward."

I looked at him and nodded. "Okay."

"And unclench your fist."

I nodded. "Okay."

He gave me a hug. "See you on the other side."

"If I make it."

After he left, I looked down at the brown bag. I put my finger through the tape and reached my hand inside. It was a tube of green mud.

Great, I thought. *Just what I need to solve the world's problems.*

If all else fails, at least I'll have replenished skin.

Jim was late to pick me up. Poetic justice. All my pretentious ways, yet I still ended up on a curb outside a rehab facility with nothing but a bag full of dirty clothes and face mud.

I checked my watch for the second time in two minutes. *Where are you, Jim?* I couldn't stand to look like an unrushed and mellow civilian a second longer. But just as I was conjuring up new strings of insults about my large Mongolian friend, my strange Jesus-looking mentor pulled up instead.

"Nathan!" Landon's car door was open, almost dragging on the ground, his body hanging out of the vehicle, "Nathan!"

I stood motionless with my humble bag of items. "What is happening here?" I asked, "I appreciate the urgency, but this isn't normally your style."

"Nathan! Get in!"

"Okay but, where is Strong Jim? He was supposed to pick me up."

"Would you just get in for heavens-sake, Nathan!"

"Don't have to ask me twice."

We drove all of five minutes in silence before Landon could look over at me.

"What?" I asked, "oh come on, don't tell me you guys are throwing me another surprise party. I can't handle that right now."

Landon gripped the wheel like a new father driving his first-born home from the hospital.

"You are acting weird," I pressed, "what's going on with you?"

He mumbled a few incoherent words and wiped sweat beads off his forehead.

"Landon? You obviously have something to say! Just spit it out!" I shook my head, waiting anxiously for this uncomfortable car ride to be over.

He nodded. "Okay."

I nudged my chin forward. "Okay?"

He nodded again.

I rolled my eyes and put a cigarette in my mouth.

"I've… I've been practicing all day how to tell you this, and, and-"

"And?" I pulled my lighter out and sparked my dart, rolling the window down.

"There just isn't a proper way to tell somebody something like this-"

"Jesus, Landon," I said, "did you convert to Catholicism or something? You're making me nervous."

"Nathan," Landon looked over at me, the steering wheel slipping out between his clammy hands, "Strong Jim…" he trailed off.

"Yes?"

He took a long inhale and then when no exhale came, I yelled, "Strong Jim what?!"

"Strong Jim passed away."

The wet cigarette between my teeth dried up.

"What do you mean?" I asked.

"He had a heart attack, Nathan. Last week while you were in rehab. I wanted to come and tell you, I wanted to take you out so badly, but I couldn't. You know I couldn't."

Ash from my cigarette flaked off and cascaded to the floor. I bent over and picked it up.

"Nathan," Landon looked over at me, "I know how upsetting this is-"

More ash fell off. I bent over and picked it up again, this time rolling it around between my fingers.

"Nathan?"

Ash. It kept falling.

"Nathan I-"

I put the cigarette out in my hand.

"Nathan!"

"Could you pull over please?" I asked.

Landon looked at me with concern.

"Pull over please." I said again.

"Nathan, I'm taking you to Cindy's right now- everyone is there with her, we can go together, let's just-"

I opened the car door.

Landon slammed on the brakes. "Nathan!"

I got out of the car.

"Nathan come back here!"

And then I started walking.

Luna Elrod Journal Entry
Date: July 10th, 2017

<u>Floating</u>

That's the word Dr. Kennedy uses.

I've never been much of a floater.

I've always *flown* or *drowned*.

Floating was always the less exciting alternative.

You can't see the entire world when you're floating.

You can't feel the entire world when you're floating.

Ah, but that's where you're wrong. Dr. Kennedy said. When you float, you can look ahead into the great big sky and stare right into your future. The world is bigger than you, more daunting than you. Let it present itself to you from a new angle.

I threw my book at him again.

I walked.

And I walked.

And I walked.

I walked until the bottom of my feet bled into the daisies.

I walked until I saw the bright yellow gas station on the corner of Alfalfa Plant Rd. and Brunk Rd.

The clerk was sitting behind the counter mindlessly reading an instruction manual for a soft drink dispenser, entirely unaware of the broken bits of me that had no instruction manual written on how to put the pieces back together.

I grabbed a pack of Miller and walked to the counter. "My best friend died," I said.

"I'm sorry Pal, but just to let you know, these Miller are half off today."

"That's because nobody likes Miller," I said.

I paid him in cash and then left.

I walked all the way to Folsom Lake.

I walked to the edge of the water, carrying my shoes.

The breeze slapped my face, stealing what little heat was left in my cheeks.

The cold water nibbled at my toes. It bit my bare skin like a rabid dog.

The sun sat on its pedestal in the sky. Watching over the universe. A big ball of fire that could come crashing down at any moment, destroying the very thing it lit up. Yet, it chose to stay put.

I stood barefoot at the edge of the lake, holding the pack of Miller.

Some people feel pain their entire lives.

And some are numb for most of theirs and have one moment that is an entire lifetime of pain.

& finally, I chose pain.

All the anger and the sadness that I held back with rigid routines.

All the control.

All the ego.

I finally let go.

My best friend was gone.

And no regimen was going to change that.

No formula could conceal this type of pain.

I fell to my knees, put my head in the sand, and wept.

I wept until my tears became their own oddly shaped oasis.

I put my head in the water and let it beat itself over and over into my eardrums, forcing myself, for once, to listen to the planet. I let madness consume me.

My gut tied itself into a knot and hanged my soul.

And when I finally had enough bandwidth to sit up, I ripped open the Miller package and cracked open a beer.

And then I dumped it into the lake.

And then I did the same with the next beer.

And then the next.

And then the next. Until I had dumped every beer in that case into the lake.

"Nobody fucking likes Miller!" I shouted, into the dark, oddly shaped oasis.

Luna Elrod Journal Entry
Date: July 13th, 2017

Mania makes you forget that death is in the equation of life. When I'm manic, the curiosity of the universe floods my mind. I fly dangerously over a roaring ocean with no safety precautions to save me when I inevitably fall. There is no safety raft. No life vests. No promise of finding land.

And once your wings are cut, you fall deep into the depths of an unfriendly sea. One that will gladly eat you alive and leave you to decay as a carcass. There is no escape from the agony. And the suffering. And the helplessness.

But stability? After the life I've lived and the feelings I've experienced, how could anything compare? How could normality and a lack of adventure not lead to melancholy?

So, what do you do?

You fly. You fall. You ruin your life in unstable haste. You suffer alone in a low. You love. You hate. You turn everyone against you. You turn yourself against you. You're a hero. You're a villain. You beg for peace. You beg for help. You beg for freedom. You finally seek help. You feel nothing. You feel peace.

And then you crave. You crave for that one little manic episode. That one little feeling you used to get at four in the morning when you felt like there wasn't anyone in the world flying but you.

It's an addiction of sorts.

But after a while, addiction manifests itself into loneliness.
And being lonely is enough to make someone want to heal.

The meds are working. I feel stable.
I feel bored.

But I don't feel lonely.

Chapter Fifty-Two: the funeral
Date: August 2017

The only other funeral I had been invited to, was my mothers. And if you recall, I slept through that one.

But up until Jim's funeral, I hadn't slept at all.

In a more theatrical world, his funeral would've been filled with the vile noise of wailing, almost as loud as his voice was. But in this world, his service was quieter than a cunning wolf sneaking up on its prey. Silent enough to hear the leaves rustling from outside the building. Everyone, completely unaware of how to make a sound.

Cindy had asked me to give a speech, but I hadn't prepared anything because I couldn't sit down and write something if I tried. My words wouldn't do the existence of Jim justice. How could I authentically portray the creation that was Strong Jim? It wasn't feasible. And neither was my sanity when it came to typing it.

But I couldn't say no to Cindy.

I stood on the podium, the microphone positioned under my lips waiting for my voice to bring it to life. I stared out at the guests. They stared back at me. Everyone waiting for someone to speak.

"I, uh-" the microphone squeaked, "sorry."

The silence resumed.

I cleared my throat. "You know, when I first met Jim, I wasn't all that into him. I thought, why is this guy *so* loud and *so* invasive?"

Small chuckles came from the audience. I smiled, wiping sweat from my forehead.

"But I was also drunk and completely unlovable at the time. Or so I thought." The audience silenced.

"That was what was so beautiful about the large bastard, he didn't care who you were or what your story was, he just looked right into your soul and fell in love. He saved my life before he even knew my name. I never imagined a world without Jim because I never imagined I'd be able to survive one without him. But Jim's not the kind of person to ever leave someone stranded, no. He made sure he lived so large that he left parts of himself everywhere, for everyone. He taught everyone in this room not only how to survive, but how to love. He is everywhere, always, looking over all of us. But now he's up there, protecting the one he cared about the most, his daughter."

I raised my water glass. "To Jim. I'll see you all around me, forever."

"To Jim," everyone repeated, raising their glass.

After the service, there wasn't much I had left to offer the mourning crowd. I let people pat me on the arm and say a few words I didn't listen too. My tongue was burnt from the cigarettes I let malt in my mouth all morning and the bags under my eyes were darker than my black suit.

But when I felt a punch in the arm instead of a pat, I came too. "Go talk to Cindy," Landon whispered harshly at me.

I looked at him with empty eyes. "I don't know what to say."

"Oh Nathan," he said, "you never do."

Jim's wife stood feebly in the corner. I wondered how she was able to dress herself that morning. Or any morning that had followed the incident.

My fingers unclenched at the side of my untucked shirt. I walked over to her.

She was listening politely to a nervously rambling guest when I approached. When she saw my awkward looming, she graciously hugged the invitee and sent her on her dreary way. I stood fiddly and large before her. Silent.

"I don't know what to say," I said.

"I know," she responded.

I nodded.

"How about a hug?"

"A human touch is fleeting, nonetheless," I responded.

"Ah," she said, moving closer to me, "but effectual."

She wrapped her arms around me.

We stood there, hugging. And I cried into her arms over her dead husband.

Luna Elrod Journal Entry

Date: August 6th, 2017

It's my last week here.

And so far, all I've learned is how to survive.

Not how to live.

I found my AA family hanging out near the deli-meats and the non-alcoholic refreshments. I walked over to join them.

Daniel had a square cheddar cub held in the air, up for observation.

"What are you a mouse?" Sofia asked, grabbing the cheese from him and eating it.

"Hey!" Daniel shouted, "I was making sure it wasn't associated with the government cheese stockpile!"

"Has anyone noticed there's no open bar?" Mateo asked.

"Yeah, no shit man," I responded.

"Nathan!" They all cheered when they noticed my awkward hoovering.

"Hi guys."

"Nathan," Sofia reached out and put her hand on my arm, "how are you, *un hombre*? Your speech was beautiful."

"I am so sorry bud," Mateo said, "we are all just completely devastated."

I nodded. "Yeah."

"How was rehab?" Daniel asked.

"We missed you, man." Xavier chimed in.

"I missed you guys too," I said, "there's an odd bunch of people in those rehabs."

Sofia laughed. "Yeah, as if AA holds a more normal crowd."

"At least we're a family," Elizabeth said, "one that can't leave each other."

I looked over at her as she started to give me a hug. *So much hugging*, I thought, reluctantly embracing the physical contact.

"Family forever," Mateo said, joining in on the hug.

"Family forever," Daniel said, joining.

And then Sofia, Xavier, and Max repeated, "family forever," and wrapped their arms around me.

"Family forever," I grumbled, hugging them all back.

Cindy was right, the human touch is effectual, nonetheless.

Chapter Fifty-Three: finding Luna
Date: August 2017

After Jim's funeral I sat on my floor and ate a piece of pie alone. A large mural of an Alfalfa plant watched me eat. I was typically used to a large, silent, *human* starting back at me as I ate pie, but tonight a slightly less heavy breather and an endearingly less indulgent sharer looked back at me.

"What do you want?" I asked it.

Silence.

"You know, herbage like you is what makes me eat so much fucking pie in the first place," I said, sticking my fork at it.

Silence.

"Oh god damn you!" I threw my fork at it, "fine!"

I called every psychiatric facility in the state. I asked for every one of her aliases. At every hospital. I did this until I found where she was. Husband privileges helped here, considering these institutions love to throw around the word, "confidentiality."

She was being discharged the *next day*.

I had today and today only to figure out how to apologize.

But I told myself, *I have the rest of my life to make it up to her*.

With Jim gone, I needed her.

Needed.

And thus began *the 13th Floor Elevators* from track one and it didn't turn off until the next day when I left to get Luna back.

--

I ironed my suit with my hands. I turned around and looked at the daises in my back seat. *This had to work.* A man only picks his wife up in a suit and tie from the psych-ward once. I grabbed the flowers and got out of the car.

A lady in a pink dress working the front desk greeted me with a troubled look, "are you okay sir?" she asked.

"I think so…? Why?"

"Sorry," she said, "I just- this is a psychiatric hospital you know? You look dressed for the Prom."

"I'm a little old for the Prom, lady."

"Is there an occasion then?"

"Yes actually," I fixed my tie, "I am here to pick up my wife."

She twinkled. "That's cute, actually."

"This is not cute," I said, "this is business."

"Yikes," she responded, "trouble in paradise?"

"Yes… actually," I laughed at the uncanniness of the innuendo, "that's *exactly* what happened in fact."

"What's the name of the lucky girl?"

"Luna Elrod."

She nodded and started typing on her computer. I gripped onto the flowers, suddenly feeling self-conscious about my appearance.

"Oh, I'm sorry," the front desk lady in the pink dress looked up from her computer, "it says Luna Elrod has already been discharged?"

"What!?" I encroached upon the desk, "that can't be? I called yesterday and was told she'd be discharged at this time today!?"

Pink dress shook her head. "It says she checked out an hour ago. I'm sorry sir, but she's not here."

"Well, where is she?" I asked.

"Uh," she shrugged, "how am I supposed to know that?"

"Dammit!"

"You might be in more trouble now," pink dress said with a captious undertone.

"You know, I actually don't think that's possible, but I appreciate the positivity."

"Well, what are you going to do?" she asked.

I looked down at the flowers I was clutching. "I have to go find her."

Pink dress nodded. "Good luck sir."

I handed her a singular daisy. "For the trouble."

She smiled and reached for the flower. "You know, for working at a psychiatric hospital, this is still one of my weirder moments."

"You know, for being an addict, I can still say the same."

Luna Elrod Journal Entry
Date: August 12th, 2017

I left today.

I went to the corner of Alfalfa Plant Rd. and Brunk Rd.

I sat on the corner by the dull yellow gas station and looked at the daisies.

The wind tussled the flowers around.

But this time, I didn't think about running over barefoot to save them.

And I didn't think about running inside the filling station and buying everything I wanted.

I didn't want to fly up to the sun and feel its hot wings burn my precious, fair skin. I didn't want to run down the street and feel the wind against my back, or strip naked and dance with the poppy flowers.

I didn't want to soar.

But I also wasn't being held under by waves that drowned me on a cigarette burnt mattress.

All I could do was sit in silence and watch the daises grow.

Her apartment was the first place I went. I ran up the entryway calling her name but the only thing that greeted me was an eviction notice on her door and a pile of untouched packages scattered across her welcome mat. *This can't be right*, I thought, *I had been paying her rent*. Or had I forgotten?

Fuck.

In the state of my panic, I noticed an elderly Filipino woman slowly making her way up the stairs holding an assortment of coupon clippings.

I took to any help I could find.

"Excuse me, ma'am, do you know where the resident of this apartment might be?" I asked.

She shook her head. "She hasn't been here in ages. And trust me, I've been alive for many of them."

"What are they planning on doing with her stuff if she doesn't come back soon?" I asked, frantically.

She shrugged. "Probably donate it."

"Are you serious?" I asked.

"Is everything okay? What's got you all strung out of order?"

I disregarded her inquiry. "Do you know if there is a way I can get into this apartment?"

She looked at me, discontent. "Do I need to get the landlord, sir? Or the police?"

"No, no! Please don't, uh- this is my girlfriend- I mean- my wife's apartment. Long story. And I would hate for all her beloved items to be put into the hands of strangers."

She put her hands on her fragile hips. "I don't see a wedding ring?"

I sighed loudly. "What's with the wedding ring thing?!"

"It's normal protocol for a wedded couple."

I smiled insincerely. "Like I said. *Long* story."

"If she actually is your wife, how do you not know where she is? Or have a key to her apartment? Or live in the same place?"

"Long story!"

"I'm calling the landlord."

"No, ma'am," I gently grabbed her shoulder as she tried to turn, "how much for you to help me get into this apartment?"

She puffed. "You think I can be bought?"

I itched my forehead apprehensively. "I'm so sorry ma'am, look, I'll do anything-"

"I'll take a gram of weed, a pack of cigarettes, and the latest edition of Playgirl."

I raised my eyebrow.

"What? They have the best coupons."

"Deal."

Luna Elrod Journal Entry
Date: August 13th, 2017

The last thing Dr. Kennedy said to me before I left was,

Luna, you said that you've always viewed yourself as an ocean, right? Untamable and unpredictable?

Yes, Dr. Kennedy. I responded.

Well, there is one thing that does control the ocean. He said.

And what would that be? I asked.

Ah. He said. The moon.

Rosamie, the divinely aged Filipino, grabbed a ladder from her apartment and took me to the back of the building where Luna's balcony was. We adjusted the ladder until it was in place under the balcony and then argued for twenty minutes about who got to go up first. I finally relinquished and let her go.

She sauntered her way up the ladder and then by the grace of God, swung her body over the railing and onto the balcony. I'm not sure what inspired her more, proving me and my disapproval of her behavior wrong, or the joint she insisted on smoking beforehand. Either way, she then started yelling at *me* to be careful.

I ungracefully pulled my body up each step. "I got it, Rosamie!" I shouted, trying to disarm her farce commentary.

"It sure looks like the ladders got you!"

Once I made it to the top and got my more robust body over the railing, Rosamie pulled at the back door, which opened with no struggle.

"Why do I have a feeling you've broken into this apartment before?" I asked.

Rosamie raised an eyebrow. "Sometimes I need a little privacy from my husband. And she's got an excellent collection of magazines."

"You know, you are far more interesting than one would expect, Rosamie."

"And you're a lot less dangerous than one would expect."

We entered her apartment. Her place looked ransacked, so I knew it hadn't been touched. The last time we were in here, we had made a complete mess. Our drinking glasses were still out, pancake mix was all over the counter, and the lipstick she applied right before we left was still by the front door.

"She hasn't been home," I said.

"I know," Rosamie responded, "I was just in here having my morning tea."

I gave her an antagonizing glance.

"Well, what now?" Rosamie asked.

Luna's typewriter was on the ground next to half-typed sheets of paper that consumed most of the floor. Shriveled, unloved plants broken at the stems were making the place reek. Fabric bits that Luna would often turn into clothing items floated around various furniture pieces. An aquamarine-colored cloth hung from the microwave handle (she called it 'micro-wave' fiber). Pots and pans were in the sink, a half-full coffee pot sat on the dining room table, and a pair of gold high heels poked out of her Chinese Evergreen plant.

"This is not good, Rosamie," I said.

"I know," she responded, "her place is a disaster. I had to cut my morning tea short because of the goldfish I found in the toilet. I *really* had to go to the bathroom but didn't have the heart to do it on Marlin."

"What? No, Rosamie. It's not good that she hasn't been home. That means she could be anywhere, without anything."

"It also means I still have privacy from my husband," she looked me up and down, "as does she."

I examined the space in hopelessness until I felt a Luna twitch come over me. "I got it," I said.

"What?"

I grabbed all the half-typed sheets of paper on the ground and collected the dead rose petals. "Thanks for your help, Rosamie, but I have to go."

"You are either a lousy robber or a lousy husband. I am having trouble deciding which is worse."

Rosamie went back down the ladder first (she refused to just go out the front door) and then she guided me with her harsh words as I struggled to get down myself (you really learn how unattractive the quality of being uncoordinated is when you have a high and grey-haired woman shouting at you from down below).

"Good luck with whatever it is you are going to do now," she said, waving me off.

"Thanks Rosamie. I'm really going to need it."

"If it's robbing, hopefully you take something of value next time. Try the master bedroom jewelry boxes or look under a mattress."

"Bye Rosamie."

I knew exactly how I was going to apologize.

In good, old, Luna fashion.

Luna Elrod Journal Entry
Date: August 15th, 2017

La Luna.

Chapter Fifty-Four: finding Luna part 2

Date: August 2017

I had never written anything sober.

All my best work came during substance abuse.

But I had also never been in love sober.

I laid out the sheets of paper and rose petals from Luna's apartment and then I searched everywhere in between for a place to put my apology.

And that's when Jim's Secret Santa gift resurrected itself. It had fallen under the couch during an intense affair with writer's block and suffered a long-winded journey of neglect.

I had yet to write in it because I had yet to find the courage of words in this phase of my life.

"Thanks Jim," I said.

And then I went to work.

I was more of writer than a craftsman, considering my fingers were too long and thick to properly maneuver scotch tape and scissors didn't seem to fit in my grip. But this was a project that needed more than words.

When it was done, bold black letters stared back at me.

"An abundance of Luna's mind. The one I want back."

Her poetry clung onto Jim's journal next to glued rose petals that substituted blank spaces.

And I begged for her mind back so she could spare me from my own.

"An abundance of Luna's mind. The one I want back."

                                      --

The parallels between me and the sea are few and far between. I don't wish to be feared but I do desire to be admired.

I admired you, Luna. And you made me fearless.

Of all the daisies blooming in the world, I wish to be yours, growing right between your toes.

You grew straight into my mind. And now I can't think without you.

My boyfriend is a remarkably informed person. Nobody would ever accuse me of that.

Your mind expands information. Your mind is the genesis of creative liberation. Nobody would ever accuse me of that.

Why would the universe make my body so small but my emotions so large?

Because you live outside of your skin. You live in a world that surpasses your exterior. You're the only person I know who can exist outside the constraints of your size.

I felt my wings get cut this time... I was soaring, and then before I knew it, the dark ocean water underneath me was coming formidably fast. But this time, the falling was the scariest part. Because I knew what was under those adoring waves. I knew what would be waiting for me. It was the most terrifying plummet of my life. And all I could do was hold onto my wounded wings and brace myself for the darkness.

Let me catch you, Luna. Please.

I love you.

I wrapped the journal in white cloth and safety-pinned the edges.

Now I just had to *find* her.

Chapter Fifty-Five: Columbo
Date: August 2017

"Come on Jim," I said gripping onto my kitchen table, "I need your help again."

There weren't many strings I hadn't pulled to find her. I had broken into her apartment, called her old job, ran up and down every street she used to rave about, went to every café, art museum and dumpster she had ever mentioned. I even went to the bright yellow gas station.

She was nowhere to be found.

He was silent.

"Jim?!"

Silence.

"God dammit Jim, the one time you decide to be quiet!"

I sat down on the floor.

Then I laughed to myself.

I laughed some more.

And then I laughed until I choked on the warm water that was coming out of my eyes.

I got up, turned *the 13th Floor Elevators* on, and sat back down on the floor. I closed my eyes and leaned my head against the wall, listening intently to the lyrics. It didn't happen quickly, but eventually, the raspy voice of Roky Erickson turned into Jim's.

Did you ever tell her? He asked.

I shook my head.

Why not?

"Because I wanted to be seen for Nathan and not anything else."

Nathan, she saw you for Nathan before you saw yourself for him. You didn't even have the confidence to make a resume by yourself a year ago, man. Now look at you.

I laughed. "Yeah, but-" I sat up straight, "wait a minute. Jim. You are fucking brilliant."

There was one place I hadn't looked.

One with very good reason why.

One where Luna knew I sure wouldn't go.

Susan was standing behind the front desk in a black pantsuit. I advanced gradually.

"Nathan. I see you. You don't have to walk towards me like a mutilated cat like-creature."

I stopped in my tracks. "Are you going to call the police?"

She sighed. Heavily.

"That doesn't answer my question."

"No," she said, "I dropped the charges."

I stood up straight. "What? Why?"

"Because" she said shrugging, "the city gave the library a *very* large donation after the fire. We got all new books for our non-fiction section. You know more than anyone how deficient our last one was. I mean, we didn't even have *Living the Good Long Life* by Martha Stewart.

"Oh," I said, astonished, "so, you aren't going to call the police because of Martha Stewart?"

"I also got a raise."

"Oh."

She raised a shoulder. "So, no. I am not going to call the police."

"Is that advised though? You have a suspect right in front of you-"

"It's handled, Nathan."

I held both my hands up nervously. "Okay."

"That doesn't mean we are friends again though."

I smiled. "I wasn't aware you ever thought of me as your friend."

"Don't push it, Nathan."

I nodded. "Okay."

We stared at each other a minute or two.

"Is she-" I eventually asked.

Susan nodded and pointed to the fireplace. My eyes followed her finger.

There she was. In her chair, reading *In the Vein of Feeling Something.* A Cutty classic.

I pinched at the white cloth wrapping.

She had gone back to her sanctuary. A place even safer now that I shouldn't have been let in (unfortunately for her, Susan was easily bought).

I was shocked however, that Susan had forgiven her so easily. The one who *started* the fire.

"Why did you let her back in?" I asked, unfiltered.

Susan winked. "She's our best customer."

I laughed. "But library books are free-"

"Just go talk to her, Nathan."

I nodded and then took a deep breath.

"You know what I do when I'm scared?"

"What?"

"Nothing, because I'm not a fucking pussy."

I walked up to her.

Her sweet beachy aroma wafted from her strawberry blonde hair. A gold chain hung from her neck, a freshwater pearl in the shape of a moon at the end of it.

"Hi," I said, bracing myself for a tidal wave.

"Hi," she said.

I opened my eyes. *Just hi? That wasn't much like her. I had been anticipating the scene from Halloween all over again.*

"I think I deserve a lot worse than a 'hi,'" I responded.

She shrugged.

The back of my throat itched for a longing taste of Luna's exploits. This causality was a lot crueler than outrage.

"Can I sit?" I asked.

She nodded.

I tried to get comfortable (although it seemed comfortable was an oath that would never be delivered). "Here," I said handing her the wrapped journal, "I need you to read this."

"Nathan-"

"Luna please," I said, breaking down, "I am so sorry. Can we please just go home and fix this?"

She looked at me with genuine confliction. "I haven't even been to *my* home."

"I know."

She tilted her head. "How do you know?"

I quickly corrected myself. "What I meant was, why have you not been home? I've been looking for you everywhere."

She sighed. "I haven't been able to go back. There's too much of... me... I guess. And I'm too scared to see it now."

I didn't understand what she had meant yet. "Where did you sleep last night?" I asked.

"At my neighbor's. Rosamie and her husband. They are an older, very sweet couple. Rosamie said I could stay with them for as long as I need seeing I supply her magazines and cigarettes."

"What?! That scheming stoner," I said under my breath.

"What?"

"Nothing."

I couldn't wrap my head around what was happening. This calmness was contradicting the usual method needed to kill my guilt and sorrow. I needed an explosion so this would blow up and we could piece it back together. I needed to tear into this situation, so it was left raw and unfiltered and only fixable by its original creators.

I needed something to make us, us again.

"Can we go somewhere?" I asked.

--

We sat on the corner of Alfalfa Plant Rd. and Brunk Rd.

We sat in silence for a long time.

And then Luna started sobbing.

I waited for her to talk.

"You see those daisies?" She asked.

I nodded.

"Those daises I used to wholeheartedly admire?"

I nodded.

"Well, I don't feel like that anymore."

"What do you mean?" I asked, befuddled.

Tears landed on the pearl moon around her neck. "I'm on medication now, mood stabilizers. I can't *feel* like I used too anymore."

A volt of rage took over and I threw the journal on the ground. "This is exactly why I didn't want you going to that place!" I shouted, "I knew they would try and change you! There was nothing wrong with you! Why would they take my Luna from me-"

She grabbed at my sleeve to try and pull me down.

"You're going off those fucking meds, Luna, I swear-"

"Nathan," she begged.

"I can't believe-"

"Nathan!" Luna was standing up now, "I'm bi-polar!"

And that's when I realized I had switched my addiction.

And the very thing I had become addicted to, was the very thing that was destroying her.

Luna's mental illness had become my addiction.

I understood then, why she couldn't go back to her apartment. She didn't want to be reminded of the times when she was Luna: the barefoot blondie. Or Luna: the girl being held under her blanket of hopelessness.

She didn't have a choice. Living like that wasn't sustainable. It would ultimately destroy her.

But it was addicting.

And if she was reminded of all the times her illness made her fly, she'd want to go back.

She had to create a new version of herself. She had to find a new way to love life again. A life that would be stable for her.

She had to find a new Luna to love.

And that was a mission for herself alone.

Luna and I were each other's hell and dream. And there was nothing in between.

Tabitha was right, some things do have clear answers.

"I'm leaving California tomorrow," she said.

"Where will you go?"

"Back home for a bit. I think my family deserves an explanation and a chance to learn."

"Will you be okay?"

She hesitated before answering. "One day. Yes."

We stood on the sidewalk, eyes locked in adjoining forgiveness before setting each other free.

Luna chuckled a little, overpowering her tears. "Good thing we never got rings, right?"

I wiped my eyes. "Damn rings."

She enfolded herself around me. I lifted my hands, anticipating them to be clenched, but they weren't. I wrapped my arms around her.

Our hug fleeting, but affectual.

A moment breaking two hearts but healing many minds.

"Can I still have that gift you handed me earlier and then took back to throw on the ground?" She asked.

I looked down at the journal that was now unkempt and unwrapped. "Oh," I said frantically, "I don't know if you are going to want that-"

"I think it'll be okay," she nodded and bent down to grab it.

I wanted to stop her, but I didn't. "Okay," I said.

She turned to go.

I closed my eyes.

I didn't think I'd be able to watch her leave.

And I had to let her.

"Oh," she turned around.

I opened my eyes.

"By the way, the whole world *can* be one person. And it's yourself, Cutty."

"What?! How'd you-"

But she didn't hear me, or rather, she absolutely, did not care.

Luna Elrod Journal Entry
Date: August 17th, 2017

I've been an ocean my entire life. Uncontrollably crashing around, looking for somebody to subdue me.

The thing that humors me, however, is that the moon controls the ocean.

The name Luna originates from the Roman goddess who personified the moon.

Luna means moon.

I was once an ocean tide, lashing against the shore, waiting to be saved.

And now,

I'm the fucking moon.

Chapter Fifty-Six: a proper send-off
Date: August 2017

The next day, I was coming home from Cindy's house. She had made their bedroom a sanctuary for anyone who needed to talk to Jim. And I really needed him at this time.

When I arrived back at my unit, a gaping hole formed at my mouth, unironically, due to the gaping hole in my door.

Despite my relentless asking, my landlord had replaced my entryway with yet, another wooden door ("something like that won't happen again," he droned on. "You don't understand," I pleaded. But my queries were not granted. Leaving us with yet, another implication).

As I stood in front of my wooden door, dreading the future conversation I was going to have with my landlord, I couldn't help but gleam. Because the giant hole staring right back at me meant there was still a tiny bit of Luna left, even if she didn't think so.

I opened the door bracing myself. But nothing had changed. The walls were still painted from her last escapade, herbage still lurked around every corner, and her décor was still very much present. She hadn't taken anything back.

The only difference was that there was a little blue bag in the middle of my kitchen island.

I stared at it, hoping it would have something to say for itself. But when it didn't, I pulled out the stuffing and dumped the contents of the bag onto the island. Only one thing came clanking onto the countertop. A gold key.

A very familiar gold key. One that I had much forgotten about.

There was one more mission to be had.

--

I opened the door to the red brick building and went down the hall. I kept walking until I stopped in front of room 112.

"Luna Elrod"

I held the gold key in the palm of my hand.

I had forgotten about this place I rented for Luna (on purpose), and I assumed she had too (not on purpose). There was never any further mention of it after the last time I left here with my heart hanging out of my chest due to the ineffectual reaction I had received.

I took a deep breath.

"You know what I do when I'm scared?"

"What?"

"Nothing, because I'm not a fucking pussy."

I turned the key.

I've heard from unreliable sources (my mother after an acid trip), that when you pass away, your body releases a natural DMT. That everything becomes windless. No ruffles shake the ungovernable atmosphere, no riffs splash water. For a glimpse of a moment there is no fear, or fame, there is no regret, affliction, or confusion. You are temporarily in a stormless state of tranquility and shamelessness. Every mistake, horror, vexation, and exasperation you have ever felt, all instantly becomes worth it.

For you have lived.

And that is a task done by damn few.

And in the very fragile moments between the key slipping into the lock and the door pushing open.

I died.

And I fell into the category of the damn few.

For my life had been worth it.

Luna's paintings covered the walls. Even the floor had endless sketches from her notepad. My face, Jim's face, trees, flowers, oceans, and moons enveloped me inside her mind.

As I looked around the room, a kaleidoscope of memories revealed themselves to me in a manifestation of watercolors and oils. Dancing at Big Bear, dumpster diving, swimming in the lake, searching the graveyard. Sitting on the corner of Alfalfa Plant Rd. and Brunk Rd., sneaking onto the cruise, Cutty the dogfish, The Pastor and Cordelia.

Our wedding day.

All our moments spent together as tangible works of art, alive in a room captured by a genius.

And on the table in the center of the room, sat another little blue bag.

I grabbed it. I ripped it open. I couldn't take the anticipation of her wild presence still around me. Silver and gold wrapping paper, hardly crinkled, filled the bag. I tore into that too. And what was left, after the gift-opening massacre, was her journal. The orange and white floral embroidered, hardcover journal. A card lay unblemished in what was left of the bag.

My journal, in exchange for yours.
P.S. This is how you properly wrap a gift.

She had given me her journal. And she had given me her artwork.
She gave me what I truly wanted,

      her mind.

Luna Elrod Journal Entry
Date: August 20th, 2017

Enough about flying. Let's learn how to float.

Present day- February 7, 2022

A universal fear of the thirteenth floor has caused many hotels and buildings to omit it altogether.

The 13th Floor Elevators, however, are fearless. I suppose I interpret the meaning of their name to suggest that they aren't afraid of going places that are daunting. Places perhaps, most people would not choose to explore.

Growing up, whenever I needed to feel fearless, I would listen to *the 13th Floor Elevators.*

And then the power those albums had over me, switched. To alcohol.

And then it switched again.

To a barefoot girl in a fur coat.

I asked myself a long time ago, when I was hiding behind the mask of an infamous drunk author, "can the whole world be one person?"

Never did I think it could be myself.

--

I moved into an apartment with a steel door. You can never be too safe. I painted the walls a very specific shade of yellow. A green sofa with corresponding green throw pillows (intentional matching) and a tasteful rug both fill my apartment with conventional charm. And I *may* have one or two potted plants around (but someplace I don't stumble upon regularly).

Cindy announced her pregnancy not long after Jim's funeral. Jim's risotto efforts turned out to be successful in many ways. I am now a godfather to a four-year-old girl named Lucy. She has the same head shape as Jim and is starting to pull the same antics as well. I don't know how much longer I'll be able to hold off on telling her that hats and comedy may not be her strong suit. We get pie together once a week at the local diner while she tests out her new jokes on me. She's confident that she'll be able to make me laugh by the time the diner features their seasonal spring strawberry pie. I'm not banking on it.

Landon was helping Cindy out a lot during her pregnancy and I guess his hippie, eccentric ways won her over (Jim would either roll over in his grave or high-five him... hard to tell). Cindy seems happy however, and that is something I would never take from her.

"He smells like shaggy," Lucy said once over pie.

"That's your best joke yet," I responded.

I got my job back at the library. Susan and I made amends (turns out she can also be bought with well-made expresso). I join her and her lady-friend/roommate/secret-lesbian-lover for meatloaf and milk every Sunday. We call it Saucy Sunday. She came up with the name. My Christmas this year was spent with Susan, her very legal and accepted concubine, Cindy, Landon, Lucy, and a burnt meatloaf.

Susan and I have plans to open a bookstore together. One that sells adequate literature and bagels the way they should be: dry and lightly touched with cream cheese (we still haven't agreed upon that part yet), but we have agreed on making it barefoot friendly, just in case. I suppose I could put my assortment of degrees to use in a stimulating way. A PhD in literature would come in use for a bookshop owner.

Once a week I go grocery shopping with Cindy and Lucy. I pick out the frozen food, Cindy picks out the produce, and Lucy sneaks the baking products into the cart. After Cindy replaces the refined sugar with cane sugar, we all bake a pie together, in honor of Jim. And then we eat it in silence. This week it was cherry pie. Lucy didn't fancy the cherries too much. She's just like her dad.

I see Aiyden once a month at the spa. Not only do they put mud all over my face, but they also put rocks on my back. Who knew dirt and rocks could be so alleviating? If I had known this years ago, I would've just rolled around in a riverbed instead of a bottle of gin. We lay by the pool and tan afterwards. Twenty-nine minutes on our stomach. Twenty-one minutes on our back.

My AA group hasn't changed much. Landon swapped our coffee pot for hot tea. He said it was better for our soul and the entire group agreed, which is how I know it was their way of getting me to stop drinking so much caffeine. Prudes. I mean, who wants the sweet fragrance of lemon and berries circulating the high-strung air at 7am as we all bond over our experience with Malört's? Every addict has a run in with Chicago (and not the musical). It's an absolute nightmare. (Little do they know I'm hitting the black coffee *before* and *after* meetings).

Weirdly and uncomfortably, Max and I often jam out together. Turns out he likes psychedelic rock music (who knew he had good taste in anything?). We've started swapping albums and I've even gone to a few underground gigs with him (though, if anyone caught us head banging together, I would relentlessly deny it was me). Funny enough, he had me for Secret Santa this year. He somehow got his hands on a signed poster of *The Thirteenth Floor Elevators*. He's not that bad, I suppose. I should probably make up for that inadequate gift I got him all those years ago.

Elizabeth now hosts very uncomfortable family parties once a month to try and get her daughters to like her again. She insists we all go to show her family that she's not the only alcoholic that has ruined their life. So, every month, I find myself in Elizabeth's backyard, drinking apple juice, making small talk with strangers who pity me. Oh, and she got a new pair of tits.

Mateo has recovered from his fear of knives. We aren't sure if he's telling the truth or not, but he did use a plastic knife this year at our holiday party. Although, he was in the bathroom for twenty minutes afterwards… but we aren't entirely sure if that was due to a panic attack, or the undercooked Chicken Piccata Elizabeth made.

Daniel is still a conspiracy theorist and now argues that we are living in a computer simulation created by an advanced civilization.

Sofia got remarried. But not to the old guy, unfortunately for him, he passed away. Fortunately for Sofia however, she got a new man who is appropriately aged, handsome, and rich. They adopted a baby girl. As far as I'm concerned, she's madly in love, sober, and mother to beautiful Isabella.

And Xavier finally found enough gumption to leave pharmacy altogether and went back to school to become a general practitioner. He finds less stress in writing the prescriptions than he does filling them. The outcome of which has not helped his student debt, however.

There is a large shrine in our AA room for Strong Jim. I put a cigarette on the table every morning and share a dart with him. "This is awesome," I laughed once, "you would never have smoked with me in real life." I keep him updated on the high jinks that go on around here and the new conspiracies Daniel has discovered.

"We can hear you!" Sofia shouted one morning when I was talking smack about Landon's new man bun.

"Oh," I muttered, turning my volume to a whisper, "they still have the same restless nosiness around here." I rolled my eyes.

I bought a new gray hardcover journal. One that looks exactly like the one Jim got me. I write in it every day. Some days I write to Jim. I ask him things like, "have you discovered female anatomy up there yet?" and, "it better not have been my mothers."

Speaking of which, I went back to the graveyard by myself to try and find my mother. Turns out, she was cremated. According to her will, her ashes were spilt up into multiple canisters and given to her ex-boyfriends. The ex's including those by the names of: Mick Jagger, Rod Stewart, Eddie Vedder, Eric Clapton, Bill Wyman, David Bowie, and a few others I won't bother getting into. I guess that explains the money and the naked guitar players in my living room growing up. One of those unfortunate bastards must've had the sperm that made me and got suckered into a *large* payout. Big thanks for the addiction gene and not the talent gene by the way.

I hung a photo of her in my living room. She's standing next to a lake, holding me as a baby. Her youthful smile larger than life. Even in death her radiant energy fills my heart. I smile back at her.

Oh, and Cutty B. Sands? He is more alive than ever. He wrote his first 'sober' novel titled *Running Barefoot Through Sands* and dedicated it to someone named Jane. It was alright.

It's been five years since I've seen Luna. It's also been five years since I had a drink. My longest stretch of sobriety yet. I've made a lot of changes in my life since I said goodbye to her, but, as we all know, some old habits die hard.

Which is perhaps why I still only like black coffee and plain bagels and will never succumb to an alternative milk option. Or it's why when I feel a craving come on, I go to *The Little Shack* and order a non-alcoholic beer on tap, a slice of pie, and talk to Jim. Or why when I need to feel fearless, I read her journal (which I always carry in my back pocket... just in case). It might also be why I keep resigning the lease on the art studio every year. Just so I can go back and behold it, whenever I need.

It's also possible that's why I'm here, now, on the corner of Alfalfa Plant Rd. and Brunk Rd. inside the gas station painted a bright shade of yellow, muttering, "can the whole world be one person?"

--

"Can the whole world be one person?" I mumbled, again, looking for a bag of peanuts that wasn't roasted in chipotle or chili lime (do they make anything plain these days?)

The gas station cashier glanced up from behind his stool. "Is that Cutty B. Sands? Who you're quoting?"

Startled, I looked over to him. "...what?"

He nodded. "Yeah. I believe it is."

"How do you know that?" I asked. It's not as if I was quoting a line from Forrest Gump.

The cashier put down the book he was reading. "Some chick was just in here, an hour or so ago, saying the same thing."

"What?" I asked again.

"Yeah," he continued, "I thought it was a cool quote, so I asked her what it meant. She went on for a while, talking about some dude named Cutty? She seemed a bit insane, pretty hot though-"

"Hold up," I said, raising my hand, "you said she was just in here?"

The cashier nodded. "About an hour or so ago."

I grabbed a bag of chili lime peanuts. I had a sudden urge to try something new. I walked up to the register.

"Just this?" the cashier asked.

I nodded, digging around in my pocket for cash and then paid him.

"Alright, you're all set," the cashier picked his book back up, "have a good rest of your day."

I remained stationary, holding onto the peanuts.

He glanced up at me. "Everything okay?"

I couldn't move.

"Sir?"

I looked out the door.

The cashier watched as I tried to catch my breath.

"Can I tell you a story?" I asked.

The cashier sighed, looked around, and bookmarked his page. "Alright. I suppose I'm not too busy."

"You'll have to forgive me. To be honest, I have a long history of telling cashiers about my business, buying bland food from gas stations, and expressing how I feel using a string of vague metaphors. And in fact, that's exactly how this story begins..."

We tell stories so history doesn't repeat itself.

The end.

"A love like that was a serious illness, an illness from which you never entirely recover." - commonly attributed to Charles Bukowski

Message from the author:

Even though you are the only person who can ultimately save yourself, this book is inspired by all the things you learn and love from the people that come and go throughout our lives.

Be kind. People are beautiful, complex human beings and listening to someone's story might change your own.

ABOUT THE AUTHOR

b.p. grew up with a deeply creative family from whom she first learned the value of artistic expression and uninhibited imagination. She adores traveling, reading, music, and of course, turning the human condition into words on a page. *hell, dream, and nothing in between* is her debut novel.

www.ingramcontent.com/pod-product-compliance
Lightning Source LLC
Chambersburg PA
CBHW020004120726
47903CB00004B/1131